One Texas Night

SYLVIE KURTZ

SILHOUETTE

INTRIGUE

All the characters in this book have no existence outside the imagination of the author, and have no relation whatsoever to anyone bearing the same name or names. They are not even distantly inspired by any individual known or unknown to the author, and all the incidents are pure invention.

First published in Great Britain 2000
Silhouette Books, Eton House, 18-24 Paradise Road,
Richmond, Surrey TW9 1SR

© Sylvie Kurtz 1999

ISBN 0 373 22527 X

46-0008

Printed and bound in Spain
by Litografia Rosés S.A., Barcelona

Before he could stop himself, he kissed her fiercely, protectively.

She sent a jolt zinging through him like an arrow on fire. He heard her murmur his name against his lips and he deepened the kiss. He wanted more of her…all of her…

What am I doing? I don't want this. I don't need this. Not now.

He released her, backing up one step until his hands cupped only her elbows. Her dark eyes were wide with confusion, with longing. It would be easy to take advantage now, to seduce her. Blurring the lines of his boundaries with the investigation was one thing; sleeping with the primary witness was quite another…

Dear Reader,

Welcome to Intrigue™!

A new trilogy by popular author Amanda Stevens begins this month, **GALLAGHER JUSTICE**. In *The Littlest Witness* we meet the first of the three Gallagher brothers, all raised to uphold the values of honour and integrity.

In this month's **LAWMAN LOVER**, *For His Daughter*, Officer Lee Garvey has some protecting to do—his daughter and the woman he loves are in danger. The pressure is most definitely on.

Strange things are happening in *Dream Maker*—Jared Slater's dreams are coming true. But when his lovely research assistant is murdered in one of his dreams, Jared knows it's time to get to the bottom of his nightly adventures... And in the first of our **AMNESIA** mini-series, *One Texas Night*, Lieutenant Grady Sloan's key murder witness has amnesia...*and* the most beautiful eyes he's ever seen!

Come back next month for another four thrilling romantic suspense novels.

All the best,

The Editors

ABOUT THE AUTHOR

Flying an eight-hour solo cross-country in a Piper Arrow with only the airplane's crackling radio and a large bag of chocolates for company, Sylvie Kurtz realised a pilot's life wasn't for her. The stories zooming in and out of her mind proved more entertaining than the flight itself. Not a quitter, she finished her pilot's course and earned her commercial licence and instrument rating.

Since then, she has traded in her wings for a keyboard where she lets her imagination soar to create fictional adventures that explore the power of love and the thrill of suspense. When not writing, she enjoys the outdoors with her husband and two children, quilt-making, photography and reading whatever catches her interest.

You can reach Sylvie at P.O. Box 702, Milford NH 03055, USA.

For Chuck—My anchor in the storm of life.

A Special Thanks—To Joanne Moriarity of Lee Valley for all her help in putting together Melinda's catalogue.

Chapter One

Murder didn't happen in this slice of Texas. In the twelve years since Grady Sloan had been an officer with the Fargate Police Department, there hadn't been a single homicide. Now, less than twenty-four hours into his tenure as interim police chief, Angela Petersen lay dead in the Tarrant County morgue, awaiting an autopsy.

As he'd inspected the small brick home on the edge of town, no bold clues had jumped up at him, saying, "I did it!" There was only blood—a lot of it—splattered over the lace curtains, ruffled pillows and other feminine frills strewn about the living room. No muddy footprints had marred the pink carpeting. No bloody knife had lain close by with accusing fingerprints on its handle. No signs of forced entry had marked any of the doors or windows.

There was nothing, except the strange woman. And the indecipherable drawing she'd held.

He'd have to use every ounce of his resourcefulness to crack the case.

A lot of fun that would be, with the critical town council breathing down his neck and watching his every move. After his fiasco with Jamie—his otherwise spotless record notwithstanding—they'd expect mistakes, and be more than ready to point fingers.

In three weeks, Fargate would hold its annual Fall Festival. The council had planned Seth Mullins's retirement celebration and the announcement of his replacement as the crowning event.

That didn't leave Grady much time to prove the town council wrong. Or to get answers from the woman who claimed not to remember her name.

His office door blustered open.

"What took you so long?" Grady snapped at his sister. Tension had him strung tighter than sun-dried leather.

"Well, hello to you, too." Desiree Sloan dumped her briefcase and large leather purse on top of his desk, ignoring the pile of papers she scrambled in the process. Flyaway wisps of light brown hair escaped from the French braid that couldn't be more than half an hour old. While she removed the jacket of her bright red business suit, she juggled a cup of coffee between her hands, sloshing drops onto the carpet. Good thing it was the color of industrial grime.

His sister was a brilliant psychologist, but grace had never been one of her attributes. She plowed through life like a scatterbrained bull in a china shop, but when it came to business, she focused single-mindedly as if in a ring facing a matador's cape. No one garnered more professional respect than Dr. Des. Which is why he'd sought her opinion this morning.

"I got here as fast as I could." She plopped into a chair, popped the loose cover from her cup of coffee and blew on the hot liquid. "You know I'm not a morning person." She leaned back in the chair and crossed one leg over the other. "So, what windmill's got your shorts in a torque this morning, brother dear? Vigilante cow-tipper? Mad doughnut snatcher at Mamie's?" She slapped one hand on the chair's armrest. Her blue-gray eyes twinkled with amusement. "No, don't tell me! Some low-down snake took off with the high school's royal blue street sign again.''

"That's enough, Desiree. I'm not in the mood for your sass today.''

"So it's Desiree, huh? I guess I'm really in trouble now.''

He loved his sister to death, but she could push his buttons faster than anyone he knew. Her irreverent humor and lightheartedness had helped him through a lot of rough spots, but this wasn't going to be one of them.

"I didn't mean to snap.'' He threw his pen onto the blotter, then tipped back his chair until it leaned against the wall. "I've been up all night.'' He dragged his hands over his face and rubbed his burning eyes. "Someone murdered Angela Petersen.''

"Oh, no!'' Desiree jammed her cup onto the desk, staining his report with muddy-brown coffee. "Angie's mother must be beside herself. And the reverend. She was the apple of his eye. I'll have to stop by and see them on my way to work. What happened?''

Grady plucked tissues from a box on the black metal credenza and mopped Desiree's mess. "Lena Strong called in late last night, saying she thought she heard someone screaming at the Petersens'. I thought it might just be the storm. The winds were pretty strong last night.''

"I know. I think I lost some shingles.''

He lobbed the sodden tissue into the wastebasket beside the desk. "Anyway, there was no answer when I got there, but the front door was ajar. I found her stabbed to death on the living-room floor.''

"God, Grady, how awful! Do you know who did it?''

"Not yet.''

"Angie had a voice like an angel's.'' Desiree shook her head slowly. "She was supposed to sing Seth's retirement song at the Fall Festival. It's going to be a grim affair now. What is it you need me to do?''

Now that Desiree was here, Grady found himself hesitating. If she confirmed the woman truly suffered from amnesia, it would complicate his case no end. He didn't have time for gentle proddings. He needed to solve a murder.

''We found a woman at the scene. When we tried to question her, she attacked us.'' Absently, he rubbed the bandage covering the bite mark on his left hand. ''Now she claims she can't remember her name.'' He slipped the drawing they'd found in the woman's hand toward his sister. ''She was holding this. Des, in all the years I've been a cop I've never had to deal with someone like her. Is it possible?''

''Amnesia?'' Desiree half shrugged as she concentrated on the drawing. ''It depends on a lot of things. If she suffered a trauma to the head, or if she was on drugs, or if she had a syndrome called 'complex partial seizures,' yeah, it'd be possible. It's hard to make a diagnosis with so little to go on.''

''That's why I asked you here. I'm going to take her to the interview room. While I ask her some questions, I want you to watch from the one-way mirror. I need to know if she's faking it.''

Desiree ripped her purse open, then flipped through her agenda. Finger sliding down her calendar, she nodded. ''I've got to make an appearance downtown Fort Worth in court this afternoon, but I don't have anything that can't wait this morning. What makes you think she's faking?''

''That's it, Des. I just don't know.'' He tipped the chair back again and crossed his arms over his chest. ''Two years ago, I would have gone with my gut.''

''And what does your gut say?'' she prodded when he hesitated.

"It says she was at the right place at the wrong time. Now, I have to wonder." The chair snapped down. He leaned forward, placing both his forearms on the desk, fingers entwined, uncertainty riddling holes in his usual confidence. "I smelled liquor on her breath. The other officer didn't."

The woman hadn't answered his question. She hadn't blinked. She hadn't moved. She'd simply sat huddled on the ground at the back of the woodshed with the same unfazable glare in her eyes that he'd seen much too often on his mother's face.

"And?" Desiree asked.

"The test came back with a count of zero. I mistook the smell of wet oak chips for alcohol, the glazed look in her eyes for drunkenness. I jumped to conclusions... because..."

"Of Jamie." Desiree's eyes softened. "Grady, why didn't you tell me you were still having problems?"

He looked away from his sister's too-knowing gaze. He would never dream of talking to anyone about his shortcomings, but Des had the knack of coaxing things out of him. It was easier to give in than to go through one of her digging sessions. "I thought I'd gotten over it."

She placed her agenda on the desk, reached forward and covered his hands with hers. "You're good at what you do, Grady. Who knows how screwed up Aimee and I would've turned out without you." She squeezed his hands. "Not everybody's Jamie. And you're not some superhero. You can't save the whole world. Nobody even expects you to save this little corner of it. It's impossible. Stuff happens. And if you need someone to talk to, you know I'm always here. We've all got our talents. Yours is finding the truth. Mine is listening. Give the rest of us mere mortals a break, will you?" She grinned at him. "Besides, you know how much I love to meddle in everybody's business.''

He looked at her over the protective barrier of his desk. ''I'm still second-guessing myself.''

''There's nothing wrong with being careful.''

''Unless it gets in the way of the job. You know how much I want to take over the chief's seat.''

She chuckled and nodded. ''Can't imagine you working for Winnin' Wayne Dillon, either.'' She straightened and put on her serious face. ''Since we can't burden the town with a bootlicker like Wayne, let's work on your mystery woman. What else can you tell me about her?''

Grady tipped his chair back and drummed the heel of his boot against the metal leg, reflecting on his first glimpse of the woman. Her eyes, mystery dark, had seemed impenetrable and definitely glazed. Her white skin contrasted sharply with the long black hair stuck in wavy strands to her head and cheeks. Dry, with a little makeup, those high cheekbones, aristocratic nose and elegant mouth, she could have passed for one of the society ladies whose smiling pictures plastered the ''Life'' section of the Fort Worth newspaper when they promoted one or the other of their do-gooder affairs. He'd learned to regret regal features like those. Yet something about her depthless eyes had drawn his attention again and again.

''She's good-looking,'' he said tersely, losing patience with himself over the attraction he had no right to feel. ''And she says she can't remember anything. I think it's pure manure. But then I find her searching through the phone book as if she *were* trying to figure out who she was. There's something about her.'' He shook his head. ''I don't know, Des....''

Desiree dropped her leather-bound agenda back into her purse and offered him a slow smile. ''So which part are you hung up on—the 'good-looking' part, or the 'manure' part?''

He knew she expected him to brush her off or argue with her, but too much was at stake. Murder wouldn't go unpunished in Fargate. Not on his watch. He'd find the culprit and bring him—*or her*—to face justice. "Both."

She shook her head and clucked her tongue. "You get too personally involved. It's your strength, Grady, but it's also your weakness. You're asking for trouble."

"I know."

THE OFFICER TOOK HER TO A small room disguised as an office. It held two padded vinyl chairs—one with arms, one without—a battered metal desk, a cheap Monet print in a black metal frame, and a token dieffenbachia in need of watering in the corner.

The large mirror on one of the sidewalls betrayed the room's true purpose. He hadn't brought her here simply for a pleasant morning chat. She swallowed hard, trying to sort through the layers of gray still fogging her mind. As she took a seat in the armless chair he offered, she wondered if anyone stood on the other side of the mirror, and she shivered. What had happened? What had she done? Why was she here?

He sat across from her, the big desk separating them. She recognized the ploy for what it was. The officer was asserting his dominance. He needn't have bothered. She already felt small and raw. He took a tape recorder out of the drawer, set the machine up on the desk's immaculate surface, and labeled a fresh tape.

His controlled ease irritated her, probably because it contrasted so wildly with the restlessness gnashing at her nerves. And he no doubt viewed her as a criminal—like the rest of the nasty people he dealt with every day.

''Do you mind if I record our little talk?'' He snapped the newly-labeled tape into the machine.

Wondering if she truly had a choice, she shook her head. ''I have nothing to hide.''

''Good, my name is Lieutenant Sloan,'' he informed her, then spoke the day and date into the microphone. He tried to smile, but she recognized the gesture wasn't a familiar one for him.

''For the record, why don't you tell me your name?'' he asked.

She'd become resigned to her fractured memory in the hour and a half since she'd woken up in a jail cell. This had happened before. How she knew, she couldn't say, but she knew. Which didn't mean she accepted the unnerving fact that she couldn't remember much of anything else. To tell the truth, her insides were shaking. She felt very much alone and defenseless. She needed a friend—someone on her side.

But nothing about the sharp planes of the lieutenant's face suggested friendliness, except the hint of dimples in both of his cheeks. From the directness of his gaze and his grim expression, she had a feeling she wouldn't be privy to a full display of those dimples today. She'd find no friend there.

His rich-brown hair looked shower-damp, and his blue uniform smelled freshly starched. Everything about him appeared calm and controlled—the direct opposite of the distress threatening to explode into full-blown panic inside her. He looked like the type of man who left nothing unfinished, and she had the nagging suspicion she fell into that category. He would pry and he would press and he just wouldn't let go until he got what he wanted.

She looked away, feeling the current of dread accelerate, and concentrated on her hand with the torn nail tip, which hung half on and half off her finger. How had she gotten here? What had happened? Why couldn't she remember?

Instinct told her the memories would return if she didn't force them, but instinct also told her her own time wouldn't be fast enough for Lieutenant Sloan. She *wanted* to tell him; she just couldn't.

"Miss? Your name…"

"I don't know right now."

"When will you?" His tone seemed to aim for the casual, as if he were asking her what she planned to eat for dinner, but he couldn't quite cushion the scalpel precision of his words, or the shimmer of tangible impatience in his voice.

"I'm not sure." She held her head up, folded her hands neatly in her lap, and placed both her feet solidly on the floor. He could try to intimidate her, but he wouldn't succeed. She knew her rights; she was…

But the last part of the sentence escaped her before she could grasp it.

"Has this happened before?" he continued.

Closed-in spaces made her edgy. *He* made her edgy with the room he appropriated by his mere presence. Did he have this effect on all his prisoners, or just her?

"I—I'm not certain." She concentrated on the slashes made by the promise of dimples in his cheeks. They seemed so much friendlier than his hard gaze.

"Do you know where you live?"

She shrugged. He had a fascinating face, filled with contrasts, hard and soft angles, sharp and smooth planes. "I must live in Fargate. I don't think I normally leave the house without shoes."

"What's your date of birth?"

As she thought, the wrinkles forming on her forehead hurt. "Winter, I think. I vaguely remember it being cold when I blew out the candles on a cake as a little girl."

"Where do you work?"

She took in a deep breath and ventured a look into his eyes once more. They were an incredible blue, almost navy. Could anyone have eyes that deep a color? Like bluebonnets in the spring, she thought. "I don't recall at this moment."

"What about hobbies? Can you remember any?"

She looked down at her hands, twisted them back and forth, and noticed the calluses at the base of her fingers. "I think I do something with my hands." She rubbed her thumbs against her fingertips. "I don't know."

He watched her as if he knew things about her—horrible things. "Guess it's hard to remember after a hard night of partying."

"I *never*…party." *I'm a good girl,* she wanted to add, but it sounded so childish, she kept silent.

"Are you sure? You don't seem to be able to remember much of anything else."

She sought the contact of his gaze once more. His good looks might make him eligible for the policemen's pinup calendar, but she'd bet her last dollar he'd be Mr. December. And right now, she needed the warmth of Mr. July. Had she ever felt this cold before? She rubbed her arms, hoping to inject warmth into her body with the friction. Emptiness rang hollow inside her.

"I don't think I like you very much," she said.

"Having you like me isn't part of my job description. Having you tell me what you know about Angela Petersen's murder is."

"'Angela?'" The name sounded familiar. Bits of shredded images rained across her mind. Soft blond hair. A quiet smile. They'd shared tea and scones in a garden. Whose? Where? She licked at her lips, tasting the memories trickling in. Angela's husband, Tommy Lee, had left her two years ago for Dallas and a new life with a new wife. Angela Petersen. Her neighbor. More. There had to be more.

"Angela was the woman murdered?" she asked tentatively. If she'd felt cold before, she was positively icebound now.

"What can you tell me about it?"

"I don't know my name. I don't know where I work. I don't know where I live." She flung her head back and closed her eyes to intensify the bits and pieces popping into her mind. "I know I like Orange Zinger tea and a toasted English muffin with crunchy peanut butter for breakfast. I know I like the feel of the earth on my fingers. I know I like movies that require a box of tissues to watch." She almost laughed at the absurdity of her fractured recall.

Tears itched the backs of her eyes. Her throat tightened. Her fingers rolled into fists. "But I don't know anything about Angela's murder. Don't you think I'd tell you if I did?"

The officer rose and dragged his chair around the desk. After he'd turned her chair to face the mirror, he sat until their knees almost touched. The tips of his black cowboy boots rested a fragment of an inch away from her bare toes. She curled them protectively away.

A shaft of panic invaded her. He was too close, much too close. She was aware of the heat emanating from him, of the fresh scent of soap carried on those heated waves, and of him—of how much his physical presence disturbed her already shaky balance, and of how much she needed to be held right now.

"I know how frustrating it must be for you not knowing who you are." A measure of warmth crept into his voice. "But it's important you give remembering a real good try. A young woman died, and you might have witnessed her murder."

"'Witnessed'?" She jerked in surprise. "You don't think I murdered her anymore?"

"Let's just say for the sake of argument that you didn't." He reached forward and placed a sheltering hand over hers. The warmth of his skin felt good on her icy fingers. The directness of his gaze, unnerving as it was, also reflected a clarity of character she wanted desperately to trust.

"I want to go home," she said. It was getting harder to breathe in the thickening air. She had to get out. But whom could she call? Did she even have anyone who cared about her?

"Where is home?"

She lowered her lashes and sighed. "I don't know, but anywhere has to be less claustrophobic than this room."

He leaned farther forward. Anxiety snapped and crackled along her overloaded nerves, tightening her chest. "You don't like closed-in places," he said. "Is that why you were wandering outside in the middle of the night?"

Once more, she allowed her gaze to meet his. She held it steady this time, not letting the piercing quality of it trouble her. "You could irritate a saint."

He shifted back again, his mouth curling into a half grin. "I've spent hours developing that very quality. But I have a hunch you're no saint, so why don't you just make it easy on yourself and cooperate with me. I don't want to hurt you. I want to find Angela Petersen's murderer."

She removed her hands from the protective cover of his and crossed her arms below her chest, scrunching back as far as she could in the chair. "I don't know anything."

"I can protect you," he promised. Something deep inside knew she needed protection, but from what? Or from whom? "There's nothing to be afraid of."

Nothing to be afraid of. But she knew there always had been something to be afraid of. A fear like a monster in the closet who banged to get out, who had haunted her days and nights, year after year. What did it want? She didn't know, and wasn't sure she wanted to find out. But this fear had nothing to do with Lieutenant Sloan's investigation. It was far too old to be part of this fresh nightmare. It was a private one—one she'd have to deal with on her own. She lifted her shoulders and shook her head. "Why would I need your protection?"

A trace of irritation flickered in his eyes. His jaw flinched once before he spoke again. "Listen, it's very important that you—"

A knock on the door interrupted him. He got up to answer. Someone out of her line of sight offered him a piece of paper.

"Melinda Amery!" He said the name with such hatred, she recoiled in her chair from the booming concussion of his voice. "Is she related to Ely?"

She couldn't hear the muffled reply. He skewered her with his narrowed gaze, and as he left, he slammed the door. Why did that name bring such hatred and anger out of him? What had this Melinda Amery done to him? Her heart thudded hard, once. Was *she* Melinda Amery?

Melinda Amery. She turned the name over and over in her mind, but it struck no chord of recognition. With a sigh, she rested an elbow on the desk and propped her head on her uplifted hand. Her free hand traveled over the dried mud on her leg, then tucked her feet beneath her.

She wanted to get out of here. She wanted a shower and a good long nap. She wanted to forget this episode. Tomorrow, things would start falling back into place and she could resume her normal life as if nothing had happened.

Except that "normal" wouldn't be the same. Angela was dead. Angela who had been her neighbor. The image of flowers and the sound of laughter flicked like wet paint onto the opaque canvas of her mind. The quiet companionship they'd shared was gone forever. And like dominoes, when one thing fell, others were bound to follow.

She knew without being told that she had a lot of questions left to answer. And none of them would bring out Lieutenant Sloan's charming dimples.

Chapter Two

Grady paced the hall outside the interview-room door. Rage, hot and red, boiled deep. He swallowed the scream of frustration hovering at the base of his throat. Melinda Amery, Ely Amery's daughter! Of course, God forbid this case should be easy to solve. God forbid the past should stay in the past. God forbid he should get anything without a trial. But this situation was simply ridiculous. Why Melinda Amery, for heaven's sake? This town had thousands of other souls. Why lock away the key to this case in *her* mind?

Once ''Daddy'' got wind of where his daughter had spent the night, Grady wouldn't stand a chance in hell of discovering what she'd seen—or what she'd done. Her unfortunate breeding placed her back high on his Suspects list. After all, her father was the biggest snake in the state of Texas. No other human being, let alone any other lawyer, could match the lowness of his slither. Why would his daughter have inherited better morals?

He fisted his hand, swiveled and punched the wall. His knuckles smarted and the blow reopened the bite wound on his hand. *Great, just great!* As he pressed the bandage back into place, he heard a door open down the hall.

Ely Amery was half the reason he distrusted his instincts. Ely Amery had used him, made a fool of him. He and Jamie had tarnished a reputation Grady had worked a lifetime to build. Now, because of them, the town council doubted his merit. And with Ely back in the picture, he risked proving the council right. It would mean fighting both sides of the battle to make sure Angela wasn't forgotten in the shuffle. Justice meant nothing to Ely. And the town council simply wanted the problem to go away— correct killer optional.

"Grady?" Desiree placed a comforting hand on his arm. "Are you all right?"

"What do you think?" He snapped away and slumped against the corridor wall, trying to regain control of his arsoned emotions. This wasn't like him! "She's Ely Amery's daughter!"

"Take a deep breath. It's okay."

He shook his head. "This case has gone straight to hell, Des. Was she faking?"

Desiree matched his stance against the wall. "I saw no signs of alcohol detox, no shaking. She sounds intelligent, even if she is a bit mixed-up. She doesn't seem like she's tough enough to have fought with you last night."

"Well, she did."

"I don't doubt it, Grady, but she has a sweet, old-fashioned quality about her. You could almost picture her dressed in lace, sitting in a Victorian parlor having afternoon tea."

"Looks can be deceiving. Don't the society pages describe Ely Amery as 'dashing' and 'charming'?" He didn't bother trying to disguise the puslike oozing of disdain in his voice. Anger was healthy, or so Des kept trying to tell him. But this anger didn't feel healthy; it felt vindictive and destructive. Focusing on the red-and-white Exit sign, he counted to ten.

"That's not the point," Desiree said. "Are you going

to listen to me, or have you already made up your mind? You're the one who asked for this consult.''

''Go ahead.''

''After reading the arrest record, the incident report and looking over the blood test, I don't think she's faking it.''

''Then why can she remember some things, but not her name or what she saw?''

''Dissociation involves episodic memory. She retained all her knowledge and all her skills, but lost all consciousness of her life's events, the people she knows and her personal identity.''

''It doesn't make sense.''

''Dissociative disorders are like that. Let me talk to her for a bit.'' She grinned up at him in that teasing way of hers. ''And you can look from the other side of the mirror and practice those cop instincts you've honed for all these years.''

Without introducing Desiree, Grady let her into the interview room. He took his spot in the observation booth.

The booth was dimly lit and crowded with two hard chairs, but he didn't sit. He wanted to pace, but there wasn't enough room. He needed to run until his lungs couldn't take one more breath, until his legs had turned to rubber, until he'd left the betrayal behind. But he couldn't, so he leaned to one corner of the glass and observed his sister with his archenemy's daughter. He had to concentrate on the woman sitting on the other side of the mirror.

A hidden microphone carried and magnified every sound in the interview room. If he concentrated enough, he could hear the gentle intake of her breath, the rustling of her green silk top when she moved, the rich and elegant textures of her voice—as complex as his feelings toward her.

Melinda Amery sat stiff-backed in her chair, her carriage refined despite the dirty clothes she wore. Oscar, his fellow officer, had been right; she was a lady born and bred. Unfortunately, her breeding didn't ensure the truth. Her father certainly didn't care one way or the other about it.

"You're related to Lieutenant Sloan, aren't you?" Melinda said. Once again, the sweetness and purity of her voice struck him. It was velvet-soft and strong at the same time. Like her eyes. Like her mouth. Like the whole damned package.

"I'm his sister. How can you tell?" Desiree asked.

Melinda waved a long finger like a paintbrush. "The bone structure is similar, your coloring..." She dropped her hand back into her lap with finishing-school propriety. "Are you a police officer, too?"

"No, I'm a psychologist. Are you an artist?"

"I don't know." Her eyes rounded with a hint of fear before reassuming their dark, mysterious depth. "He's watching, isn't he?"

"You've been in a situation like this before?"

"Maybe." She turned, and with unnerving accuracy, intercepted his gaze. Involuntarily, Grady shifted his weight back, away from her direct line, then chided himself for his foolishness. She couldn't see him. "I can feel his eyes on me." She turned her attention back to Desiree. "Yours have that same keenness without the bite."

"He's the grouch of the family." Desiree had the nerve to giggle. "But his bark is definitely worse than his bite."

Melinda's head tilted, hiding the Mona Lisa-like smile on her lips. Her hair drifted forward in a graceful cascade, and even rain-dulled, it came alive with blue highlights. He couldn't remember ever seeing hair that black.

She was good. Too good. He wanted to believe her. Part of him already did. But he hadn't trusted that part of himself in a while, and she was Ely Amery's daughter. No matter how haunting her dark beauty was, he couldn't let himself be distracted.

"Do you know what happened last night?" Desiree asked.

Melinda straightened and shook her head. The motion outlined her breasts against the water-stained silk. His next breath hesitated and he crossed his arms over his chest. Her gaze averted from Desiree's to her lap, then it snapped up as if she'd remembered something. "It was raining."

"It was. Try to tell me whatever bits come into your mind. Don't worry if it doesn't make sense."

She rubbed her arms with opposite hands. As if she were cold, her nipples pebbled beneath the silk. He forced his gaze to return to her eyes. "The rain. It came in through the screens and pinged on the patio table. It made an awful noise on the roof. I—I can't..."

Melinda shook her head, making light run through the black hair like blue ribbons. Where was this sudden memory jog coming from? Was it just part of the act? The fear in her eyes, the halting motion of her hands as if she wanted to break the coming flood, seemed real. But then so had Jamie's tears. He'd believed her, and look where that had gotten him—labeled sucker of the year, and his judgment called into question.

"It's okay," Desiree said in her warm, comforting voice. "Take it easy. Start at the beginning. You were on your patio, and it was raining, and..."

Melinda took a deep breath before she spoke. "I'd come back from work late because we'd made so many changes in the layout."

"What kind of layout?"

"For the catalog!" Melinda spoke fast, as if capturing the thoughts in flight. "A couple of suppliers couldn't meet our orders and we had to scramble for replacements. I run a gardening-catalog business with my partner, Dolores Flint. I design the catalog. She handles the business end.'' She smiled shyly, and the whole room seemed to brighten. ''I guess I am an artist of sorts.''

''What did you do when you got home?''

The room's fluorescent lights had paled her skin, but the returning memories drained all the remaining traces of color. For a moment, he feared she would faint and he stepped forward, only to have the glass stop him.

''I opened all the windows to let the breeze in,'' Melinda continued. ''It was hot, but I don't like the closed-in feeling of the air conditioner. I went to the kitchen, but I couldn't decide what I wanted to eat, so I made tea. Then the rain started and it wouldn't stop.'' Her fingers twined nervously in her lap. Their movement had him wanting to break through the glass and still them.

''You don't like rain?'' Desiree asked, without judgment.

Melinda shrugged. ''Most of the time I don't mind it.''

''What was it about last night?''

''I don't know. It was so strong, and the thunder, and the lightning.'' Her hands moved in time to the staccato sound of imagined thunder.

''Thunder can be frightening sometimes. I usually turn the radio up loud so I don't have to hear it.'' Des paused. ''Go back to your house, now. It's about eleven in the evening. What made you go outside?''

Melinda jumped up from her chair and moved about the room with the agitation of a caged gazelle accustomed to running wild—graceful even in fear.

Quit! Concentrate on her face. You're supposed to be looking for the clues of a liar. Watch her movements. Listen to her voice. Find the person beneath the refinement and the silk.

''Something was going to happen. I could feel it.'' As if she were listening for a predator, she stopped for an instant. ''The monster!'' Her eyes grew wild. Her hands snapped to her chest, clutching the silk in her fists. "I couldn't breathe. The open screens felt like fortress walls." She resumed her restless pacing. "And I felt the crush. I had to go out. I had to leave."

"What monster?"

For a time he thought she wouldn't answer. Her eyes glazed over. Just as suddenly, they cleared again. He searched for signs of subterfuge, of calculation, and found nothing but the improbable impression that she was elsewhere, reliving a nightmare.

"I thought if I went to the park to see the ducks swim—" her voice cracked with emotion "—I could forget. I could disappear. I'd be okay when morning came. The ducks, they like to swim, and watching them relaxes me." As she spoke, her arms twitched and jittered.

"What monster, Melinda?"

He had to strain to hear her whisper. "I don't know."

"You never made it to the park," Desiree reminded.

Melinda stood still like a gazelle who'd spotted the lioness trailing her. "Everything was black."

"Except when the lightning flashed. What did you see then?"

She shook her head in short, snappy strokes. "I had to run. I had to hide."

She still wanted to run; he could see it in the tautness of her body, in the way she held herself prisoner with her arms, in the fear he could smell even through the glass. She wasn't faking, but what did this fear, this imaginary monster, have to do with what she'd seen at the Angela Petersen's?

"Where did you hide?" Desiree asked. "Retrace your steps."

"I ran to the shed." Melinda slunk back to the chair. Her body rounded itself into a tight ball—the same position he'd found her in at the bottom of the woodshed.

Again he got the impression that part of her was elsewhere, and he found himself believing in her unseen pain.

"The rain wouldn't stop. I couldn't see anything. I waited. I knew he'd find me. He always does." She rocked herself gently back and forth, and closed her eyes.

"Did he find you?"

"Yes!" Her eyes grew round with fear once more. Her fingers curled around the chair seat until the knuckles turned ghastly white, as if she were trying to keep herself from fleeing. "I tried to get away. He caught me. I had to fight." One hand flew to her mouth. "Oh, no! That was the police officer, wasn't it?"

"Yes."

"Oh, my! Oh, my! He looked like a dark blob, like the monster. I thought, I thought… I thought he would hurt me."

"Why did you think Lieutenant Sloan would hurt you?"

Melinda's face blanched, her eyes grew impossibly wide, but she didn't answer.

"Then what did you do?" Desiree asked, her voice soothing.

Melinda's chest rose and fell in jerky motions. "After he caught me, I left. I couldn't stay. I couldn't watch."

"Watch what?"

"I don't know." She closed her eyes tight. "Something horrible. Something horrible always happens when the monster comes out. I wish this whole mess would disappear. I wish I could just vanish."

Monster? Was she trying to put the blame for her actions on someone else, or was she simply crazy?

"Where did you go?" Desiree asked.

"Away, just away…"

Large tears shone in her eyes, magnifying their dark beauty. Grady wanted to believe the innocence he saw in them. He wrapped his fingers tightly around his biceps. But he couldn't. Not yet.

Desiree pulled a tissue from her purse and offered it to Melinda. She dabbed at the moisture and clamped the wet tissue into her closed fist.

Jamie had been beautiful, too. Bright and perky whereas Melinda was dark and mysterious, but beautiful nonetheless. They shared the same refinement, the same socially impeccable breeding. He'd been drawn by Jamie's eyes and her tears, too. And he'd let himself be lured into the honey of her voice, the soft tangle of her arms, the twisted web of her lies. He'd believed her, and she'd used him, lied to him.

Desiree's voice brought him back to the present.

"You're doing fine, Melinda," Desiree said. "The picture you drew, is that what you saw in the window?"

"I don't know." She shook her head slowly and lifted her arms in a helpless gesture. "Everything else is just like fog. I can't see through it. I can't remember how I ended up in jail." She wiped away the tears forming anew in the corners of her eyes.

Desiree retreated. "It'll take time and thinking to put all the pieces of the puzzle together. I want you to relax now, okay? I'll see what I can do about getting you home again."

"Thank you."

Desiree patted Melinda's knee. "It's important that you try and stay in the present. Try not to drift away." She pulled a business card from her purse. "This is my phone number. Call me if you want to talk again."

Melinda took the card and nodded.

A moment later, Grady met Desiree in the hall. Station noises filtered through the closed doors all around them. A burst of laughter erupted from the officers' locker room. The odor of coffee and Lois's cinnamon cake drifted from the briefing room. A radio crackled from the communications desk.

"Well?" he asked impatiently.

Desiree blew back a stray strand of hair from her forehead. "When you found her, she was exhibiting massive dissociation. She'd stepped aside from herself and turned off the apparatus that allows a person to fully perceive. She saw you as a monster. That's why she fought you."

He rubbed the back of his neck. "Why couldn't she remember what she saw in the window?"

"My guess is that it triggered something from her past that she couldn't deal with. She may have seen something, then repressed it, or seen it in an altered state and won't be able to retrieve it because it never fully registered, except maybe as fear and therefore something to avoid."

"How do I know which?"

"You don't."

"So how do I get her to remember?" Frustration hummed along his skin like the charge of electricity through a wire.

"She'll have to remember on her own." Desiree gave him a sharp look to emphasize her point. "Not everybody knows you as well as I do. To others you can come across as intimidating. You can't push her, Grady. It'll just delay the process because she'll be fighting."

"I don't have time to wait." He let out a long breath. A couple of cycles in an old-fashioned washing machine wouldn't have left him feeling as wrung out as he did at the moment. "Isn't there anything I can do to speed up the process?"

She shrugged her shoulders noncommittally. "There's hypnosis or Amytal."

"Can you do that?" He sensed he grasped at slippery straws.

"I'm not a psychiatrist. I can't prescribe. You can't try

either procedure without the patient's permission, and I doubt she'll give it to you. She doesn't want to remember.'' Desiree sighed. ''You could try taking her back to the place where you found her and see if that triggers her memory. Sometimes it works. Sometimes it doesn't.''

''What else can I do?''

She slung her purse over her shoulder and placed one hand on her hip. ''My professional advice is twofold. First, I'd advise her to go see a good therapist and let him deal with her. Dissociation takes practice. It has to have happened before, which means there's something unpleasant in her background. Second, don't get personally involved. Let someone else handle the case.''

''I can't.''

''You have to. With Ely—''

''—I'm the interim chief. It falls under my duty.''

''You'll get other chances.''

''Not in this town.''

She glanced at the oversize watch on her wrist. ''I've got to go, Grady. I want to check on Angela's parents and I've got to go over my notes before I testify in court this afternoon.''

''Thanks for your help.''

''Any time.'' She gave him a light kiss on the cheek. ''And get Doc Martin to look at that hand. Human bites are notorious for their infection rate.'' She took two steps down the hall and turned. ''Oh, I forgot to tell you. Aimee got her own class. Herb Findlay finally found a job. They're moving to Mississippi. Rosalyn had to give up her first-grade class and Aimee's taking it over. Isn't it great? She's been waiting so long to teach in her hometown.''

''That's terrific!'' He felt an ounce of genuine pleasure, and a touch of pride, for the first time that day. ''We'll have to celebrate on Sunday. It's your turn to cook, right?''

''I cooked last Sunday. It's your turn. Aimee really likes

that coconut cake you make. Keep me up-to-date on Melinda.''

With a wave of her hand, Desiree bustled out of sight.

Grady started to return to the interview room, when the telegraph-sharp click of heels drew his attention. He didn't need this now. But he turned anyway, and tried to present a pleasant front to Betty Brasswell, a regular busybody and general pain in the behind, not to mention Fargate's mayor. To give her her due, she did keep the town on its toes, and if something needed to be done, you could count on Betty to stir up the populace. Next to Seth, she was the most recognizable person in town.

Copper-colored curls bouncing, she clicked and clacked her way toward him.

''Grady, a moment of your time, please.''

''What can I do for you, Betty?''

Her long nose twitched as she spoke, sniffing trouble, no doubt. When Betty was around, nothing was sacred, and if her sharp ears or her news-sensitive nose got wind of anything, she investigated to protect her town. Abstract rotten tomatoes were tossed at her as often as flowers, but she didn't care. The town's welfare came first. Nothing else mattered.

''Is the young lady you brought in last night the perpetrator of this heinous crime the whole town is buzzing about?'' Betty asked.

''I don't think so, but the key might be hidden in her mind.''

''Then I suggest you retrieve that key immediately.''

''She's suffering from amnesia.''

Betty waved her hand in an impatient circle. ''Amnesia, pah! That only happens in storybooks. I've dealt with all kinds of human beings in over thirty years of public life, and I've never heard of a true case.''

''She's Ely Amery's daughter.''

Both Betty's eyebrows disappeared beneath the curly bangs of her hairdo and her mouth dropped open. She soon recovered from her momentary surprise. "Has her father been notified?"

That was Betty for you—town image first and foremost. Amused, he fought the smile itching to form. She'd view it as insubordination. "I don't think so. We just found out."

"Then you must release her at once."

"I thought you wanted the key extracted."

She leaned in and tapped his chest with her stubby finger. "Grady Sloan, must I remind you I don't support your position as interim chief. Your duty is to keep the peace. Do you know what kind of trouble Ely Amery could bring down on this town?"

"I'm well aware of it, ma'am," he answered.

"I assure you we do not want that kind of attention. Unless you have a darned good reason to hold this woman in custody, I want her set free."

She talked to him as if he were still the six-year-old who'd accidentally trundled right into her when he was learning to ride his two-wheeler. No wonder he got no respect; her memory was too long.

"Angela Petersen is one of ours," she continued. "It's up to us to make sure her murderer is apprehended and punished. I don't want to involve the State Police unless it's absolutely necessary. We don't want that kind of publicity. Do I make myself clear?"

"Crystal."

She gave one sharp nod. "Then I suggest you follow my orders. Let Miss Amery go. Let her believe she won't be bothered anymore. Then use whatever charm lies hidden beneath that tough hide of yours and sweet-talk the key out of her. It works for an old civil servant like me. I'm sure it will work for an officer of the law, as well."

Mayor Brasswell turned on her heel and clicked away before Grady could comment. He reached for the interview room's doorknob.

Yeah, simple thing. Charm a beautiful lady out of her secrets. Should be easy. Except this beauty had been sired by a snake. Except he didn't enjoy subterfuge. Except the prospect of seeing more of Melinda Amery appealed to him about as much as facing a plate of broken glass for dinner.

Chapter Three

Grady drove Melinda back home in silence. The semicircle that made up Laurel Court stood on Fargate's easternmost boundary, out of his regular beat, but like all of the officers in town, he was familiar with every street. When he shut off the squad car's engine in her driveway, he knew his action had taken her by surprise.

"Thank you for taking me home." She opened the door.

The dismissal in her voice sounded like a lady's to her servant, and rubbed him the wrong way. "I want you to take a little walk with me."

Her gaze snapped up at him. "I thought you said I was free."

"You are. I'd just like you to show me the path you took last night."

She fiddled with the folds of her skirt. "I—I really need to take a shower and change, Lieutenant. Perhaps another time."

"You're here. I'm here." He smiled and cocked his head. "There's no better time."

They stared at each other, but even a lifetime of ordering servants about couldn't match the intense defiance of an underdog who dared look his master in the eye. As he'd expected, she looked away first. Her downcast lashes made dark fans against the pale satin of her skin. The tiny victory rang hollow, but he cast the uneasiness aside. Finding Angela's murderer was more important than feelings—his or hers.

"All right." She sighed, slipped out of the car, and politely closed the door.

"Show me what you did when you came home last night."

She nodded and headed toward the front door. He followed, his mind cataloging everything he saw.

From the prim and proper way she'd sat beside him on the drive, he'd expected lace curtains at the windows, dark antique furniture placed in a stiff and formal fashion, and delicate doilies spread strategically on the backs and arms of velvet chairs. What he found jarred his preformed image.

Melinda had brought the outside in. She'd painted the walls the pale blue of a summer sky and left the trim around the five floor-to-ceiling windows and French doors white. A handwoven carpet, in shades of green, had been laid over a polished wood floor. The furniture was rattan with cushions in a print of light green and terra cotta. Plants, in clay pots and baskets, in all shapes and sizes, decorated the floor, tables and even a pedestal or two. Windows unobstructed by curtains opened onto a magnificent view of an enchanted garden and led the eye to the wide-open cow pasture beyond.

"I came home and went to the kitchen." As if she expected him to leave momentarily, she stood by the door.

He nodded absently and continued his slow, deliberate examination, wondering still at the odd return of her memory in fits and starts. If he played it cool, pretended it didn't matter, would her memory return faster?

After taking in the whole, he focused on the details. A cream-colored afghan lay haphazardly over a rattan footstool. A book was carelessly dropped on it. The imprint of her body shaped the chair's cushion with delectable curves. A half-drunk cup of tea rested on the table beside the single chair. Garden and decorating magazines poked up from a basket on the floor. The smell of earth and flowers scented the air. This was a room to relax in.

Almost as startling as what he saw, was what he didn't. No television sat in the room like the modern Buddha found in most homes. There were no pictures on the walls, or photographs on the tables. A solitary chair.

No signs of a man.

She'd built a private world for herself. He sensed his intrusion in it wasn't welcome.

Every surface was neat and clean, except one. Rain had fallen through the open windows and had pooled all over her expensive wood floor.

"Do you have a mop or some towels? If the water sits on this wood much longer, you'll have quite a repair job on your hands."

She hesitated and finally dropped her death grip on the front door's brass knob.

He followed her down the hall to the utility closet. She jerked it open.

"What's this?" Grady asked, spotting wads of crumpled paper tossed recklessly into the back of the closet. An odd place to keep trash in such an orderly little house.

"Nothing. Just sketches I've been meaning to throw out."

"Can I have one?"

She shrugged, but her face had taken on an unhealthy ashen color. Fear—strong and barely controlled. Once again she gave him the impression of a gazelle poised for flight. *"Nothing"* indeed!

He squelched the pressing instinct to protect, to nurture. He couldn't protect her. He didn't dare. No. This time, he'd have to press and crack. He'd have to play the hunter even if it meant hurting the prey.

She watched him with her fearful dark eyes, her breath tense in her chest. He thought she'd burst. And she did. With a flash of movement she shoved the broom aside, snatched the mop and a bucket and shot to the living room, brushing her arm against his in the process. A zing of pleasure shot up his arm. From his heightened awareness, a good cop's asset, he deduced; not from her.

Clearing his throat, he crouched to pick up a wad of paper and pressed it flat on his knee with the palm of his hand. The streaks of black pencil on the white paper startled him with their viciousness. On first viewing, they appeared like the mad slashings of an angry child. But as he kept looking, the lines below the slashes took shape.

He unfolded wad after wad to find the same mysterious layers of perception beneath the concealing surface. And in every one of the pictures, hidden in the zigzags, he found a glinting knife held high by the indistinct shape of a human figure. Male or female? When had she drawn these? Did they relate in any way to the Petersen murder? What was she hiding? And why, always why?

Tucking a few of the sketches in his pocket, he couldn't get rid of the feeling they were a silent plea for help. He shook his head. Getting fanciful wouldn't solve his case for him. Miss Melinda Amery could buy all the help she needed, *if* she needed it.

If anyone needed help, he was the one, because, God help him, even with Jamie fresh in his mind, he couldn't stop his insane attraction toward this dark-eyed woman. But he'd learned his lesson. Her father had taught him well. Beauty and innocence didn't always go hand in hand.

This time, Grady wouldn't be the one to lose. Yet, as he straightened and went back to the living room, he couldn't escape the notion he'd missed something important in those fevered lines. Something crucial. About her. About the case.

"When did you draw these pictures?" He watched the soft curves of her cheeks, the contrast of black hair and white skin, the nuances shifting like night shadows across her still face. Absently he licked his lips. Would her skin taste as creamy as it looked?

She wrung the waterlogged mop into the bucket. Her hair cascaded down, hiding her face. "I don't know. I just found them there. I meant to throw them out."

"So you said. Why did you draw them?"

She paused, resting her hands on top of the mop handle. Anyone else watching her would probably have missed the slight tremble of her fingers as she grasped the wood. How long had fear been part of her life? How long had it eaten at her this way? And his questions, his pressing, weren't helping her find the island of balance she so obviously had sought when she'd decorated her home.

Her chin lifted in a pulse of defiance. The dash of grit beneath the porcelain-perfect exterior sent a surge of excitement through his veins. She'd had enough—for now. If he continued pressing, he risked permanent antagonism. He didn't want that. The game had barely started.

He prized truth and honesty; there'd been little else to hang on to as he'd grown up. Mazes and puzzles had fascinated him from an early age. Finding the true path among the distractions brought a sense of triumph. Even now, nothing fired him more than solving a mystery.

"Unless you're arresting me," she said, "I don't think I have to answer any of your questions."

"Cooperation with officers of the law looks so much better, though."

"How far does cooperation go? I think I've done my share." Her smile didn't reach her eyes and her voice iced with polite civility. "Perhaps I should file a complaint of police harassment. How would that look on your record?"

"Is that a threat?" He matched her proper tone and rime-cold smile.

"Look, Lieutenant, I've had a bad night." A certain weariness crept into her voice. "I woke up in jail with no idea how I got there. You all but accused me of murdering my neighbor. And I came home to rainwater all over my floor. I need a shower, a meal and a nap. I suggest you leave before I call your superior and complain."

He strolled about the room, looking but not touching; not wanting to press the issue, but knowing he had to, for Angela's sake.

"Fair enough, Miss Amery." He gave her his best smile. Her weariness swam to him in a long wave. It took a stiff shrug to dislodge the sympathy for her plight that suddenly settled over him. "But be warned. I'll be on you like a tick on a dog until I get the information I need from you."

The pink of anger flushed her cheeks. Her eyes shone like the polished Apache Tears Aimee had kept in her rock collection.

"Then I'll have my father's legal tweezers remove you. Leave me alone, Lieutenant Sloan. I don't know anything that can help you, and I'm not planning on taking any trips down memory lane for your benefit."

"But you do know something," he whispered into her ear as he came to a stop next to her. Her shoulders flinched up in instinctive reaction. "As a matter of fact, I think you know everything. In here." He touched her temple and found the cool skin even softer than he'd expected. He let his finger linger for a moment before he drew it back. "And you see, it's just not in my nature to let an injustice go unpunished."

He switched to her other side with one smooth motion.

She held her ground, though the tense lines of her body betrayed her desire to run.

"An innocent woman died, Miss Amery. Your neighbor. A twenty-two-year-old girl. I imagine she'd probably been in your garden countless times, sniffing all those pretty flowers you have there. Who could resist such a pretty sight? And someone slashed her to death. Someone took a knife, jabbed her repeatedly with it, and left her to bleed to death on her living-room carpet—"

"Stop it!" The mop clanged to the floor. Melinda clamped her hands over her ears, but didn't budge from her spot on the wet wood floor.

"That's just it, Miss Amery. I can't."

He switched sides again, just to keep her off-balance—the way a good cop should—and noticed the quiver of silk over the sensual rise of her breasts. The ravenous craving of hunter for prey intensified. He wanted her with such fierceness, he knew he had to draw back. If he didn't, he'd lose what few instincts he could trust.

"I won't be able to sleep until Angela's murderer is behind bars, Miss Amery." He drew closer, his lips a hairsbreadth away from her creamy skin. "Will you?"

SHE HATED HIM, MELINDA decided. Hated the guilt he piled on top of the fear. Hated the way his voice floated around her, soft and strong, insinuating itself on her psyche like fingers of mist around the moon on a cool fall night. She didn't need this. Not now. She'd already missed a good part of a workday, during the busiest part of the year, and there was too much to do to get the Christmas catalog out on deadline to waste time.

The sooner she got rid of this annoying police officer, the better. "If I show you what you want, will you go away and leave me alone?"

"That depends on what you give me."

His blue eyes were trained on her. She didn't like the feeling of being studied, of being classified and judged. He made her feel like a piece of evidence, and she didn't like the idea one bit.

The intensity of his gaze sent her nerves haywire with awareness of him—of his clean male scent, of the power coiled in his lean body. She'd been brought up to respect authority implicitly. But Lieutenant Sloan with his piercing blue eyes and his intriguing face didn't inspire respect; he inspired something baser, something she didn't want to contemplate in the least. That much intensity was far too frightening.

Like a bomb on the verge of exploding, she felt the fabric of her intentions straining. She hated September. Maybe it was because September should mean fall and cool weather, and in this part of North Texas, the sun still burned unbearably hot. Maybe it was the pressure of putting the Christmas catalog for her gardening mail-order business together before the end of the month. Or maybe it was simple paranoia. September seemed to catch her holding her breath, waiting for something awful to happen.

And this year it had.

And she was right in the middle of it.

And Lieutenant Sloan's piercing gaze promised he wouldn't relent until he'd explored all of her deep, dark secrets.

"You've got everything on tape," she said, proud her voice didn't betray her inner turmoil. "What more do you want?"

His face cracked into a wolfish grin, displaying the utter charm his dimples could have. "I want you…to show me the path you took last night."

He paused after the 'you' long enough that a shudder shafted through her. She groaned inwardly at the faux pas of having left herself open to his gutter interpretation, and at her instant and powerful arousal. She moved away from him with a jerky, stiff-legged gait.

"I went out through these doors because the noise of the rain on the roof was driving me crazy."

"Why does it do that?"

His breath felt hot against the back of her head. Apprehension snaked through her. "I don't know. It just does." She walked across the patio to the white wrought-iron table. "I picked up my sketch pad because it was getting wet."

Her body shook at the memory of the crazed lightning zigzagging across the sky, of the thunder rumbling like a warning over the countryside, of the trees swaying like bleached ghosts in an eerie dance lit by strobe-like flashes of light. She'd known she wouldn't find solace in her haven that night.

"I was going to watch the ducks float on the pond," she said. She didn't mention the panic, the immediate need to feel wide-open spaces, that had launched her into the dark night.

She stepped outside onto the stones arranged in a curving pathway to the front of the house. She could still feel the rain stinging her skin through the gauzy layers of her clothes, and how the nettling had reassured her she was still alive and not in some sort of hell.

"I went out this door and to the front." Melinda swung open the chain-link fence gate she'd painted black. She left the rough stone path and walked onto the grass. The spiky blades prickled the soles of her still-bare feet. "I cut across Lena's yard and Angela's yard."

As she stepped purposefully onto Angela's yard, anguish crushed around her. Memories threatened to seep through the fine cracks Lieutenant Sloan chiseled with his sharp gaze and his unnerving silence. She edged them back firmly, knowing instinctively nothing good would come from remembering.

Without knowing quite why, she stopped in front of the big picture window at the front of Angela's house, bringing her hands to her chest as if to hold her heart inside her body. Yellow police tape crackled in the breeze. Undeniable now—the fact that this was real after all, not just a nightmare. Her blood suddenly seemed to run cold, chilling her, and goose bumps raced up her arms.

Lieutenant Sloan's hot breath caressed her ear. "What did you see in the window?"

A flash exploded through her mind. She startled. Like a slide in a projector, the scene burst forward, every detail sharp, then faded to black.

Mouth wide open, she froze.

"What did you see?" he asked again, more insistent this time.

Her scream of terror iced and shattered inside her. The picture blinked against another faded one. Primitive survival instincts kicked in, flooding her body with adrenaline. Her rapid breaths matched the hammering of her heart. *Hide!* She had to hide.

Strong hands held her shoulders. She couldn't move.

"It's okay." His voice soothed her. "You're all right." Little by little, Lieutenant Sloan's insistent words tamped back the terror to the dark corner from which it had erupted.

He turned her around and pinned her with the mesmerizing blue of his eyes. His voice gentled. "What did you see?"

She broke their visual connection, concentrating on the blades of Bermuda grass at her feet. The brief vision was gone, and she had no intentions of stirring it up again. "Nothing. I saw nothing."

"Then how come you're so scared?"

She didn't know. She didn't want to know.

Melinda twisted away from his grasp and headed toward the woodshed. "I guess this is where you found me. It's not very clear in my mind. Whenever I try to picture last night, all I see is a strange blob. After that, everything goes fuzzy."

"We can try again later."

She pivoted back to face him. "No, we can't. I've been cooperative. You promised you would leave me alone."

"I said, it depended on what you gave me. I don't have what I need."

Hands on hips, she flung her cresting anger at him. "Then, Lieutenant Sloan, I suggest you do what my tax dollars pay you to do." One hand left her hip and pointed vaguely to someplace away from Laurel Court. "Get out there and find the person who killed Angela. Whatever you may think of me, I'm not the one who committed the crime. Why are you wasting your time with me?"

"'Waste'?" Lieutenant Sloan crossed his arms over his chest and cocked his head to one side. "The problem, you see, is that you can't remember what happened between the time you found yourself in front of this window and the time you woke up in our hospitable little holding cell. You fought me like a banshee, Miss Amery. You bit me hard enough to draw blood. Who knows what you could have done in your state of convenient amnesia?"

Panic needled her chest, making it hard to breathe. She couldn't have. She knew she couldn't. Angela had been a good acquaintance, if not a friend. She'd shared tea with her, shown her how to care for flowers. She'd listened to the small woman's heart-wrenching sorrow when Tommy Lee had left, and shown her how to bury the pain. Not in a million years could she have hurt her.

"I did not kill anyone."

The lieutenant reached forward to touch her cheek. She

shivered despite the sun's heat beating down on her. She fought her impulse to lean into the warm flesh of his hand.

"The last murderer I dealt with had big, innocent eyes just like yours. She swore she hadn't killed, either."

As if on cue, the cavalry arrived, giving Melinda an excuse not to answer. She spotted her father's gold-trimmed Cadillac gliding to the curb. With regal smoothness, he got out of his car and came toward her. A few more gray hairs salted his black hair since she'd last seen him at Christmas. A few more lines added distinction to his tanned face. But nothing else had changed. He still wore his charcoal French-couture suit with a red rose in the lapel, and he still walked as if he owned the world. He'd always been able to solve all her problems. Maybe she could lean on him once more. Leaning on Lieutenant Sloan would prove too dangerous.

"Daddy!" She ran to her father and bear-hugged him. "I thought you were in New York."

He returned her hug, then pressed her away to arm's length. "I flew in this morning. I called you at work, but Dolores said you hadn't shown up. When you didn't answer your phone at home, I came to check on you. What's going on here? You look a mess."

Disappointment made her heart sink to her heels. She couldn't depend on her father, either. She'd have to tell him about the monster and she couldn't do that. Her father honored order, discipline and temerity. He couldn't suffer fools or weakness, and in his eyes she'd often acted too weakly. She didn't want to add to his discontentment. She would have to handle the hard lieutenant on her own.

"It's a long story. My neighbor was murdered last night, and Lieutenant Sloan, here, was asking me some questions."

Her father's gaze connected with the officer who offered

him a crooked smile and an irreverent salute. "Grady Sloan. You're still wearing the blue."

"And proud of it."

When had they met? she wondered. No love seemed lost between them. If anything, the lieutenant's eyes had grown colder.

"Chief Mullins let you investigate a murder?" her father asked, making it sound as if this particular officer wasn't worthy of the title.

"Chief Mullins has taken ill. I'm the interim chief." The lieutenant's voice had taken on that quiet authoritative quality she'd first noticed about him.

Her father whistled. "How'd you get past Brassy Brasswell?"

"My good looks and charm. Same as you." He flashed his famous dimples, but there was no warmth in the gesture.

Her father laughed. "I'll be sure and look up the defendant if you manage to arrest one."

One of the lieutenant's eyebrows rose. "Then start with your daughter, Amery. She had opportunity, and she's trying to use amnesia as a defense. How many amnesia cases win?"

Her father didn't even blink. "Depends on the quality of the attorney."

"Or how low they're willing to go. You won't get me a second time."

Her father was enjoying himself tremendously. Her uneasiness grew with each passing minute. The last thing she needed was her father and her accuser locking horns. On the other hand, it might make Lieutenant Sloan forget all about her.

"That, of course, is still to be seen." Her father wrapped one arm around her shoulder. "I certainly hope you haven't committed an error in procedure and badgered this poor witness without giving her a chance to call her attorney.''

"All the information was given on a strictly voluntary basis."

"If you know what's good for you, Sloan, you'll keep away from my daughter."

The lieutenant seemed to swallow back a remark. He nodded in Melinda's direction. "I'll be back."

He strode to his squad car, leaving her feeling as if she'd just survived a tropical storm.

"You're under no obligation to answer his questions. You know that, don't you?" her father demanded.

"Yes." But Lieutenant Sloan's presence seemed to scramble her otherwise sensible brain.

"If he bothers you again, call me. I'll take care of him." Her father squeezed her shoulder affectionately and led her back toward her house. "I have an even better idea. Why don't you come back to Fort Worth with me? Keep me company until these country cops take care of their little drama."

But Melinda needed the safety of her home. The cold, empty feel of her father's huge house would only depress her more. She needed to know she could take care of herself this time. "I can't, Daddy. I've got too much to do at work."

"You don't need that job. I never liked the idea of you working with Dolores in the first place."

She shook her head without energy. "It's what I want to do. It makes me feel closer to Mom."

"I'm afraid you'll get hurt again. Besides, I need someone to play hostess for me while I'm in town. There's going to be such a big fuss made over the Campbell case. I need you with me."

Ever since he'd considered her old enough, her father had cajoled her into playing hostess for him. Plenty of women had wanted the title, but he'd insisted no one could fill the role as well as she. She'd hated every second of her official duties. They tended to make her feel ill at ease, inadequate—a feeling her father unwittingly reinforced with his couched, yet negative comments. Which had left her with no other option but to prove to him that she could be a success in her own right.

"I'm good at what I do, Daddy. I won the American Business Catalog Association's Achievement of Excellence award for marketing last year."

He turned her toward him, holding both shoulders in his capable hands. "I don't like the idea of you being alone out here when there's a murderer on the loose. These cops down here aren't used to trouble. They can't protect you."

"In case you hadn't noticed, I'm all grown up. I'm twenty-eight. I can take care of myself."

He looked down at her water-stained silk shell, her ripped skirt and her dirty legs. "I can see that." He hugged her close. "I'll take care of you."

"No, Daddy." She pushed him away firmly, feeling in control for the first time that day. "I want to stay here."

The sarcasm in his voice had hurt her more than she cared to admit. When would he realize her ambitions didn't aim for high-profile accomplishments like his? Her house, her garden, her catalog were enough for her. She didn't want fame and fortune.

She wanted peace.

IT NEVER RAINS, IT POURS, went the old axiom. But that cliché didn't come close to covering the deluge inside her. This storm was turning into a full-fledged tornado.

Melinda, fresh from a shower and a change of clothes, toweled her hair dry. The hot stream of water hadn't evaporated her roiling anger. Nor had the cold sting frozen it out. She loved her father. He was all the family she had left. But sometimes—almost every time they spent more than five minutes together—he infuriated her. She knew he didn't mean to hurt her. He expected her to be as tough as he was. And she knew she'd let him down.

Somehow, she always did.

At least this time she'd stood her ground and refused to be swayed by him. She was still at home. He'd left. But the air inside her house still reeked with the scent of his spicy cologne and the heaviness of his persuasion. She needed fresh air, sunshine and space—lots of space.

She ran a comb through her hair and headed toward the park, carefully skirting Angela Petersen's house. Why the town council had designated this patch of land a park, Melinda would never understand. It consisted of a dip in the land between barren hills that was filled with water. The town had tried to grow grass, but the budget didn't allow for watering in the summer. Long ago burned by the sun, what little grass remained was a crisp yellow. Three scraggly trees, growing at the edge of the pond, offered their thick, gnarled roots as nesting grounds for a family of ducks. An asphalt path circled the pond and two weathered benches stood on opposite shores.

A few mothers brought their toddlers to feed bread to the ducks; otherwise the park remained mostly unused. Melinda didn't mind. She liked its solitude.

By the time she sat down on the farthest bench, she felt some of her calm returning. She watched the ducks swim in lazy circles on the water and let her mind drift.

For a moment she'd been attracted to Grady Sloan. The sure intensity he emanated seemed so stable compared to the emotions spewing inside her like springtime hail. She'd been tempted to bury herself in his arms and let him convince her that everything would be all right. She'd wanted to talk to him, to tell him about the monster. She'd half hoped he'd offer to put on armor and fight the beast himself.

A foolish move.

Another moment of weakness.

Counting on anyone but herself would only lead to heartache and disappointment. Her previous knight-in-shining armor had proved to be a toad in disguise.

She turned her face to the sunshine and closed her eyes, gaining strength from the warm rays. She prayed the sun would shine for the rest of September. Three more weeks. That was all she asked for. Three more weeks. She'd get through them just fine.

Feeling better than she had since last night's storm had caught her off guard, Melinda went home.

As she slipped her key in the lock, a voice called to her. She turned to see Kerry Merrill, dressed in her Winn-Dixie uniform, hurrying toward her. Her eyes were red and puffy, and streaks of tears still glistened on her cheeks.

Melinda's heart went out to the short brunette. Kerry and Angela had been best friends for a long time. The two girls' giggles had often drifted on the breeze into her garden, and sometimes in lonely moments, she'd envied their sisterly bond. "How are you holding up, Kerry?"

That set off another stream of tears Kerry tried to stem with ineffective swipes of her hands, soaking the bandage covering one of her palms. "I can't believe it. I just can't believe it. Angela's dead." Her voice had a strident tone to it that bordered on hysteria. "How could this happen?"

"I don't know."

Big, watery brown eyes pleaded up at her as she grabbed Melinda's wrists. "You were here. Did you see anything?"

Pressure again. It built in Melinda's chest, shortening her breath. All the relaxation she'd managed to gain at the duck pond drained in one instant. "I'm afraid not."

Kerry's grip fell away. She moved in slow, zombie-like steps until she faced Angela's house. "I—I can't go in there."

"I don't think you're allowed to until the police tape goes down."

"But Rusty, he'll miss Angela." A deep frown creased her forehead, as if amid the horror she needed to hang on to something real, something alive, and so she'd settled on Angela's cat. A living tie between them to ease some of the pain. "He won't understand she's gone. I came to get him. But I can't find him."

A look of utter dejection crossed Kerry's face and fresh tears sprang from her eyes. "I've got to find him."

Melinda's tears almost joined Kerry's. Instead, she hugged the girl who now shook with grief. "It's all right, Kerry. I'll keep an eye out for him. When I see him, I'll call you. Okay?"

That seemed to calm Kerry somewhat. She sniffed and backed out of Melinda's embrace. "I'm sorry. I didn't mean to get so blubbery. It's stupid, I know, but Angela loved Rusty."

Melinda squeezed Kerry's arm gently. "It's okay. I understand. I'll look out for him."

They spoke for a few more minutes before Kerry left, then Melinda stepped inside her home, feeling drained once more.

The green message light on her answering machine blinked feverishly. She turned away, planning to ignore its beckoning call, then with a sigh, she pressed the message button.

"Melinda, this is Dolores. Where are you? There's a problem with the mock-up. I really need for you to come in." There was a crackling pause. "Are you all right, kiddo? Call me, okay? If I don't hear from you soon, I'm coming over. By the way, did you know your father's in town?''

Beep.

''Melinda, this is your father. Dolores says you didn't show up for work this morning. Give me a call so I won't have to worry about you.''

Beep.

''Melinda! Where are you?'' Her father again.

Two hang-ups.

''Miss Amery, this is Lieutenant Sloan.'' His voice startled her. It came clear and crisp over the tape, causing a rush of emotions almost identical to the one he'd created in person. Why couldn't he be on her side? ''I need to see you again.''

Simple words that could be taken so many ways.

Fear mounted once more, tiny at first, a mere granny knot in the pit of her stomach. Then it grew into Gordian proportions.

She couldn't remember much about last night. Some parts still lay in a cloud of fog. Always would.

Maybe remembering her fear's origin could extinguish her nightmare.

But the thought of searching through the black folds of her memory had her gripping the kitchen counter's edge as if her life depended on it.

What if...? But she couldn't have. She unglued her hands from the countertop, and turned them over to look at the palms. She simply wasn't capable of killing.

Or was she?

A butcher-block knife rack stood next to the sink. She reached for the largest handle and drew out the blade. Hand fisted over the handle, she lifted the knife above her head. With a decisive movement, she sliced the air. The descending blade whooshed and caught a shaft of afternoon sunlight. With a gasp, she jettisoned the knife into the sink, heard it rattle against the stainless-steel sides. Scurrying backward, she reached for her heart with both hands to steady its racing drum. Her gaze flicked back to the knife rack on the counter. Two empty slits, dark and wide, became magnified by her awareness of them.

Two slits.

A knife was missing.

Her knife.

She turned her attention back to the answering machine, fighting the tears misting her eyes.

How long would it take the lieutenant to find the real murderer? With a shaking finger, she pressed the rewind button.

He wouldn't give up. He was too persistent.

And what if the answer he found was her?

Chapter Four

The watercolor sat propped on top of Melinda's computer terminal. It pictured the featured item, a metal Victorian rose arch, in sharp detail. Her paintbrush had stroked the pink, purple, and blue morning glories decorating the arch, and the couple kissing beneath it, against a background of misty, dreamlike haze.

She should be working on the president's letter for the inside front page of The Essential Gardener's Christmas catalog. Instead she fiddled with the copy for the rose arch that would go in the spring catalog. The letter had to be done for her two o'clock meeting with Dolores tomorrow, but she just couldn't muster the enthusiasm needed for the task. She hoped to have the Christmas catalog in final layout by Thursday and the whole thing dumped at the printer's by the weekend. Another two weeks and this catalog would be out of her hands and on its way to the customers—one week ahead of schedule.

If she was lucky, which lately hadn't been the case.

Then she'd have a day or two of breathing space before she started on the spring seed and tool catalog.

Not that she was complaining. She loved her job. Not only did she get to indulge her fancy in painting and writing, she also got to show off her organizational skills. Usually, the painting and writing parts came easily. The juggling of deadlines, office politics—even in this family-like atmosphere—and various outside support companies were the things that drove her crazy. But today she stared at her painting and didn't feel the pretty words flowing, didn't like what she saw, and didn't want the feelings she wasn't quite sure how to handle.

After a fitful night's sleep, filled with black twisting nightmares of Angela Petersen, Lieutenant Grady Sloan, herself and flying knives, she'd woken up to morning sunshine and routine expectations, and both had brought a measure of balance to her whirling mind. Work, she understood. It was concrete. Her nightmares weren't, and therefore were better off ignored. She'd arrived at the office and plunged into her work with feverish zest, catching up on yesterday's absence by lunchtime. Not until a moment ago when she'd cued up her disk to the proper spot for her write-up on the rose arch, did she realize how much Grady Sloan had infiltrated her unconscious.

The man, bending over the woman to kiss her, bore a striking resemblance to the determined lieutenant, and she knew—even though the woman's back was turned to the viewer, even though she'd painted the waist-length hair blond, even though she would never wear such constricting clothes—she knew the woman was herself. In spite of her fears, in spite of her dislike, something about Grady Sloan inspired crazed fantasies of comfort and security.

But succumbing to those fantasies would be pure stupidity. And years of growing up beneath her father's stern thumb had made sure she wasn't stupid. Grady Sloan's interest in her wasn't the man-for-a-woman kind, but the cop-looking-for-a-murderer kind. And there was just enough fog in her mind to make her think that maybe, just maybe, the killer he wanted might be her. If she'd done something as uncharacteristic as biting a police officer when she'd mistaken him for the monster, couldn't she, under the same misconception, have killed Angela?

The mere thought roiled the acid in her stomach into a nauseating wave. Why had she skipped lunch again? She closed her eyes and shook her head. She, who couldn't squash a bug, simply couldn't have committed murder— monster or not. She had to believe that, or she'd really go crazy.

Inhaling a deep breath, she hoped to clear her mind of her contradictory thoughts. With a cleansing sigh, she placed her fingers on the keyboard, focused on the painting, conveniently ignoring the couple under the arch, and lost herself in the watercolor mist.

The sky, a pastel palette... "No, no, the rhythm's wrong." Her little finger pressed the 'delete' key.

The morning was going to be special.... "No, not right. Sounds like a breakfast cereal." Delete.

In the soft mist of the purple and pink dawn, he came to her. "Yes, that's it." *She'd waited beneath the blooming flowered arch among the scent of roses, the song of birds, the lifting night—waited for him, unsure. His footprints disturbed the dew on the grass and his smile shone just for her. Alone. Finally. No phones, no interruptions, no wordly demands, as if the city had floated away, leaving them surrounded by a country paradise. She went into his open arms. He fit his lips to hers. They both remembered the kiss long, long after it had ended. They both remembered the magic they'd found in her garden beneath the rose arch on a special summer morning.*

"Victorian Rose Arch." *Beautifully hand-wrought of a quarter inch by three-quarter inch flat iron and treated with a weatherproof coating that will last for years of enchanting—*

A commotion near the front door disturbed Melinda's concentration. Recognizing the voice, she snapped her head up. She lifted herself a few inches off her chair to look over the partition of her work station.

The first thing people noticed about Dolores, her partner, was her hands. She seemed incapable of carrying on a conversation without waving them about like semaphore flags. And right now her sun-wrinkled, smiling face and fluttering hands were pointing Lieutenant Grady Sloan in her direction.

Melinda groaned. She didn't need this aggravation right now. She shuffled papers about until she found the item number and price for the rose arch.

Of course, Dolores would have fallen for his charm. He looked as gentle as a golden retriever with those deep dimples flashing. But Dolores hadn't yet had the pleasure of coming up against his pitbull-like determination. Melinda had. And she didn't like it one bit.

She reached for the phone, intending to call her father, then hesitated. No, not this time. For her mental health, she *needed* to handle this situation on her own.

Returning her fingers to the keyboard, Melinda typed the rest of the information with a speed she didn't know she possessed. But even the clicking of the keys and the low cacophony of office noises couldn't drown the sound of Grady's sure steps bringing him closer to her cubicle. The clean scent of his soap reached her before he stopped and leaned over the partition, making her type gibberish just to keep her fingers moving. *Wonderful, Now I'm acting like…like a suspect, for goodness' sake!* Not quite the poised impression she'd hoped to make.

"Good afternoon, Miss Amery."

"What can I do for you, Lieutenant Sloan?" Her fingers never paused over the keys, and she didn't look up. She didn't want to see the disturbing blue of his eyes, didn't want to know if his charming dimples creased his cheeks for her as they had for Dolores, didn't want to feel the accusation etched in every line of his face.

"Is there somewhere we can talk privately?"

"I'm a very busy woman."

"I can see that." He leaned closer and lowered his voice. "But do you really want your employees to hear my questions?"

Her heart's rhythm increased, pounding her blood in deep whooshes past her ears. She lifted her head with measured control to look at him.

The slow, deliberate sweep of his gaze over her work area seemed to take in every detail. What did he see with those piercing eyes? What conclusions was he drawing? Thank goodness he couldn't see her painting or her computer screen from his vantage point. She'd hate for him to know he disturbed her so much. "What kind of questions?"

"Regarding your memory."

Her fingers went spastic on the keyboard before they halted all motion. Her memory, or lack thereof, was the last thing she wanted to talk about. His determined gaze finished his meticulous perusal of her cubicle, then it skewered her, and she knew relief would come only if she attempted to humor him. There was nothing to remember. He'd simply have to accept that fact. The sooner the better.

She averted her gaze to the gibberish on the screen. "Give me a minute to finish my copy and I'll meet you outside," she answered, proud of the even, calm tone of her voice.

"I'll be waiting."

Though she concentrated on her computer screen, Melinda heard the teasing promise in his voice. Why did he enjoy torturing her so much? She remembered the visceral verbal sparring he'd shared with her father yesterday. *You won't get me a second time,* Grady had said. Had she become a pawn in a power play between him and her father? What had happened between the two of them? Well, she had news for both of them. She wasn't going to play. She was much too busy.

Melinda jabbed the delete key and erased the two paragraphs of gibberish she'd typed, saved the rest of the material, and printed a copy. Nodding her approval, she slipped the sheet into its proper place on her mock-up. The deepening pain on the right side of her head warned her a major headache was on its way. She wouldn't get any more work done today. She grabbed her purse and her file and readied to leave.

Dolores came around the corner, perched herself on the edge of her desk, and gave Melinda a slow smile and a curious look. "A date?"

"What?"

"The cute cop. Is he business or pleasure?"

Melinda dropped the file in Dolores's lap. "Definitely business."

"Too bad."

"He's all yours if you want him," Melinda said, knowing Dolores wasn't above taking her place when she refused to go on the weekly blind dates the older woman arranged for her. The strange thing was, Dolores always seemed to have a good time with those men who were half her age.

"Thanks, but he looks a little too starched for me. Perfect for you, though."

Melinda straightened her purse strap on her shoulder. "If you weren't my partner, I'd fire you."

Dolores waved her comment away with a sweep of her work-roughened hands. "And if you weren't Abigail's daughter, I wouldn't have to worry about you so much. Having no men in your life isn't healthy."

Melinda smiled, another part of their weekly ritual. "In today's world, having too many is lethal."

Dolores snorted and laughed. The file on her lap fell to the floor. "I don't have to have 'em to enjoy 'em." As she jumped down to pick up the strewn pages, her single white braid bounced forward over her shoulder. "So what does he want?"

"The impossible."

Dolores glanced up and gave her a puzzled look. "Are you in trouble?"

Melinda shook her head. "I haven't done anything wrong."

Dolores looked up at her with a worried expression. "Are you going to tell me what's really going on?"

"Soon, I promise."

"I worry about you."

"I know you do, and I love you for it."

"Go on, then." Dolores straightened from her crouch. Her gaze strayed to the front door. "Don't keep your hunk waiting. I'd hate to see sweat stains ruin the perfect creases of his uniform. I'll hold down the fort."

"He's not *my* anything." *Except a thorn in my side.*

Dolores cocked her head sideways, her wide grin reaching almost to her ears. "Are we protesting a mite too much?"

"No, we're not." Melinda started to leave, then turned back. "By the way, that counts as your Melinda 'fix-up of the week.'"

"Ha, that's what you think! Wait till you see the dreamboat I've got lined up for you this Friday." Her smile faded and her pale-blue gaze sought Melinda's face. "Don't let life pass you by, hon. That's not what your mother would have wanted."

Swallowing hard, Melinda headed for the glass front doors. Between Dolores's parade of suitors and her father's not-so-subtle suggestions of eligible bachelors dying to meet her, she could have a date every night of the week if she wanted. But she didn't. As much as Dolores kidded Melinda about her romantic heart, Melinda sometimes wondered if she had a heart at all, if she was capable of loving someone with the fierce passion the imaginary people in her copy and her paintings loved each other.

As she wound her way slowly around the cubicles, Melinda gave a short, sharp laugh. Whatever had possessed Dolores to believe that someone like Grady Sloan would be perfect for her? She shrugged. None of Dolores's choices of dates for her had proved suitable. Why should this one irk her so much?

Lieutenant Sloan waited patiently in the bit of shade offered by the green canvas canopy. Dolores was right; he did look neat and starched as if he were to appear at a press conference in the next few minutes. His body stood in the at-ease position of a soldier, but his gaze never stopped its sweep of the surroundings. Was he ever completely still? Did he ever relax? She had the sudden impulse to dip him in a vat of bronze just to see him perfectly still for more than a minute. A tiny smile curled the corners of her mouth. The thought did hold some appeal. Bronzed, he couldn't possibly disturb her the way he did in the flesh.

When he saw her approaching, he gallantly opened the door for her. For a moment, she almost thought she'd made up her extreme impression of his presence yesterday. But when his body moved, a certain intensity took over, making him appear bigger than life and twice as dangerous.

At least to her.

"How are you doing, Miss Amery?"

How could the sound of his voice make her feel caged and comforted at the same time?

"Fine." She had a feeling he wasn't asking about her

health for idle reasons. Everything he said, everything he did, seemed to have a purpose.

"I'm glad to hear that. And your memory, has it all come back?"

Ah, yes, the memory. As they stepped into the sunshine, he pulled mirrored glasses from his breast pocket and slipped them on. A shudder of apprehension chilled her despite the afternoon sun's strong heat. If she couldn't see his eyes, how could she read his thoughts? How could she tell if he saw her as a killer or the unwitting victim she hoped she was?

"Most of it." And that last little bit made all the difference. The last little bit sent a fear greater than she'd ever known thrumming through her, eating away her hard-earned peace, stripping away her energy faster than a snowman would melt under the Texas sun.

Melinda walked down the long, paved drive to the farm-to-market road. Her house was half a mile from the warehouse they used as a combination distribution center, showroom and office. Most days she preferred to walk. Today, she'd like to fly and leave Lieutenant Sloan far behind.

"Can I give you a ride home?" Grady offered as they passed his squad car.

"No, thank you. I like to walk." Sharing close quarters with him sounded much too confining. She needed open spaces, not his cramped cage.

Grady fell in step next to her. He kept a polite distance between them. At least a foot separated their bodies, but he might as well have glued himself to her side the way her awareness of him encroached on her senses. Heat suffused her—an uncomfortable warmth that had nothing to do with the day's torrid temperature, and everything to do with the persistent policeman walking beside her.

"I'd like to go over the details of the incident," he said,

his voice solid, stable, filled with the quiet authority she was learning to despise.

Incident! Angela's death wasn't a mere *incident.* Melinda's gaze fixed on the ground ahead of her, a sudden irritation quickening her steps. The irritation hadn't come from the words, she decided, but from the impassive way he'd said them. The ''incident'' had turned her world upside down—not to mention that it had ended Angela's altogether. But she couldn't tell him about the nightmares, and he'd never understand her silence.

''It was a murder, not an incident,'' she said. ''Someone with a life, a family, with hopes and dreams, died. Angela Petersen is not a faceless, nameless corpse.''

''I agree.'' As they turned onto the road's shoulder, he gave her one of his quick, observant glances, making her shiver in a purely physical reaction. ''I'm glad you'll cooperate. Let's start with the moment you decided to leave the house. Did you ta—''

''I'd really rather not think about that night.''

''I'm afraid you don't have much choice, Miss Amery. We can do it here or down at the station, but either way, I will get a statement from you.''

Melinda spun to face him, arms crossing under her chest. The country road's traffic flowed at regular intervals, whipping her hair into her face and whirling the rayon of her dress around her legs with each car's backwash. ''It was raining. I went out because I couldn't stand the noise. I went out to the front of my house, cut across Mrs. Strong's lawn and Angie Petersen's. Everything else is in a fog until I woke up in your jail.''

As she spoke, he nodded, and she could practically hear the clicks as every word was being cataloged for future reference. ''I need more.''

''I don't have more!'' Her fists clenched by her side. ''How can I get that through your thick skull?''

She wanted to slap him across the face and jar his computer-like brain out of whack. She wanted to stamp her feet in frustration. She wanted to growl at him. But instead, she resumed walking calmly, politely toward her house. Seeing an opening in the traffic, she jogged across the road. She'd been raised as a lady, she would act like a lady—even if he irritated the stuffing out of her.

"I'd like for you to agree to an Amytal injection," Grady said, rejoining her.

Melinda spun, forcing him to check his gait mid-stride. "No!"

"Come on, you didn't even think about it."

"I don't have to. I won't do it." She swiveled away from him, heading blindly toward the oasis of her home, wrapping her arms around herself to keep from shivering in the sudden chill.

"How about hypnosis?"

"No!"

"You're not being very cooperative."

"And you're not listening. I don't remember anything. I don't want to remember anything. I live in the present, Lieutenant Sloan. I look forward to the future. I don't have time for trips into the past. No Amytal. No hypnosis. Can I make myself any clearer?" She didn't wait for his answer, but turned into the entrance to Laurel Court.

"You're putting me in a very difficult position." Grady's breath fanned against her hair. Instinctively, she took a sidestep away from him.

"And you're putting me in an awkward one. I truly would like to help you. But digging into my psyche is something I simply cannot allow."

"Why not?"

She sighed heavily, not knowing how to answer without sounding as if her brain lacked a few vital parts. Sometimes it felt that way. As if she'd been robbed of part of her life. But the thought of exploring those black holes petrified her. What monsters would she unearth? What was so horrible that her mind had chosen to hide the memory away from her? Her life was fine the way it was. She had her work, her garden. What more could she possibly want?

Her gaze strayed to Grady's strong profile. *Having no men in your life isn't healthy.* Well, she didn't need a man. She liked being on her own. With one to answer to.

Grady reached up to lift a low-hanging branch from one of the live oaks lining the curves of Laurel Court. His fingers accidentally brushed against her shoulder, sending a small thrill all through her limbs. The aura of his strength enveloped her and a dull ache penetrated her chest.

No one to hold her. No one to share with. No one to love her.

Not that Grady Sloan was the right choice for her. He was all wrong. She needed… She needed… Well, whatever she needed, Grady Sloan didn't have it. He tormented her. He irritated her. He—

The black sedan parked in front of Angie's house caught her attention, bringing instant relief. "Angie's parents are here. I'd like to offer my condolences."

For now, she could escape the emotion-stirring self-assurance of Lieutenant Grady Sloan. But she wasn't fool enough to think the respite would last.

SHE WAS RUNNING AGAIN. Running from him. On a professional level, her disquiet pleased Grady. Her agitated state could only mean he'd hit a nerve. Yet part of him—the part he'd learned to question—sensed there was more to her agitation than the key he needed to solve his case.

He hadn't planned on stopping at The Essential Gardener, but as he'd passed the warehouse he now recognized as her workplace, he'd turned in, drawn irresistibly, it seemed, toward the building. How he'd known she was there, he couldn't have said. But he'd known. A good cop's instincts, he'd rationalized, only to have the image of her dark eyes beckon him and belie his explanantion.

Official business, he'd justified, then scrambled for a reason for his presence until frustration gave him an answer. Though he'd hoped she would, he'd known she wouldn't agree to the Amytal or the hypnosis. Desiree had warned him that she didn't want to remember. But he'd needed to prove to himself that, cleaned up and wrapped in her upper-class mantle of stiff upper lip, Melinda Amery couldn't twist his gut as strongly as she had yesterday. Then he could go back to putting his full attention on solving the case, and leave her haunting eyes behind.

Of course, reality hadn't deemed to agree with his expectations. Miss Melinda Amery had forgotten to wear her plastic smile. She'd forgotten to wear her power business suit. She'd forgotten to hide her fear from him.

His reaction hadn't been much better.

One look at Melinda had made his gut tighten. One breath of her flower-garden scent had made him forget for half a second why he'd dropped in to visit. One accidental touch had stirred his hunger for her so sharply, he'd thought it was impossible for a man to want a woman that much.

Concentrating on the details of her office hadn't helped. Her soft, flowing beige dress in a tiny-flowered print had blended beautifully with the tan walls of her functional, if not stylish, cubicle. The sketches tacked up on the padded walls, the unexpected superficial disarray of her brushes and paints had startled him for a moment, then he'd seen the hidden order and had almost smiled. Almost smiled, too, at the small stuffed monkey holding a half-deflated Mylar balloon that read Congratulations. Who would have thought Miss Melinda was the sort to go for sentimental nonsense? And in the reflection of the metal filing cabinet, he'd seen the gibberish her flying fingers had typed on her computer screen.

He'd wanted to hold her then, to tell her he would never hurt her, to promise the nightmare would come to an end. He'd wanted to kiss the fear away and replace it with desire. Why, he couldn't have said. She was everything he'd learned to loathe. Even reminding himself she was Ely Amery's daughter hadn't eased his need to comfort her. He resented all those primal needs she stirred in him—the possessive protectiveness, the ferocious anger, the lust, raw and fervent. Since he couldn't express any of those, he settled on controlled intimidation. Keeping her squirming would remind him of his duty; of the key she held locked in her head.

She wasn't his to protect. She wasn't his to have. She was his to crack and to extract the information he needed to put Angela Petersen's murderer away. Instead of strengthening his resolve, the notion left him chilled.

Grady cast his uneasiness aside and forced his wandering mind back to the task at hand. He watched Melinda as she offered Harold and Clarissa Hobart her condolences. He listened for the nuances beneath the words in the conversation going on around him as if he could peel away the layers to get to the truth.

Lies. He could feel them all around him, but he wasn't sure where they came from. Straitlaced Melinda? Or Angela Petersen's parents—the proper preacher and his meek wife?

Angie had been the youngest of twelve children. Her father's favorite. The Reverend Hobart had made no secret of his feelings toward Angie's angel voice. He'd deemed such a gift was heaven sent, and as such, was to be put only to God's service—not to encourage man's lustful spirits. He'd never approved of the sad country songs Angie loved to sing. Had he feared her power in those moments? Had he heard how she'd put her soul into them? Had his convictions been strong enough to resort to stopping the "sin" any way he could?

The reverend detached himself from the two women to face Grady. "Have you located the perpetrator of this crime?" Harold's stern features and set face showed Grady a man struggling to keep a brave front. Only the red, puffy eyes betrayed his grief.

"Not at this time," Grady said. "We won't give up until we find who killed your daughter."

"Have you spoken with that sinful ex-husband of hers?"

"We're still trying to locate him."

Harold's eyes darkened with anger. His jaw tensed. His hands encased in thin leather gloves curled into fists by his sides. Gloves? On such a hot day, they seemed out of place. But then the reverend also wore a dark jacket, a starched white shirt, and a tightly knotted tie. Maybe they'd stopped on their way to or back from the funeral parlor.

"When is Angela's service?" Grady asked.

"Tomorrow at one. We've just come from finalizing the arrangements. And to pick out a dress for her...final journey." As the reverend confirmed Grady's hunch, sadness once more enveloped the gray-haired man. "What can you tell me about the case?"

Grady felt sorry for Harold. He knew how devastating the loss of family could be. After losing his parents, he'd almost lost his sisters, too. And though he imagined the death of a child could create deeper layers of pain, he could understand a father's need to see his child's murderer punished.

"We don't have much to go on at this point," Grady said, lowering his voice to avoid adding more anguish to Mrs. Hobart's grief.

Harold Hobart often served as chaplain-on-call in cases where spiritual guidance and comfort were needed. He spent a considerable amount of time at the station reporting on his feelings and observations at accident scenes, often garnering information from grieving relatives or scared victims that helped solve cases.

"The profuse blood-spattering is consistent with a knife attack," Grady continued, knowing Harold understood the jargon of the trade and wanted its cold reassurance. "All indicators make it apparent the entire attack episode took place while the victim was in the living room. We believe she must have known her attacker. There were no signs of forced entry."

"Have you recovered the murder weapon yet?" As if the mere thought of the knife brought immense pain, Harold's jaw flinched.

"We're still looking for it. We're having some DNA tests done on blood samples we've found at the scene. We're hoping they won't all be Angie's and can help point us toward the perpetrator."

"Good. When will those be in?"

"I'm afraid they won't be back for a while. We'll need you and Mrs. Hobart to go by the station for fingerprinting, so we can eliminate your prints from the ones we've found at the scene."

"We'll be glad to oblige. You'll let me know if you find anything new."

"I'll do that."

Harold extended his hand to shake Grady's. "I appreciate it, Lieutenant Sloan."

"Please accept my deepest sympathies. I'll do my best to bring the murderer to justice."

"Thank you." Harold choked on his words and returned to his wife.

Away from his conversation with the reverend, Clarissa

Hobart had dabbed at her eyes with a sodden tissue, but did not speak a sound, except a few squeaks of utter despair. Melinda had tried to console the woman who appeared much older than her years, but Grady doubted she'd penetrated the mother's heavy anguish. The gentleness of Melinda's words, her easy compassion touched Grady. He wouldn't have expected such tender emotions from any of Ely Amery's progeny. He made a mental note to research Melinda's mother's background.

As the Hobarts' car drove away, Grady rejoined Melinda and caught her wiping tears from her cheeks. Before he could stop himself, he placed an arm around her shoulders, felt the fragile bones against his palm, and drew her to him. For a moment she leaned into him and her shoulders shook beneath his fingers, sending an answering shiver through him. But before he could analyze how good her body felt pressed against his, she inched away, and walked out of his embrace toward her home.

Mysterious Melinda of the dark eyes filled with fear, of the romantic heart reserved for her paintings—why did she hide in the refuge of her home built for one? What had the world done to her to create such an island? And why was he letting the soul-deep sadness swirling in her eyes get to him?

Could she truly be as innocent as she looked? Hadn't Jamie's big green eyes looked that innocent? But Jamie's hadn't had the underlying turmoil of fear and doubt.

The pain of the lesson Jamie had taught him still stung. His moment of weakness had forced him into the position of having to prove himself to the town council even when his record spoke for itself.

One mistake!

He didn't plan on making the same one a second time. His future, all he'd worked for, wasn't worth losing over a woman's sad eyes.

And certainly not Ely Amery's daughter!

As much as grace wasn't part of Desiree's genetic makeup, Grady knew patience wasn't part of his. And yet, just as work turned Desiree into a swan, Grady understood that only careful listening, watching and understanding would let him uncover the clues he needed to solve this crime.

Melinda didn't want to remember, but she'd have to.

And if he was going to get to the source of her fears, he'd have to start chipping at her carefully built wall now. Do it methodically. Do it without emotion.

Getting past her fortress would take patience. A lot of it. And time. More than he wanted to give.

Looking at the invisible burden weighing on her shoulders, the stiff lines of her back, the sensuous sway of her slender hips, Grady knew the task wouldn't be easy. For either of them.

Chapter Five

"Can I come in?" Grady asked.

Melinda paused with her key inserted halfway into her front door's lock. "Can I stop you?"

"I'd be back with a warrant." As if there were no question she'd acquiesce, he took his sunglasses off and tucked them into his shirt pocket.

She shrugged and feigned indifference. "Suit yourself."

He stepped into her house and overwhelmed the small space. "You can call your lawyer, if you'd like."

"There's no reason. I've already told you—there's nothing to remember." She turned away from his imposing frame, and headed toward the spacious view from the living room. In no time, she unlatched all the windows, letting the slow, warm breeze ease the stuffiness of the hot interior.

"I've got to change." Without waiting for a comment, Melinda edged toward her bedroom at the back of the house and softly closed the door behind her.

Expelling her pent-up breath and letting her purse slip from her shoulder to the floor with a thump, she sagged against the door. She hoped he'd leave. She didn't know how much longer she could keep up the appearance of being together. Already she could feel the widening cracks in her shaky front.

Hadn't she accepted his strength when she'd been unable to comfort Mrs. Hobart? She'd wanted to stay there, to turn into his arms, to feel his steady heartbeat against her hand. For a moment she'd forgotten he was here on business, that he didn't like her—not as a woman—that he wanted her memory.

Then she'd remembered.

She'd sidled as easily as she could from the solace of his arm, and had felt both like a fool and strangely bereft. Using all her willpower, she'd forced herself to step toward her house, hoping all the while he wouldn't follow.

Twisting her arms back, Melinda reached for the zipper of her dress and pulled it down. The soft rayon fell in a puddle at her feet. She grabbed a loose sleeveless top from her dresser and headed for the master bathroom. The stress of having Grady Sloan around, watching her every movement, had increased her headache to the point where she was sure the pounding could easily register a four on the Richter scale. While she filled a glass of water with one hand, the other grabbed the bottle of aspirin from the medicine cabinet. She shook out two tablets and swallowed them with the water.

Getting her father to help her out of this mess would be easy. One word, and he would see to it that Grady Sloan would keep his distance. Such a gesture would please her father, but it wouldn't do anything for her sagging self-esteem. Once again she would have failed, and Daddy would have had to rescue her.

The last time she'd stood up for herself, she'd found the relative peace of The Essential Gardener. This time, maybe she'd find salvation.

She rubbed her temples with her palms. On the other hand, Grady Sloan's presence was sweeping her in directions she didn't want to go.

He made her feel like a freak with his reminders of the

black holes in her memory—blank spots that had plagued her ever since she could remember; dark voids she associated with primal fear. Shouldn't a normal person want to find what monster filled the blanks? Shouldn't a normal person want to exorcise those hidden demons? Maybe she should accept she wasn't normal. She had no desire to uncover the past. It was dead and done.

Dead?

She shuddered.

Willing the aspirin to hurry up and work before she went crazy, Melinda spun out of the bathroom and into her room.

To make the situation worse, Grady's overwhelming presence made her question her choices. She'd seldom felt lonely before. She'd been content with the quiet life she'd made for herself. Shrugging, she jerked her closet door open. Okay, so maybe she'd envied the lives of other women her age—their marriages, husbands, children—but never for long. And never had she felt this burning need, radiating up from someplace deep inside her, for something she wasn't quite sure how to label and didn't dare examine too closely.

Something like a woman's desire for a man.

Shaking her head, she snatched a skirt from her closet and pulled it on as she walked toward the bed.

With a sigh, she dropped to the foot of her bed. To Grady, she wasn't a woman; she was a suspect. To her, he couldn't be a man; he had to remain the law. If he didn't... She shivered. Her insides churned in turmoil.

Closing her eyes, she willed the internal chaos to ease. How long would it take for the nightmares to fade this time? She'd been free of them since she'd defied her father and started the catalog business with Dolores.

Until two nights ago.

She didn't want to deal with the past. She'd spent most of her life perfecting living in the moment.

Feeling safe.

Until Angela's murder had reopened all the closed wounds of fear.

Now, the peace she'd earned had vanished. Nothing would ever be the same.

The past had come knocking. Soon she'd have to decide if she'd open the door. Not for Angela, not for Lieutenant Sloan, but for herself.

She wasn't ready. Not yet. She needed a plan. Time to think one through. Her very soul was at stake. She needed a little more time to deal with the consequences that lighting the dark might entail.

If she told him so, would Grady understand?

Probably not.

He was strong, solid, rooted in reality. What would he understand of monsters of the past, of stolen childhoods, of scarred souls? Pressed and starched as he was, what would he know of broken hearts and trodden feelings? An officer of the law, he certainly couldn't understand the necessity to hide.

Melinda let herself fall backward on the bed and stared at the ceiling, gathering strength with long, slow breaths.

Maybe if she took long enough, he'd just leave.

TWENTY-FIVE MINUTES AFTER Melinda had disappeared into the back of the house, she emerged. Grady hadn't been sure she would. He'd felt her turmoil in a tangible way; had felt it touch him, touch his heart. He told himself he didn't care. But he did. And he didn't like the idea of caring for Ely Amery's daughter. Didn't like the idea of caring for someone who reminded him of Jamie in so many ways.

The same, yet so different.

Melinda seemed to float into the room like a cloud. She wore a wheat-colored sleeveless T-shirt over a broom skirt seeded with a wildflower pattern. Her feet were bare. Nothing restrictive, Grady noted; everything flowing like a breath of wind.

"You're still here." Without giving him more than a quick glance, she grabbed a handled basket from a wicker shelf unit in the living room and headed for the kitchen.

"We haven't finished our discussion." Even her hair flowed freely, as if binding any part of her body would keep her from rapid escape. What was she so afraid of? Why did it matter?

"I thought I made my position clear." She grabbed a lunch-size paper bag from the fridge and made her way outside.

"You did. Now I need to find out why." He followed her onto the covered porch.

"I thought I made my position clear on that point also." She picked up a weed popper, a spade, pruners, a garden fork, and a bag of bulb fertilizer from a battered white table and added them to her basket.

"You did, but I'm not satisfied."

She turned to look at him then. He sucked in air as if he were being absorbed by a black star. Below the placid surface of her dark eyes lay a deep whirlpool waiting to be explored and drowned within. Disturbed by his thoughts, he looked away, falling back on his habit of analysis.

Satisfied. Two days ago, he would have said he was perfectly satisfied with his life the way it was. Now, a murder and an amnesiac witness later, he wasn't sure how to define the word.

The clinking of Melinda's tools in her basket and the *thwack* of the screen door announced she'd moved outdoors. He dogged her footsteps, breaching her space, reminding himself with every step that he was the authority, and her mind held the key he needed. He couldn't afford to see her as a woman.

In the wilds of her yard, her outfit looked like camouflage. Grady tore his gaze away from her to regroup. What was wrong with him? Had all his honed skills disappeared with Jamie's betrayal? Why couldn't he concentrate on the task at hand? This wasn't like him at all. Maybe he should talk to Desiree. He forced his attention back to his surroundings.

Stepping into her garden was like stepping into a fantasy world. Wildflowers and native plants grew as if they followed no rhyme or reason, inviting relaxation. Grady steeled himself. He couldn't relax. He had to focus on details. Look, listen, and learn.

What did he need to know about her to solve his case? How could he do it without getting involved? His position represented justice. He had to follow the law to the letter; only then would Angela's murderer get his, or her, just reward.

Dissociation takes practice. It has to have happened before, which means there's something unpleasant in her background. Desiree's words came back to him. *You get too personally involved. It's your strength, Grady, but it's also your weakness. You're asking for trouble.*

He had to find Melinda's "monster." To do that he'd have to earn her trust. That meant getting involved—getting in trouble. He could only hope that this time, the price wouldn't be his future.

As the minutes ticked by, he found his gaze seeking her once more. She crouched beside a flower bed, pulled at imaginary weeds, airing the soil with a garden fork as she went, totally oblivious to his presence.

Her delicate features invited thoughts of fragility. But fragile things and fragile people broke. Melinda had bent and adapted to whatever unpleasantness had plagued her life. The bending had left its mark, but it also underlined her strength. Looking at her garden, he knew she still believed in dreams. She'd bent, but hadn't broken. Which only made his task harder.

No gloves covered her hands, and for a moment, he envied the soil. Holding her close to him earlier had left him craving for more. Lust for her was against the rules. He sneered silently. Her father would have a picnic if he had an inkling of Grady's desires. Never mind the raking Brasswell would feel obliged to give him.

Melinda's shoulders relaxed degree by degree. The standoffish impression she'd presented at her office vanished in the magical entity of her garden. The stress lines across her forehead had smoothed down, transforming her into the picture of serenity.

And in a minute, he'd shatter that tranquillity.

Bracing himself for the task, he approached her and crouched beside her. *Get straight to the point. No sense dancing around the issue.* There was no time for gentler ways.

"What are you afraid of, Melinda?" "Miss Amery" seemed too formal for the invasion he had to make. "Melinda" rolled off his tongue much too intimately. What had happened to his perfect balance? She had him feeling like a boat in a storm, listing first to one side, then the other. Maybe the town council had been right to mistrust his abilities.

Her fingers kept moving, but tension rode up her shoulders, little bit by little bit. "I've got bulbs to plant."

"I'll help you." He reached for one of the brown bulbs in the bag.

She jerked the basket away. "I'd rather not. I plant by instinct."

Grady shifted to look more closely at her face, but her

long lashes hid her eyes. He didn't want to admit she intrigued him. But she did. The soft strength, the quiet fear, the dark beauty. They all stirred his senses in a way that wasn't mere curiosity, in a way that he couldn't afford to explore. "It hasn't been cold enough to plant bulbs yet."

"What do you know about gardening?"

Enough to understand that each plant in her garden had been sown with a mixture of love, sorrow and hope. "More than you think."

Her head snapped up. "What's that supposed to mean?"

Their gazes met—hers animated by a thousand feelings clipping by so fast, he felt sorry for the agitation he had to cause. But he had no choice.

She returned her attention to her garden, each gesture now complicated by nervous flutters.

"Is this where you bury your memories?" he asked, continuing to batter her wall while he could.

"Pardon me?"

When she looked up at him, wide-eyed, he knew he'd found the right thread to pull. "The things you can't bear to remember, do you work them into the soil?"

She dug her spade into the ground, making a hole much too deep for the bulb she intended to plant. "I don't know what you mean."

"Something is scaring you, Melinda. You live alone in this house, for one. What are you hiding from?"

Her mind seemed to drift when his message skirted toward the negative, giving Grady the impression he wouldn't ever quite reach her. Despite his resolve to break her, a strange tenderness wound its way around his heart.

"I'm sure you're mistaken." She spoke quickly, breathlessly. "I had a perfectly lovely childhood. Horseback-riding lessons, piano lessons, art lessons. I've visited the world. I lacked for nothing. There's nothing to bury."

Oh, yes, he'd found the right thread. "It would be a shame to dig it all up."

"What?" Confusion added another layer of animation to her dark eyes.

"The knife. Did you bury the knife missing from your kitchen under all those pretty flowers?"

She stared at him long and hard. As she held her breath, the scalloped edge of her shirt shivered to the rapid beat of her heart. Dumping her tools abruptly, she stood. "I don't have to answer your questions."

Grady followed, slowly, steadily. Something wasn't right. "Would it make you feel better if I came back with a warrant to search the grounds?"

Frustration crinkled her brow. "What do you want from me, Lieutenant Sloan?" she pleaded. "I don't know what it is you're expecting from me. I didn't kill Angela. I didn't bury any knife."

"I want the truth. Nothing but the truth."

"And I've already told you all I know. Why can't you leave me alone?"

"Because Angela was a living, breathing person, and someone savagely murdered her. And because it's within your power to help me find the murderer."

Her eyes were clear and deep, not simply surface mirrors to hide deceit. As she shook her head and mouthed a silent "No," he could almost feel her pain slicing his breastbone. He didn't want to feel compassion for the hurt child hiding somewhere in the woman's body. He didn't want to feel anything at all for her.

"You've told me what you want to remember," Grady said. "Now I need to find what you've chosen to lock away."

She shivered, bowing her shoulders like a protective buttress against a cold wind. Grady had to hold himself back from gathering her into his arms to warm her.

"What if I can't?" she whispered.

"The Amytal or hypnosis could help."

"I—I..."

Suddenly he understood. The Amytal and the hypnosis would put her under someone else's control. He looked around her yard. She'd worked hard to feel in control, to feel safe. He'd have to find another way.

Tentatively, he reached out to touch her arm. "Then talk to me, Melinda. I won't hurt you."

"Yes, you will." He saw the accusation in her eyes. He understood the knowledge came from experience, from pain. Who else had hurt her? "Don't make promises you can't keep."

He moved away, giving her space. He found himself near the wind chime at the corner of her porch and pulled the heart-shaped striker, setting it in motion. The chimes' soft melody filled the quiet yard. "Tell me about yourself, about your family."

She stood rooted like a prisoner awaiting execution. "What does that have to do with Angela's murder?"

"Maybe nothing." He shrugged, then tweaked the chimes into action again. His fingers itched to touch her soft skin again. "Maybe everything. Talk to me. I want to hear your story."

"It's rather boring."

"I very much doubt that." Their gazes met and burned until the collar of his shirt seemed too tight. "Tell me everything."

Her sharp laugh held no mirth. "You don't have enough time."

He eased himself into the single hammock chair. "I have all the time in the world." He sensed her calculating her options. Her expressive eyes signaled the moment of her surrender.

"I grew up with all the advantages money can offer."

She turned away from him and ambled toward the old pecan tree that acted as the centerpiece of her yard, shading the more fragile flower specimens. As if she could draw from the tree's strength, she leaned against it. "My father was successful. He worked hard and played hard. He expected a lot from everyone." Suddenly she glanced over her shoulder. "How am I doing?"

"Fine."

And just as quickly, she looked away.

"Your father expected a lot even from you?" Grady continued, pressing, pushing, demanding.

"Especially me." Her head bowed with the weight of failure. He'd let his own family down enough times to recognize the gesture.

"Why?"

"I'm an only child. He wanted me to follow in his footsteps. Study law. Become his partner."

As he set the hammock swing into motion, the cotton strings creaked and groaned a muffled protest. "You didn't want to?"

"No. He gave me every opportunity to succeed." In profile, he saw her sad smile. "Unfortunately, that didn't extend to fantasy. You see, I wanted to be an artist."

Her voice was soft, yet strong. It made him want to lean forward to catch every word even though she spoke clearly enough to be heard across the yard.

"How does he feel about your job?"

"He thinks it's below me. My awards and my successes aren't valid because they're so small." As if protecting herself from a blow, she flinched.

"How do you feel about your job?"

"I love it. Everything about it." She smiled sheepishly. "I'm rather good at it."

The love she'd poured into her garden, into the sketches tacked on her office walls, proved it. "I can see that."

She moved her head and her hair cascaded from her shoulder to hide her face, but not before he saw the pink of a blush on her cheeks. Shy? Melinda? Interesting.

"My father's done a lot of good."

How could someone who specialized in freeing criminals be considered as having done good work? All Ely's power, money and social standing made him impervious even to the law of the land. People like Ely didn't do good. People like Ely abused good for their own ends. The sour taste in Grady's mouth made him want to spit.

"He's helped so many people with his charity work," Melinda said with pride. She batted a curling tendril of hair away from her temple. "The women's shelter in downtown Fort Worth, the Angel's Gate home and school for pregnant teenagers, the help hotline for abusers and those being abused."

She turned slowly, shifting her position against the tree to look at him. "Don't get me wrong. I don't think Daddy's perfect. I know about the rumors. I hear what some people say about what he does. But he's a good man. All he's ever wanted for me was the best."

Good and Ely Amery simply didn't add up. Seeing no point in pursuing this line of conversation, Grady shifted topics.

"What about your mother?" He rocked the swing with one foot. The other rested on his knee.

Melinda straightened away from tree, eyes darting about as if she were looking for a lost object. "What about her?"

"What do you remember about her?" Her sudden agitation set off flags of warning. Another thread to explore.

"I was young when she died." Melinda stooped to pick up her tools and her basket. "She was wonderfully loving. I don't remember much else." The bag of bulbs fell from her hands, spilling its contents in a semicircle around her. "Do you remember your mother when you were eight?"

"Some days I remember every detail as if it were yesterday."

His father had been gone, trudging somewhere south, selling some sort of machinery. His mother, unable to deal with the long absences, had sought refuge in cheap red wine. His sisters, two and five, hair in knots, dressed in dirty clothes because no one had done the laundry, had scrounged through the lower kitchen cabinets for nonexistent food. He remembered eight only too well. And ten. And seventeen. How helpless he'd felt, how scared, how angry. *You're the man of the house while I'm gone, son. Take care of your mother and your sisters.* And he had, because there had been no one else to do it. And every action, every decision, had been filled with doubt. And now the doubt he'd tamed was back, full and strong.

"Well, good for you." With an anger mirroring his own, Melinda launched each bulb she retrieved into the bag. "Does this discussion have a point, Lieutenant? If not, I have work to do."

"Everything I do has a point."

"I figured as much," she mumbled. As she whipped around for an errant bulb, she knocked over her basket, tumbling the garden tools onto the ground. He rose. The swing shook behind him.

Sensing something was about to erupt like a boil in need of lancing, Grady pressed. "How did she die?"

Melinda scrambled for the dropped tools, but couldn't seem to get a solid hold on them.

If he pushed her much further, he'd lose whatever ground he'd made. He changed tack. "What do you want out of life?"

"Peace and quiet." She breathed the words like a prayer.

Grady knelt beside her, picked up the tools and steadied her hands with his. Soft, warm and smooth, her skin felt good against his. "Do you ever think of children and a family of your own?"

She averted her gaze, gingerly removed her hands from his grasp. Grabbing the paper bag with one hand, she gathered a handful of bulbs with the other, spilling as many as she'd retrieved from the ground. She was silent for so long, Grady didn't think she'd answer.

"Sometimes."

Grady heard the yearning, heard the half-formed dream, heard the hope she didn't quite dare believe in. She was a set of contradictions—soft and hard, frightened and strong. What kind of life turned a beautiful woman into a practical recluse? What kind of experience had gone into building an armor, leaving so many holes for arrows to find the soft tissue?

As he watched her surreptitiously wipe a tear from the corner of her eye, Grady knew that whatever Melinda had seen or done on the night of Angela Petersen's death held the key to her future as well as his.

He also learned something he didn't want to.

Her silent questioning told him she was sincere. She truly couldn't remember.

Grady righted the basket, took the bag from her shaking hands and stuffed the bulbs inside. "You spend a lot of time and energy in this garden."

She shrugged and moved away to pick up the last bulb at the base of the pecan tree.

"It's a great place to relax." Grady walked over to her and gently took the bulb from her hand with one hand, leaving the other beneath hers, enjoying the softness of her skin, hating the invisible connection forming unequivocally between them.

She swallowed hard. "It's peaceful and quiet."

"And you need that, don't you?" She averted her gaze, but with a finger on her chin, Grady brought it back to meet his. "You need the peace and the quiet to balance against all the noise in your head."

She took in a sharp breath and held it. Without warning she ripped her hand from his and turned away, moving toward the lush greenery around the little pond in the back corner of her yard. As if to cleanse herself, she buried her hands in the gurgling waterfall, letting it wash over her fingers. "A garden doesn't yell, talk back or hit. It creates. It's beauty. It's life."

Yell? Talk back? Hit?

Her anguish tore at him. He pushed the sentimentalitly aside.

Finally, the break he'd been waiting for. One step closer to her monster. Who was it? The father she so obviously adored? The mother whose mere mention sent her into a state of upheaval? Or someone else altogether?

If she weren't Ely Amery's daughter, if Jamie's betrayal weren't still fresh in his mind, if he weren't a police officer sworn to obey the law, he'd take her in his arms and love the pain away.

But he'd already had enough heartache to last him a lifetime, and he certainly couldn't afford this one. Not with his future at stake.

Was she guilty? There'd been no blood on her clothes. No blood on her feet when they'd found her at the scene. There was innocence in her eyes. And fear. Then there were the missing memories. And there was the knife he'd noticed missing from the block on the pristine counter of her neat little kitchen.

And to find the knife he was sure was buried somewhere in this beautiful garden, he'd have to destroy the last remaining link to her feeling of security. He couldn't explain his regret at the thought of upheaving this peaceful oasis.

Guilty or innocent? He saw traces of both in her deep, dark eyes. She'd done that to him. Planted doubts. And the good cop's instincts that had brought him so far had deserted him along with his common sense.

As if he were a wrecking ball aimed at a condemned building, every second he spent with her brought him closer to disaster. It was getting harder to remember he was the hunter and she was the prey.

Chapter Six

"What happened between you and my father?" Wiping her wet hands on her skirt, Melinda sprang to her feet and marched purposefully toward the house. She needed tea to soothe her dry throat, her tense nerves.

Grady stopped her with a hand to her shoulder—a statement of power and control. She looked into his piercing blue eyes and knew she didn't have a prayer of escaping. Even for tea.

Why did he have to touch her? Every time he did, she felt a protective layer slip away like an outgrown skin. Did he know his touch made her tremble to her very core? The headache that had faded as she'd worked the soil returned with a vengeance.

"Okay," Grady said. "Quid pro quo. I'll answer your question, if you answer one of mine."

She broke their connection, inching away from him. "I think I've answered enough, don't you?"

He wasn't giving her time. He was forcing her to make a decision now rather than later. She resented him for that. The invisible band around her head tightened.

"One gut-wrenching story for another." He cocked his head and flashed her his dimples, but the warmth didn't extend to his eyes. "Deal?"

She shrugged. Wariness pumped adrenaline through her

body, priming her to flee like some Stone Age ancestor chased by a woolly mammoth. She'd already said too much, but Grady wouldn't give up until he had her completely eviscerated. "Why not? You go first."

"This little story isn't pretty. Are you sure you want to hear it?"

"I'm sure." She folded her arms under her chest and looked for a spot to sit.

"There once was a beautiful girl." Grady reached out and touched a strand of her hair. Melinda forced herself not to move, not to blink, but her insides trembled like Jell-O on a spoon. "Much like you. Everything about her spelled class, except where you're midnight dark, she was sunset bright."

His eyes darkened with the memory. "She had high ambitions even before her Daddy struck it rich and moved the family out of Fargate. When you look at her today, it's hard to believe she was ever a small-town girl."

His gaze refocused, sharp with implied accusation. Melinda tried to move out of range, but found her maneuver useless. Those dark-blue eyes followed her wherever she went.

"Don't look at me like that," she said. He saw too much, came too close to the mark with his guesses. "Whatever this woman did to you, I'm not like her. I'm not like anybody you've ever known."

As if he could read her heart, her very soul, his gaze sliced into her. She needed to leave, but couldn't move.

"You're right about that. I've never met anyone quite like you."

He turned abruptly, and she prayed he hadn't heard her sigh of relief.

"One day, her brother was killed," Grady continued, his voice remote and clipped as if he were reciting facts for one of his police reports. "Murdered in cold blood.

Like Angela Petersen. Only this murderer had used a hand-gun to do the deadly deed. It was a crime of passion, you see, and when the evidence started pointing in her direction, she phoned the state's most famous attorney.''

As if he expected her to fill the void, he paused expectantly.

"My father."

"Give the lady a prize." Without turning to look at her, he lifted his arm, signaling to an invisible assistant in the wings. "The great Ely Amery, champion of lost causes, accepted the case."

He swiveled to face her, eyes ablaze with potent anger. "Do you know what this brilliant attorney advised her?"

"No, I don't pay attention to my father's affairs."

"How interesting."

Melinda didn't know what to do with herself. She settled on resting her backside against the waist-high stone wall separating the flagstone patio from the small patch of grass and the rest of her garden.

"What did my father tell her?"

Her question set him in motion. The tightness of his movements gave life to the storm of anger brewing inside him. "He told her she needed to find somebody the jury could trust."

"She came to you."

He came to an abrupt stop in front of her. She inched back along the wall and had to look up to meet his gaze.

"Yeah, the socialite remembered the hometown boy. The one who wouldn't back down when they tried to rip his family apart. She remembered his loyalty and the crush he'd once had on her, and decided to set her claws into both."

His finger trailed along her cheek following the path a trail of tears might take. Her heart beat as if she'd just run a mile at top speed. Trapped. He had her trapped again.

Her shoulders rounded, but she couldn't bring her legs up to hug them with him so close.

"Like you, she cried pretty tears. Like you, she swore her innocence. 'Please, Grady, you've got to help me. I can't trust anyone else,'" he mimicked.

"I still don't see how that ties in with my father."

"You will."

He crowded in on her.

"She wooed me." He stroked her hair, following the flow past her shoulders, pausing ever so slightly on the rise of her breast. Her nipples pearled under his touch. She shivered.

"Kissed me." He bent toward her so swiftly, she didn't have time to dodge his kiss. A hard, vengeful, threatening kiss. A kiss that gave her fears a brand-new definition.

"I don't think this is appropriate." Melinda scooted sideways, knocking down one of the clay pots lined on top of the wall.

"You wanted to hear the story." Grady's deep-dimpled grin held no warmth.

"I don't need the demonstrations." She folded her hands primly on her lap. "My hearing works just fine."

"Too bad. I was looking forward to the seducing part."

Melinda edged a few more inches away from him, then straightened her stance, holding her ground. His crooked grin was filled with satisfaction this time, and she could have slapped him for it.

"She even showed me how much she loved me. And I fell for it, promised to help her out of her bind. I knew her. I liked her. I let my guard down. That was my first mistake."

Grady stared out at the grazing cows in the pasture. "The murder was out of my jurisdiction, but I had friends in the Fort Worth police department. I questioned the evidence. I poked holes in their theories. That was my second mistake.''

Arms folded across his chest, he turned back to face her. ''Your father was brilliant. He took the tidbits I fed him and spat them into huge stains with borders so indistinct, the jury had no choice but to say they had reasonable doubt. I became the defense's best witness. That was my third mistake.''

Melinda gulped. ''She got off. Isn't that what you wanted?''

''Yeah, that's what I thought.'' He kicked at a loose piece of flagstone with the toe of his boot and sent it skittering down the small incline toward the fence. ''We went out to celebrate—her, your father and me. That's when I realized I'd been had. Your father mocked my stupidity.''

Grady crouched and snared a daisy from the flower bed. ''But it wasn't until she kissed me good-night and dumped me that I understood I'd been used.''

One by one, he ripped the white petals off the daisy. ''You see, she *had* killed her brother. Admitted as much with her last kiss.''

He squashed the flower's golden heart between his thumb and index finger and shook his head. ''Over an argument about money.''

''I'm sorry.'' Melinda recognized the hurt in his voice, felt the deep emotions he couldn't quite bring himself to express, but she didn't know what to do, what to say.

He rose and stretched. ''Just remember it won't work twice. Unlike an old dog, I *can* learn new tricks.''

''Not everyone's like her.'' Melinda flicked her hair off her face, tilting her chin up ever so slightly in defiance.

''Your father's known to stretch the truth. What makes you think you're so different?''

''I never learned to lie. My father expects the truth from everyone around him.''

Grady sneered. ''Typical lawyer.''

''Maybe, but he's still my father.''

He gave her such a weird look, that for a second, she thought he'd understood what she'd meant. Suddenly, the tension disappeared from his body.

''Point taken.'' He moved one of the clay pots out of the way and sat beside her. ''Now, your turn. Tell me about your monster.''

Panic jolted her heart. She couldn't face ''it'' yet.

''Sooner or later, you'll have to trust me,'' he said.

Trust. The idea terrified her almost as much as the horror playing hide-and-seek in her mind. No one—not even her father—knew about the monster and the terror he'd wrought over the years.

''You've already made up your mind about me.'' Melinda jumped up and trailed her hand along the line of cool clay pots spaced on the wall. ''You've already judged me guilty.''

She gently reached out for one of the many pots of herbs, gently cupping one of the fading pale pink blooms in the palm of her hand. It was cool and smooth, whereas Grady's skin was warm and rough. ''Sap from the leaves of this plant can treat eczema, but a bite from the roots can be deadly. Does that make the plant good or bad?''

''It depends.''

''My point exactly. Everyone has good and bad inside them. Everyone lives their lives in shades of gray. Even you, Lieutenant. The difference between you and me is that you see only the black and the white.''

''That's not an answer.''

''What were you expecting? A murder confession?''

His cool, searching gaze never wavered, rippling uneasiness through her. She put the pot down before she dropped it.

''I'm one of the good guys, Melinda.'' He paused, letting the silence grow between them until it crammed the space separating them like a tangible presence. She wanted to fill the silence, end the nervy edginess it caused, but she wasn't sure where or how to start.

"Tell me about the monster, Melinda."

Shaking her head, she turned from him. "I can't, I just can't."

When he rose, she heard the brush of fabric against stone. His soft whisper warmed her ear. "I'm right here. I won't let anything happen to you."

Like a comforting blanket, his fingers molded themselves to her shoulders, oozing warmth into her shivery body. She closed her eyes, shutting out the safety of her garden. "Don't make promises you can't keep. Those are always the ones that hurt the most."

"Tell me...." His whispers enticed. Because she needed him to leave, because his voice drifted over her like a shower of downy feathers, because part of her needed closure, she let him convince her to lower the drawbridge in her mind that kept the monster prisoner. He wrapped his arms softly around her, and the embrace felt strong and secure—solid. "Tell me, Melinda...."

Fuzzy flashes penetrated the black behind her closed lids. Her memory tumbled faded images like old photographs drained of color, with blurry edges. She gasped and opened her eyes wide.

"You're fine." Grady's voice....

Her heart pounded wildly against her ribs. Sweat formed along her hairline, prickling her scalp. Air refused to flow through her tightened chest. Her hands grasped at her shirt, trying to keep her heart in, willing her lungs to function. The yard swirled with muted colors, growing brighter by the second.

An explosion charged her mind, sending her reeling down a steep spiral. Her body tensed against the imagined fall. She vaguely felt the bolstering arms keeping her solidly in place. Bits and pieces of a jumbled puzzle came to her like a slide show stuck in Fast Forward.

Black, red, green, yellow.

The colors flashed by too fast to comprehend.

And noises. *Lindy. Swish. Poof.*

And heat. Piercing heat. Terrible heat, burning deep inside her like a funeral pyre.

As the colors, sounds and sensations formed into a vortex settling over her, the stench of blood and sulfur permeated her senses, overwhelming them.

''No!'' Like a spectator at some horrible play, she heard her own muffled scream.

Melinda prided herself on her intelligence, her self-control, and hated the effect this almost-forgotten nightmare had on her. Hated herself for reacting to it. Hated the way it left her feeling empty and overcome with sadness. A tear rolled down her cheek.

''It's all right.'' Grady's steady voice penetrated the whirling cloud, dispersing it. His strong arms shawled her, creating a living boundary between her and her mutating monster. She sought contact with him the way someone lost in a dark cave sought light. All pride fell aside.

''I can't.'' She couldn't stop the sob. Turning in his arms, she sought his solidity.

''Shh, it's all right.'' He touched his lips softly to hers. Starved for reality after her brief encounter with hell, she responded, sliding her arms around his waist. Her breasts flattened against his chest. Her hips pressed against his. As if he breathed life into her, she deepened the kiss, reveling in their physical connection, in his strength, in his warmth. She wanted him to touch her everywhere, to bring her back to life. He smelled like Ivory soap. He tasted like black coffee and breath mints. He felt like…heaven.

Then panic set in.

What was wrong with her? She was acting like some desperate woman. And maybe she was. Desperate for the fear and the nightmares to go away. Desperate for the life of a normal woman—with nothing more complicated in it than her family and her job.

Her brain pulsed inside her cranium, bringing pain and nausea. Remembering propriety, she stumbled away from him. She didn't dare look at him. She was too close to tears to find regret in his eyes.

"I'm sorry." She pressed her fingers against both her temples. "I've got to lie down before my head explodes. I trust you can find your way out."

As Melinda moved forward, she wobbled. Grady's hand slipped under her elbow to steady her. He guided her inside her house to her bedroom and helped her beneath the cool lavender sheets. She rolled onto her stomach, burying her head in the soft feather pillow. The mattress sagged beside her with Grady's weight.

"Go away," she said, her voice muffled by the pillow.

His fingers massaged the tense muscles of her neck and shoulders. The pain eased. *Ah-h-h.* His touch felt so good, so warm after the numbing cold of reliving her nightmare. She didn't want him to stop. She needed him to leave before the tears came. "Go away."

"Can I get you anything?"

"Just go away. *Please.*"

She counted the seconds of Grady's silence by the pounding in her head. His touch slowly lightened, then disappeared. Her eyes burned. Her throat tightened.

"Melinda." He stroked her hair so gently, the first tear seeped into her pillow. "You're going to have to remember. There's no way around it. But I promise, I'll give you some breathing space. Not forever. Just for now."

As Grady rose, the mattress returned to its original position.

When she heard the front door shut, Melinda let her dammed emotions burst.

He had the power to change her life, and he was using it. And she didn't know which frightened her more—her monster's invisible claws scratching to be free, or Grady Sloan's gentle kiss.

GRADY CURSED HIMSELF WITH every step he took to reach his car still parked in front of The Essential Gardener.

He'd touched her.

He'd kissed her.

Knowing who she was, what she might have done, what her repressed memories kept from him, he'd still wanted to take her right there in her garden.

All of it was against the rules.

If the town council ever got wind of his blunders, he'd lose the chief's seat to Winnin' Wayne faster than old Brasswell could blink.

He yanked his cruiser's door open, plopped into the driver's seat and jerked the door shut with a satisfying slam.

She had him feeling like a rope in a tug-of-war contest. He was losing control of the situation and doing it fast. The truth was, he hadn't felt in control since he'd first set eyes on her. She made him feel exposed—in a hail of bullets without a vest. Which wasn't a feeling he cared to own.

He ground his teeth in a tight circle. He had to get a grip. If he didn't, he might lose all propriety and do something he'd really regret. Something stupid like let himself be drawn in by the mysterious aura surrounding her, by her beauty—and by his hormones, which were raging like a teenager's, for crying out loud!

He snapped on the ignition and the engine roared to life.

Melinda was right. In this case, even the law wasn't black-and-white, but an awful shade of gray.

Tests were trickling in with inconclusive data. Alibis of other possible suspects were checking out. And each person he questioned seemed to open more doors than he or she closed.

Though evidence, or lack thereof, appeared to point in Melinda's direction, technically, she hadn't done anything. Her loss of memory was real and, thanks to Desiree, supported. Between that and the immunity her father's power gave her, it left him mired in that huge gray area he hated so much. And with precious little time to sort through the muck.

All in all, a dangerous spot.

And he'd gone and promised her time he didn't have to give.

As he sped by the high school, he saw the slim figure of a boy walking with a baseball-equipment bag slung over his shoulder. At seventeen, the towheaded, freckled-faced Carson Crews was the county's best pitcher, good enough to earn a sponsorship on the select league. Not only could he throw strikes, he could throw them with smoke. Batters never saw the ball coming. Grady figured he imagined his father's face hovering over the plate and aimed for it with all his tamped-down anger. In Carson's place, that's what he'd have done. Grady slowed the car and rolled the passenger-side window down.

"Want a ride?"

Carson hesitated. "Sure."

He tried to hide the right side of his face, but Grady saw the purpling mark. Grady's anger billowed into a thunderhead, but he couldn't let it explode. Not in front of Carson. He shoved the car in gear. "Quite a shiner you've got there."

"Got hit with a baseball at practice."

Yeah, right, Grady thought. *A baseball with knuckles attached to that bastard who's your father.*

Ninety percent of Grady's calls were false alarms or dealt with domestic disputes. Too many of those calls had come in from the Crewses neighbors when Jackson, Carson's father, decided to vent some steam.

Frustration twitched through him like a snake looking for a strike. Every bruise he saw on Carson made him want to slam his fist into Jackson's face and let Jackson feel what it was like to be on the receiving end and not be able to do a thing about it. But his badge forbade him.

He'd beaten the system once.

Now he was part of it.

So much for all the changes he'd imagined he'd achieve when he'd entered the academy.

Grady felt for the boy. Saw a lot of himself in him. Knew the boy took the blows aimed at his kid brother, too. But the only thing Grady could do was let Carson know he was on his side, and wait until the boy wanted help to fight back.

"How's your old man?" Grady's jaw twitched.

"The usual."

"Drunk?" He'd wanted to use more disparaging terms, but curbed himself.

Carson shrugged and looked out the side window at the passing view. "He got a job last week. Some carpentry work in Fort Worth. Says he's got something else lined up, too. It'll pay big bucks, according to him."

"I'm glad to hear that." With Jackson busy and out of the way, Carson would get a break—until the next bender. "What's Jody up to these days? Haven't seen him around lately."

"Moved to Oklahoma with Aunt Liv. Goin' to school there this year."

That was a relief. At least one of them would be safe. "Why didn't you go, too?"

Carson shrugged. "Someone's got to take care of Pa."

Yeah, somebody had to pick up the pieces after a drinking binge. Someone had to make sure he didn't choke on his own vomit. Someone had to make excuses. Grady had done that often enough for his mother to know. But at least his mother had never laid a hand on any of them.

At the curve of the street leading to the Crewses trailer, Grady slowed. "You need anything, you call me, you hear?"

"Thanks, Grady."

Face drawn much too sternly, shoulders hunched and back straight, Carson hiked down the dusty lane leading to his hell of a home. Grady checked for traffic, jerked the steering wheel to the left and whipped the car onto the road.

Melinda with her monster. Carson with his bruises.

Two reminders in one day.

The past was doing its best to catch up with him.

WALKING INTO HIS HOUSE, Grady couldn't help contrasting his static living space to Melinda's peaceful retreat. Compared to her garden paradise, his home was lifeless, empty.

The nondescript brown-plaid couch blended with the sand-colored carpet. The chocolate leather recliner offered no relief from the monochromatic arrangement. Neither did the battered walnut coffee table, end tables and television console. Not even a plant brightened the gloomy room. Desiree had given him a fern of some sort when he'd bought the ranch, but through neglect, the fern hadn't lasted more than a couple of months.

The room looked like a cheap hotel suite, for all the individuality it had. Yet, before today, he'd never noticed how dull his quarters looked—and felt. He found himself longing for the small touches of home Melinda had created in her house. How would she transform these dull walls into a welcoming refuge?

Home. The word implied so many things. A wife. Kids of his own. Someone to return to at the end of the day. Before today, he'd never thought it was something he wanted for himself.

Shaking the stray thoughts out of his mind, he changed out of his uniform into jeans and a T-shirt, and headed for the barn to feed his two horses. Ironsides, the gray gelding, pawed the ground for his dinner, making a noise like a locomotive impatient to run. The sorrel mare, unimaginatively named Red when he'd bought her, preferred to be summoned. She looked up, acknowledging his arrival with a whinny, then ambled leisurely toward the corral, nibbling at the grass all the way.

He usually enjoyed his chores around his miniature ranch, but tonight, not even grooming the horses' coats to a polished gleam could relax him.

After a quick dinner, Grady decided to head for the station and vent some of his frustration catching up on paperwork and going over the facts he'd gathered on Angela's death. Halfway there, he changed his mind, and continued toward the hospital.

Seth dozed in a sitting position. His gray hair, still thick on his head, was in its usual mussed state. His grizzled mustache made too wide a broom under his nose. His beefy jowls drooped on each side of his square chin. For the first time since he'd known Seth, Grady noticed a fragility beneath the pale skin, and the thought saddened him. Seth had been his rock; the only person who'd stood by him, who'd understood how important keeping his family together was to him.

Just as Grady decided to let his old friend rest, Seth opened his eyes.

"Grady! How'd you get past the missus?"

"Sent her down for a well-deserved breather. How are you feeling?"

"Like I got stomped on by a mule with studded shoes." Seth waved one of his square hands at him. "Come in, son. I'm glad you stopped by. I'm dying of boredom here. I was just fixin' to call you. No one in that danged station'll tell me what's goin' on. Where've you been, anyway?"

"Hasn't Brasswell stopped by to liven up your days?"

Seth's eyes, the same warm color as the butter toffee he kept on his desk in an Arby's Christmas glass, twinkled with amusement. "Unfortunately! That woman could talk the ear off an elephant. But you know her. When she wants to, she can dance around any situation."

Grady grabbed the lone chair nestled under the window, dragged it beside the bed, and straddled it, his forearms hanging from the chair top's back. "Did she tell you about Angela Petersen?"

Seth's smile disappeared. He shook his head in short, sad strokes. "Poor thing. I was lookin' forward to hearin' her pretty voice at the Fall Festival. How's her family holdin' up?"

"Not too well. The reverend's concern about the investigation is getting a tad obsessive. He's been calling every day for updates." His thumb rubbed the chair back's smooth metal. "I don't suppose Brassy had anything good to say about the way the investigation's going."

"Well, you know her." Seth pulled the thin blue blanket higher over his round belly. "She thinks the whole town'll fall apart unless she holds it together."

"She doesn't want me to take your place."

Seth paused, looking deep into Grady's eyes. "She doesn't make the decision by herself."

Grady looked away and studied the blue-and-orange geometric design on the curtains. "You think those sniveling councilmen won't follow her lead? They usually do."

Seth cleared his throat and worried the blanket's satin trim. "You gotta understand. For her it's personal, Grady. It's that smart-mouthed kid who stole her thunder she can't forget."

"I couldn't let them take Des and Aimee away. I was responsible for them."

"You made her look bad. She's not the kind to forget losin' out to a seventeen-year-old boy. And being proven wrong."

Grady stood and paced the length of the bed. "So I'm supposed to roll over and let Wayne take the spot I've more than earned?"

"What's really on your mind, son?"

That stopped Grady cold. As much as he trusted Seth, he couldn't bring himself to mention Melinda and her effect on him. The uncharacteristic indecision. The lust so hot it practically had his blood on fire. The fear he wasn't supposed to feel, now that he was a grown man, the "law," and not a boy of seventeen. "Nothing I can't handle."

As if Seth could read his mind, he nodded understanding. Somehow the accepting gesture calmed the storm raging inside Grady. Whatever happened, Seth would be there for him.

"I have confidence in you, son. I know you'll make the right decision."

A nurse poked her head into the room, interrupting them. "Visiting hours are over," she announced perkily.

"I was just leaving." Grady returned the chair to its position beneath the window. "Take care of yourself, Seth."

"Next time you come, bring me some real food, will ya. Nothing's got any flavor around this place."

Grady smiled. "What's your pleasure?"

"A sampling of Mamie's desserts would be a good start."

"I'll do that."

He stuffed his hands in his jacket pockets and strode out of the room.

The right decision. For once, Seth's faith in him might be misplaced. And was the right decision always the better one?

BACK IN HIS OFFICE AT THE station, Grady ignored the stack of messages from Brasswell demanding proof of results. As he caught up on paperwork, he worried about recovering the murder weapon with its possible clues of fingerprints and blood. The longer it took to recover the knife, the less likely the evidence would be usable. Though he hadn't seen any evidence of fresh digging in Melinda's garden, he couldn't quite shake the feeling that the knife might be hidden somewhere in the floral fantasy. The heavy rain might have washed the signs away. There was no way around it: To eliminate his doubts, he'd have to get a search warrant.

Concentrating on the crime-scene pictures, he lost track of time.

He went over the gory photographs time and time again, analyzing the patterns of tear-shaped blood spatters, the slitlike stab wounds, questioning the lack of tool marks on the doors or windows, the lack of footprints on the carpet and floors, searching for the one thing that could help him solve his case, or at least point him in the right direction.

He went over the lab reports trickling in daily. So far, nothing conclusive. He looked over the reports filed by fellow officers on interviews made in the neighborhood of the crime, and with the relatives and a few suspects.

He found nothing.

Whoever had committed the crime had covered his...or her...tracks well. That fact niggled at him like a sand spur under a saddle pad, irritating his already sour disposition. It was too neat. Too perfect.

He knew the what, when, where and how. The why and the whodunit remained a puzzle. A crime of passion committed by someone who knew her. Not exactly the solid answer Brasswell expected.

Grady flung the folder of pictures aside. The photos scattered in a fan over his desktop. He reached into a drawer and pulled out the wrinkled sketches he'd found in Melinda's closet. He propped one booted foot on the edge of his desk, and unfolded the papers. Smoothing the paper down, he tried to decipher the drawing beneath the vicious, masking scribble.

It was almost as if she'd tried to *X* out the event she'd drawn, the way an angry child might do with something she didn't like.

A real event? An imagined one? Or the monster itself?

He picked up the next sketch and found it just as indecipherable. Before he went cross-eyed, he refolded the drawings and returned them to the drawer. Plopping his foot back on the floor, he ground his fists into his eyes, then raked his hands through his hair.

The sketches made no more sense than the photographs; and the photographs, no more sense than Melinda's hole-ridden memory.

Nothing made sense.

He called up a file on his computer, entered Melinda's name, and waited for the information to process. She'd been reluctant to discuss her mother, the way her mother had died—which aroused his curiosity. Maybe he'd find a clue there.

As he waited for the computer to find the information, he closed his eyes. His mind drifted.

His jumbled thoughts formed pieces of images. He tried piecing them back together, but the shreds floated out of his grasp like leaves in the wind. Then he glided along with them. They curled and curved until scenes whirred by like clips from a black-and-white movie—Wayne trotting up to the stage at the Fall Festival, his grin wide and sloppy, accepting his promotion to chief; Angela's sightless eyes, her body scored with slashes, advancing toward him, her disjointed voice saying, "Help me! Somebody help me!"; and Melinda, laughing. He turned around. She came to him, her hair rippling in the wind, her smile aglow, her eyes vivid. She kissed him, stealing his soul, and when he was soft in her arms, her lips nibbled at his earlobe, and she whispered, "I did it, Grady. I killed Angie."

He awoke with a start and shook his head to clear the dismal pictures. Forewarned was forearmed. He would not fall under Melinda's spell.

As he stretched to work the kinks out of his back, something on one of the photographs spread on his desk caught his attention. Some of the dots on the kitchen slice in front of the back door didn't match the perfectly spaced rust periods around the pink and blue-ribboned geese.

Dried blood?

Drops that had struck the surface and left slightly elliptical markings. Which meant the killer might have gotten hurt in the struggle.

And the only way blood could have gotten there was if the murderer had used the back door to flee. The rain had washed away the outside evidence, but the half-moon-shaped piece of carpet had trapped at least three good drops and absorbed them into its pile.

He made a note to call the lab in the morning.

Finally, a break.

Chapter Seven

Melinda placed a saucer of cat food and a bowl of water outside her back door for Angela's cat. The big orange tom had taken up the habit of visiting her daily since his mistress's death. He refused to come inside, but did accept food before he resumed his vigil two houses down. Melinda had tried to hold him for Kerry, but Rusty skittered away if she got too close. With a heavy heart, Melinda secured the rest of her house.

As she opened her front door, ready to leave, her father had his hand up, about to knock. "Daddy, what are you doing here?"

Her father smiled and hugged her. He looked as impeccable as usual in his dark suit with its red rose in the lapel. "I called your office and Dolores said you took the afternoon off. I decided to treat my little girl to a late lunch."

"Oh, I can't, Daddy." She rummaged through her purse for her keys. "I was just leaving for Angela's funeral."

He frowned. "Why are you going at all?"

"She was my neighbor." Less than five minutes and she was tense. That had to be a record. Melinda inserted the key into the lock and turned it sharply. She wasn't going to let him get to her today, not when the funeral, the reason for it, and the determined Lieutenant Sloan already had her nerves on edge.

"Were you close?" he asked gruffly.

Following the narrow stone path, she strode to the garage door. "Not really. I had her key in case of emergency, she had mine. She liked my flowers. We talked once in a while—but no, we weren't close."

Her father trailed her. "I thought you didn't like funerals. You wouldn't even go to your Aunt Lorinda's three years ago."

"I *don't* like funerals." She unlocked the garage door and pulled the door up. The door wobbled on its tracks but with an extra push finally settled in the open position. "It's just I feel I have to go."

"For the life of me, Melinda, I don't understand your logic." One hand on his hip, the other cutting the air to pieces, her father brought her down like a prosecutor cross-examining a witness. "You don't like funerals, you barely knew the girl. Why attend at all?"

Familiar anger flared, but she swallowed it and sighed with resignation. There was no point in getting herself all worked up. In her father's eyes, she was still eight and couldn't think for herself. Under her father's watchful gaze, she fiddled with her keys. "There's no logic in death."

"Are you all right? You look a little pale." His forehead crinkled with worry.

"I'm fine. I just haven't been sleeping well."

She'd dreamed again last night. The blotches of color and cacophony of noises had formed into semicoherent images. Though she couldn't quite decipher their meanings, it wasn't so much the images that had caused the dark circles under her eyes, but the whirlpool of emotions that had risen from the images' depths like the phoenix from the ashes—the profound fear, the all-consuming anger and mostly the heart-wrenching betrayal. She shivered at the memory of the dream that had kept her looking deep into the corners of her room for most of the night, even with every light blazing.

"Is that country cop bothering you?"

Her father had his attorney's voice on, and Melinda couldn't help the smile. Grady was responsible for a lot of her confusion, and for her more pleasant dreams. He might have been the catalyst for her nightmares, but she knew he wasn't the cause. "It has nothing to do with him."

"I can take care of him," her father insisted.

The determined lieutenant had a way of making her shake with fear and tremble with desire all at once. He was opening windows and doorways she'd barred for too long. But this time, she wouldn't take the easy way out. "*I* can handle him myself."

At her show of autonomy, her father flinched. The movement was almost imperceptible, and after a good look into her father's frosty glare, Melinda decided she'd imagined it. Her father never flinched—not for any criminal, not for any authority, and certainly not for her.

She leaned against the open garage-door frame, turned her gaze to her shoes and worked the tip of one foot in a semicircle in front of her. "Daddy, how did Mom die?"

"Don't you remember?"

Melinda shook her head, helpless in her ignorance, feeling the blank holes in her memory had stolen an important part of her. "No, I don't."

"She died in a fire in her greenhouse."

Remembered heat from her nightmare doused her like a wave of fire. Unconsciously, her hand went to her heart to steady its beating. Licking her dry lips, she looked up and met her father's hard gaze. "Where was I when it happened?"

Her father's gaze narrowed. "You were safe in bed where all good little girls should have been."

Was there an edge of sarcasm in his voice, or was her imagination skewing her hearing as well as her memory?

Her father cocked his head in the arrogant way she'd never liked. That attitude might be an asset in the courtroom, but as far as she was concerned, it only put a wedge between them. Why was he on the defensive?

"Why the sudden interest?" he asked tersely.

She shrugged, feeling a need to defuse her father's tension. "I don't know. Since Angela died I've had some…dreams." She played with the clasp on her purse. "I know Mom died when I was eight, but I couldn't remember, and it bothered me."

"How could you?" Her father wrapped an arm around her shoulders. "There's nothing for you to remember. The sound of the fire truck woke you up, but your nanny shielded you from the horrors of the incident. You never saw any of the flames, or your mother's body. Aunt Lorinda came right away and took you to her house until after the funeral. And when you came home, all signs of the disaster were gone. There's nothing for you to remember."

Her breath hitched in her constricted throat. All the commotion surrounding her mother's death, and leaving her imagination to fill in the details between the snatches of adult conversation she more than likely overheard, must have sparked her childhood nightmares. Had she built them up to such a feverish pitch that her mind had shut down and left blanks?

"Would you like me to make an appointment for you to talk to someone?" Her father's voice softened and he squeezed her shoulders tenderly.

"No, I'm fine." Feeling tears welling up, she pushed out of his embrace. "I'm hoping if I go to the funeral, I can make peace with Angela's death. I'm hoping it'll stop the nightmares."

Her father nodded his understanding. "Maybe going to

the funeral will help. Nightmares are just distortions of fears. They have nothing to do with reality.''

''I know.'' She shrugged and ran a finger through the dirt on the back window of her old Volvo station wagon.

''Do you want me to go to the funeral with you?''

''Thanks, Daddy, but it's something I need to do on my own.''

His eyebrows dipped and his mouth turned down in exaggerated hurt. ''My little girl doesn't need me anymore.''

Melinda hugged her father. ''Yes, I do. I always will. You're the only family I have left.''

''I couldn't bear to lose you after losing your mother.'' He hugged her back, and she felt need in the gesture. She'd always thought of him as strong, as someone who didn't need anyone else. The fact that he needed her to need him touched her.

''I don't remember much about Mom at all.'' Melinda pushed out of his arms enough to see his face. ''What was she like?''

His eyes took on a faraway look, as if he'd turned back the years in his mind to a time he remembered with fondness. ''You're becoming more like her every day. She was—'' He stopped himself and smiled sadly. ''Come by the house and we'll take out the old photo albums and share some hot cocoa. Just like the old days.''

''I'd like that.'' Her father's mellow moods came rarely, but were precious moments to treasure. Their shared evenings of cocoa and stories were her fondest childhood memories. ''You loved her very much, didn't you?''

''More than she ever understood.''

The pained look on her father's face brought a lump to her throat. She glanced at her watch. ''I've got to go.''

''Melinda?''

''Yes, Daddy.''

He shook his head slowly. ''Nothing. I'll see you soon.''

As Melinda got in her car, she had the feeling her father had left something important unsaid, and that wasn't like him at all.

MELINDA TOOK A SEAT in the last pew and watched as most of Fargate's residents crowded into, and overflowed out of, the small church. Lieutenant Sloan, in full dress uniform, stood at attention by the church's ornate front door. His quiet stance didn't fool her for an instant. His sharp gaze scrutinized the massed population, searching, analyzing, watching.

His gaze met hers, lingered, then returned to its methodical observation. The thump of pleasure in her chest at seeing him surprised her. The instant muddling of her senses unnerved her. And though she was keenly aware of every movement he made, Melinda forced herself to look at anything but him.

In contrast to the mournful tears being shed inside the church, the sun streamed through the stained-glass windows, dappling Angela's white coffin in a rainbow of colors. The Reverend Harold Hobart outdid himself. Never had a service been so moving. By the end of the eulogy, not a dry eye remained in the church. After the service, in a grim procession down Prairie View Drive, the whole congregation followed the hearse for the three blocks to the Fargate Cemetery.

As the last prayer faded on the stiff breeze, the grieving mass broke apart and slowly dispersed. Loath, it seemed, to leave their beloved daughter, their little sister, in the dark ground all alone, the Hobart family, a sobbing black cloud huddled under the maroon canopy, remained in place. Melinda wound her way through the crowd toward them.

Just outside the family circle, Kerry, Angela's best friend, dabbed at her eyes with a wet tissue. Impulsively,

Melinda wrapped an arm around her. "I'm so sorry for your loss."

"I just can't believe she's gone, you know." Kerry shook her head.

"I can't, either. I already miss her laughter."

A soggy smile lit Kerry's tear-reddened face. "She sure could laugh. I don't think I ever saw her cry, except when Tommy Lee left her. I don't know why she married him in the first place. He was all wrong for her."

"The heart doesn't always understand logic." Reflexively, her gaze sought Grady's form, walking toward her along the fringes of the thinning crowd.

When he reached them, Grady acknowledged Melinda's presence, then turned back to Kerry. "Is there anything I can do for you?"

Fresh tears streamed down Kerry's plump face, melting her makeup into dirty smears. Her sodden tissue couldn't absorb the moisture; it only spread the wetness until Kerry's cheeks glistened in wide ovals. Melinda fished in her purse and handed her a fresh one.

"Thanks. I'm sorry."

"Don't be," Melinda said.

"It's all right," Grady said. "You and Angie have been good friends for a long time."

Kerry nodded, swiping the tissue beneath her eyes. "I've known Angie since we were in kindergarten."

"Was she seeing anyone?" Grady asked in a low voice.

Melinda's head snapped up. She threw Grady a questioning gaze. What in the world was he doing? Questioning Angie's best friend at the funeral? There was a time and place for such things, and this wasn't it.

Leave her alone, she mouthed.

Over Kerry's head, he silently cautioned her not to interfere. "Did she have a boyfriend?"

"No, not really." Kerry sniffed and touched her tissue

to the corners of her eyes once more. "Not unless you count Mike. Tommy Lee's leaving hit her hard. Mike's been a good friend to her." She blew into the tissue. "I'm sorry, Grady, but losing Angie was like losing a sister."

"I know." His tone was soothing, yet firm. Melinda clenched her jaw at the continuance of his improper invasion. "How serious was it between Mike and Angie?"

"It wasn't anything like what you think. Mike has this band, you see. Angie liked his sound, and he liked her voice. He works at Halloran's ice-cream shop during the day, but that's just to pay the bills. His heart's in the gigs he plays at night with his country band."

This was ridiculous. Couldn't Grady see how hard this was on Kerry? What was he up to? What did he hope to get from her?

Kerry shredded the wet tissues in her hand. The bits stuck like dandruff to the skirt of her simple black dress. "Angie was going to be his ticket to the big time with her voice. Angie, well, she was kinda torn between loving to sing country songs and the promise she'd made the reverend to sing only for God. Mike was smart enough to convince her that any time and anything she sang pleased God." Kerry looked up at Melinda. "Remember when she asked you to look after Rusty about a month ago?"

Melinda nodded. She'd gladly taken care of the cat for the night Angie'd been out of town.

"Mike took her down to Austin to cut a demo. It's great. You ought to hear it." Kerry smiled, her pleasure genuine. "She truly had an angel's voice."

"Yes, she did," Melinda said.

"Old man Halloran would give Mike a hard time when Angie went there after work to wait for Mike's shift to end," Kerry continued. "Halloran didn't even have anything to complain about. Angie always bought ice cream, and Mike—well, you know Mike—he's never cheated anybody out of anything, especially not a minute of work when he was getting paid for it.''

"Mike's a good man," Grady said. "I didn't see him anywhere today. I would've thought he'd be at Angie's service. Have you seen him?''

Kerry shook head slowly back and forth and brought a hand to her mouth. Her fingers shook against her lips. "He doesn't even know she's dead. He's been on the road trying to get anybody who'll give him half a chance to listen to the demo." Her eyes shone, heavy with tears again. "Oh, Grady, when he finds out, he'll be crushed." The tears sprang free. As she sought to control her sorrow, her lips trembled. "I—I've got to go.''

Tissue dabbing uselessly at her tears, Kerry rushed away from them.

"Kerry!" Grady called after her.

She turned and wobbled like a top.

"That cut on your hand, how'd you get it?''

Did the man not know when to quit? Melinda wondered cynically.

Kerry looked down at the bandage. Her face contorted with pain. As her head bobbed with the tears she tried but failed to repress, she worried the bandage with her other hand. "It was an accident. I sliced it at work when I found out about Angie.''

"Let me know when you hear from Mike.''

She nodded and hurried away.

"Was that necessary?" Melinda couldn't keep the crispness out of her voice.

Grady slowly turned to face her. "There's never a proper time to talk about death.''

Her hands spread wide before her. "But an interrogation right here in the cemetery?''

"It's often the best time to catch people off guard.''

Melinda shook her head incredulously. "Don't you ever go off duty?"

"No. I'm on call twenty-four hours a day, especially when I've got an unsolved murder on my caseload." His gaze strayed toward the Hobarts. He turned his blue eyes on her once more, and she saw the deep sorrow in them. "What better gift can I give her parents than finding out who killed their daughter?"

"I'm sorry. You're right. It's just that you seemed so callous, grilling Kerry with Angie's coffin barely in the ground."

"Miss Amery!"

They both turned around to see Harold Hobart striding boldly in their direction. "Do you remember yet?" he asked, before coming to a halt. His voice cracked with anguish. "Do you remember who killed my daughter?"

Melinda's heart raced and she felt the blood drain out of her face. Without thinking, she shrank away from him, closer to Grady. "I didn't see anything."

Reverend Hobart grabbed her arms in a tight grip and shook her. "What did you see?"

Panic ran rampant, snatching her breath away. Something flashed in her mind. She instinctively sought something solid to protect her. Her back, firmly against Grady's side, gave her security. The panic washed away. For an instant, the reverend's unexpected charge at her had, brought her nightmare to life.

"I'm terribly sorry." The reverend let her go and backed away. "I was completely out of line. I'm—"

"I understand." Melinda's breath hissed out in one long exhalation. Gradually her shaking subsided and her balance returned. "Your daughter has been killed. You want to find out who killed her. I swear, Reverend, if I knew, I'd tell Lieutenant Sloan. But I didn't see anything."

Contrite, the reverend bowed his head. "Angela spoke

well of you. I'm certain you would do anything in your power to find her murderer. I'm sorry." He looked up again, sadness pulling at the corners of his eyes. "Will you let me know the minute your memory returns?"

"Of course. I would do anything to ease your sorrow."

Shoulders hunched, the reverend returned to his family clustered around his daughter's freshly dug grave.

"Are you all right?" Grady asked, his arm still pressed along her spine.

Melinda moved away from his burning touch and faced him. "I'm fine. He caught me by surprise."

"It's grief."

"I know." Suddenly uncomfortable in his presence, she clutched her purse strap. "Well, I'd better get going."

He nodded, and she moved toward the cemetery gate. She felt his disconcerting gaze following her progress. It wasn't until she was back at the church, in her car, that she felt safe.

She drove aimlessly for what seemed like hours. She followed every street, studied every house in the town she'd picked as home, learning with wonder about the individuals who peopled it. She'd chosen Fargate because it was small enough for her to feel secure, yet large enough to offer a measure of anonymity. Would they have cried for her as they had for Angie? Or would her funeral have been attended only by her father's circle of influential friends?

With work being so close to her house, she'd hardly gotten to know the people of Fargate. She shopped at odd hours to avoid crowds, or drove into Fort Worth to get lost in them.

Today, a good part of this small town had come out to grieve for one of their lost members. She'd felt a community in the gathered people and envied their closeness. Of the hundreds of people at the service, she'd recognized only a few faces. Even after having lived in Fargate for more than two years, she was an outsider. The thought saddened her.

She hadn't exactly set out to live a closeted life. It had seemed easier at first. Now it was simply habit. Though she felt safer here, more settled than she ever had in her life, after two years, her roots were still tentative—almost as if she expected she'd have to run, as if the broken ties she'd have to leave behind would hurt too much.

But from what, exactly, would she have to run?

As the sun dipped below the horizon, Melinda found herself back in her own driveway. She turned off the ignition and listened to the engine's pings as it cooled.

She'd waited too long for a life of her own. It was time to find out what her mind was hiding from her.

GRADY HAD PROMISED HER breathing space but didn't give her any space at all. While she'd never noticed him before Angela's murder, Melinda now saw him everywhere she went.

During the day, she tried to lose herself in her work, and found her mind constantly drifting toward him. At night, she imitated his style and interrogated her memory, questioned her nightmares, analyzed the images and sounds coming invited into her mind, always careful to skirt the monster's cage. She needed to build a little more courage for that.

A trip to the Fort Worth library had given her a handful of articles about her mother's death—dry facts about the woman who'd given her birth and left her much too early. She filled page after page of impressions, feelings and memories, of anything that came to her mind, hoping that something, anything, would somehow glue all the tangled pieces of her jigsawed memory into a picture she could recognize.

And when she fell into an exhausted sleep every night, it was Grady who crowded her dreams.

He stopped by every day after work. Had done so for the past eight days. Their shared iced tea had become a ritual she anticipated. She thought she might even have to invest in a second chair if his visits continued.

Disasters at work took on less meaning. When the printer called to tell her the disk she'd sent him had spewed out gobbledygook, she'd taken it in stride. When she'd had to send the blues back to the printer for more corrections, it hadn't fazed her. Even when the irises had shown up with flipped photographs, it hadn't daunted her. All she could think of was Grady and their afternoon tea in her garden.

Not even her father's daily phone calls and chidings could dispel her buoyant mood. She couldn't remember when she'd ever felt this alive.

Today, she'd found herself brushing her hair, touching up her lipstick, putting a sprig of mint in the cooling tea. Now, she was getting down her best glasses, adding a plate of cookies to the ivy-painted tray, and listening for the purr of his car.

He didn't touch her.

He didn't talk about Angie, or the murder, or her father.

He was Grady. She was Melinda.

They talked of inconsequential things like the weather, her garden, his horses. They talked about everything and nothing—she, perched on the wall; he, swinging in the hammock chair. He promised her a horseback ride. She promised him a Christmas cactus in bloom.

She wanted much more, and thought he might, too.

The first time he'd stopped by, he'd had a search warrant in hand and had kept her company while two officers sifted through the contents of her garden. She should have been angry. She should have been hurt. But she wasn't. He'd simply been doing his job. Now he knew she had nothing to hide. And she came closer to believing she was as innocent as she believed.

The second time he'd shown up, it had been as if the visit hadn't been planned. His "Can I come in?" hadn't been a command. As a matter of fact, his hesitation had pleased her more than she cared to admit.

The promise she saw daily in his eyes permeated her sleep and meshed with her nightmares. His unspoken promise of passion had her aching so desperately, the tension nearly drove her mad. The way he looked at her so hungrily made her feel special, fully feminine for the first time in years.

She wanted him to touch her. She wanted him to kiss her. She wanted him to love her with a fierceness that frightened her as much as it excited her. Never had she wanted a man the way she wanted Grady Sloan.

But part of her feared for her heart. When he had what he wanted, would he leave? She remembered his punishing kiss when he'd spoken of the woman who'd betrayed him. Would he do to her what the woman had done to him? She couldn't bear the loss. And so she couldn't bring herself to cross the line.

In her driveway, his engine's soft purring rumbled on for a minute before it died. She licked her lips in anticipation, smoothed the front of her dress, and forced herself to take calm, even steps to the door. At his knock, her heart gave a small lurch. With a pat to her hair, she answered. Both her hands remained twined on the knob to keep herself from reaching for him, from touching the five o'clock shadow darkening his jaw.

"Hi!" Genuine pleasure shone in his eyes.

She smiled and her delight at seeing him fluttered all the way down to her stomach.

"Hi!" Did she sound as breathless as she felt?

"Can I come in?" He removed his sunglasses and twirled the temple between his fingers.

"I wish you would." She felt schoolgirl giddy, first-date clumsy, and cat sinewy all at the same time.

As she brought the tea tray out into the garden, she caught him looking at her with naked admiration, and she had the strange feeling he'd kept his uniform on to remind himself that he was the law and not a man. As if he needed the reminder of authority, his hand stroked the gun holstered at his hip.

She almost smiled at his unconscious gesture. The idea that she could make him nervous had an intoxicating impact. She'd never had much of any effect on a man before. A new feeling of power surged through her.

"If I didn't know better, I'd think I'd scared you," Melinda said, embarrassed by the coy laughter that followed.

She set the tray down on the small wrought-iron table she'd dragged out several days ago for that purpose, and felt his piercing gaze trail her every movement. She should be used to his intensity by now, but she wasn't.

"You do." His relentless gaze forced her to look up from the task of pouring tea into glasses. The blue of his eyes had never looked so bright, so transparent. "I want you. You have to know that."

So intense, his gaze. So sharp, the answering pang deep in her. Her hand involuntarily braced her abdomen. His admission shocked her, but didn't surprise her. She'd seen the truth of it in his face for a week now. "I do."

As she handed him a glass, their fingers touched, hesitated and separated once more. She sat primly on the wall's edge. He settled himself in the hammock chair.

So civilized.

Melinda wanted to scream. But she was a lady. Why did she have to remind herself so often these days?

She held her glass tightly with both hands to keep them

still. She wanted to use her fingers to loosen his collar, to run her palms over the muscles of his chest, to feel if the hard lines molded by his uniform were from more than starch. But she didn't. She hitched in a shaky breath. It was amazing, the wanton feelings just looking at him aroused in her.

She looked away, suddenly embarrassed by the train of her thoughts. "I—"

"I'm afraid I'll forget who I am and give in to my basic instincts," Grady interrupted. As he settled the glass on a flagstone by his chair, the ice cubes clinked loudly. He raised one foot to rest on his knee and laced his fingers behind his head. "Do you know what would happen if I did?"

Oh, yes. I'd melt like strawberry jelly on a hot short-cake. She shuddered with anticipation. Her throat went dry. She had to clear her throat before she could speak. "Tell me."

"It would ruin my career."

"Oh." Condensation from the glass in her hands pooled between the hammock of her thumb and index finger. "And if I wasn't a...suspect—a witness. What then?"

As if nothing important was happening in her little garden, as if today were just an ordinary day, birds twittered in the background. The breeze blew the wind chimes into a pleasing tinkle, belittling the small drama taking place between them.

"That would be a whole different story."

Her hands wobbled in her lap, spilling tea on her cream-colored dress. She sprang up like a wound spring and batted at the wet liquid spreading into a stain.

"I—I'll be right back." She practically ran into the house.

He made her nervous. He made her edgy. He made her want to relieve the primitive tension strung to near breaking between them. And that voice of his—sand on silk, raw with desire—was driving her crazy.

With a cloth she wet at the kitchen sink, Melinda worked at removing the stain on her dress. Frustrated, she hurled the cloth into the sink.

They were crossing a line, admitting to cards they held tightly, or perhaps just calling a bluff.

Maybe nothing would come of starting a relationship with Grady. Maybe once the initial fire of sexual need was flushed, they'd find there was nothing at all between them.

She could tell herself time and again she couldn't be falling in love with someone she barely knew, someone who thought of her as an obstacle to an investigation. She could stay up night after night, day after day, counting the reasons why their relationship couldn't work. But like death, love knew no logic.

And as surely as autumn followed summer, she was falling in love with the dangerous lieutenant.

If there was any way they would get an opportunity to explore this disturbing attraction hovering so potently around them, she'd have to prove her innocence to him. Not with drug-induced trips into the past, but with the cold, hard facts Grady's analytical personality craved.

And, as much as she feared the prospect, she'd have to face the monster hiding somewhere in her head. For that, she'd need help. This past week of solitary digging had taught her she could only go so far on her own. Taking the last step to open the monster's cage felt like jumping blindly over a cliff. She needed to know that someone would catch her, should she take the plunge. Though his presence had a definitely disquieting effect on her, she trusted Grady.

But if they were going to pry into her memory, they were going to do it her way.

Before she lost her nerve, she returned to the garden.

"I'm ready." She said the words fast and sharp. They felt like a bitter pill swallowed without water.

There was dead silence in the oasis refuge she'd created for herself and didn't often share. Even the birds and the breeze stilled for a moment as if they, too, could feel the situation spinning in a whole new direction. She waited, twisting her fingers, one around the other.

"What are you ready for, Melinda?"

"To let you into my world." She didn't give him a chance to respond, but sped on. "Do you own a tuxedo?"

"Why?"

"From what I could gather from the library, investigations have steps. One of the first is background. I'm taking you to the party being given in my father's honor tomorrow night. I'll pick you up at six-thirty. I promised Daddy I'd be there early."

Another silence stretched between them. The length and weight of it made her jittery all over again, shaking her resolve.

She'd been wrong. Still and focused on her, his gaze was much more nerve-racking than while in motion, sweeping his surroundings for cues and clues.

"You don't know where I live."

She'd caught him off guard. Choking back her smile, she realized that for once, *she* held the upper hand. "I'll find you."

She'd taken the next step.

She'd agreed to face her fears.

Now there was no turning back.

Chapter Eight

After a hard-running game of soccer in their Friday-night league, Grady and Oscar went to Mamie's for their post-game meal. At nine, the dinner crowd was long gone and they had the restaurant to themselves.

Except for Melinda.

Grady spotted her right away. She leaned against the counter, chatting with Maggie, the cook.

Take-out bag in hand, she almost ran into them at the door. She smiled at Grady, and the foreign surge of softness clunking in his chest like an out-of-whack engine baffled him. He made quick introductions.

"Tough game?" she asked, looking at his grass-stained shorts and socks.

"We've played better."

"Speak for yourself," Oscar quipped. "We could've won, if you'd made the last shot."

The game had ended up tied. As Oscar had said, they could have won, but Grady had missed an easy shot on goal, kicking the ball too hard and sending it flying over the net instead.

The type of shot he'd never have missed if he hadn't been concentrating so hard to wipe thoughts of Melinda out of his head.

But he couldn't get her out of his mind. He thought

about her day and night. And when he wasn't thinking about her, he was dreaming about her—erotic dreams that woke him with a painful yearning. He'd tried to label the deep itch, but no word came close to describing the hunger devouring him deep inside. And he didn't like the lack of control such a fact implied. Looking at her, he couldn't find an answer, either.

"Dining alone?" His chin pointed at her bag.

As if his gaze burned her, Melinda blushed. "No, I've got a date."

The thought of someone else kissing Melinda good-night brought an unexpected surge of something that had him seeing an unpleasant shade of green. He shook his head. *It's none of your business.* "A date?"

"With a stack of pricing reports and a calculator." As if aware of the straying track of his thoughts, she smiled. "I've got to go. I'll see you tomorrow."

As Melinda walked out the door, Grady caught Oscar's low whistle and cut off Oscar's view of her softly swaying skirt by urging him inside.

"What did I do, man?" Oscar asked with a chuckle.

"Nothing." He wasn't about to explain anything about Melinda to anyone, let alone someone as observant as Oscar. They'd known each other too long. He headed toward the booth at the back of the restaurant.

Grady's afternoon-tea sessions with Melinda had started because he couldn't keep himself from driving by her house. He hadn't planned to stop. But he had. He'd simply wanted to check on her, make sure she was all right, give her a chance to talk. As he would have for anyone else, he'd rationalized. But would he have continued the afternoon ritual if it had been old Lena Strong who'd been found in front of Angela Petersen's home with holes in her memory?

The mystery in the dark maze of Melinda's eyes had

drawn him in. He couldn't help himself; he needed his daily dose of her. The way an addict needed a fix. The way his mother had needed wine. Melinda would perturb him until he solved the enigma wrapping itself in layers around her.

But this driving need was starting to affect everything he did, even his soccer game. And if he kept going on this track, he might as well just call the State boys to take over the investigation, and hand the promotion over to Wayne himself.

Each visit left him more frustrated than the last. Questions hovered on the tip of his tongue, but he'd promised her space. He wanted to touch her, but he'd promised her space. He remembered the inebriating taste of her, the exhilarating touch of her, but he didn't make any moves toward her. He'd promised her space.

He was still in control—detective to hostile witness.

Funny how he didn't believe a word of the baloney he was feeding himself. There was nothing detective-like about what he'd like to do with her, nothing hostile about the way Melinda looked at him, her eyes filled with desire.

But he couldn't accept her silent invitation. He was the law. She was, at the very least, a material witness. No matter how much he'd like to trust the innocence in her deep, dark eyes, when all the evidence was analyzed, they were left with just her as their best suspect.

"I can't believe you missed that shot," Oscar said, as he slid into the booth by the window. The red vinyl seat squeaked from the sweat on his thighs, and his gym bag caught the corner of the red-and-white-checked plastic tablecloth, dragging half of it off before Grady could straighten it. "I set it up perfect for you. I told you, man. You gotta use your left foot."

Grady set his own gym bag on the floor and sat opposite Oscar. "I've got a lot on my mind."

Oscar's mustache rose into a wide grin, showing off his white teeth. "Pretty, too."

"The case, *hombre*. The case."

"Oh, yes. The case." Oscar roared with laughter. "And if I believe that, you've got a bridge to sell me."

"Maybe I do." Grady smiled, feeling his heavy mood lift for the first time in days. "It comes with all the amenities, including flood, fire and pestilence."

"With an offer like that, how can I resist?" Oscar snatched a menu from between the sugar shaker and the catsup bottle.

Without a look at the menu, Oscar signaled he was ready to order. "So how's it going? The case, that is."

"Not too well." Grady ran a hand through his damp hair in a frustrated zigzag. "Practically every soul in town's been interviewed. Practically every stone's been turned." They'd found nothing, not even under the pretty flowers in Melinda's garden. "The lab results are inconclusive. No new leads have turned up. It's all come to a dead end. Excuse the pun."

"Murder weapon turn up yet?"

"Not yet. Not likely to, at this point. My only hope is for Melinda Amery to recover her memory." Grady unwrapped the silverware from the paper napkin and put the napkin in his lap. "How about you? Anything unusual show up on your rounds?"

"Nada."

Silence fell over the table like a pall. Feelings or not, he'd deal with Melinda and recover her memory. He had too much at stake not to. So why did he have to remind himself of the fact yet again?

Two water glasses in hand, Janet—Maggie's twenty-something daughter—sauntered over to take their orders, keeping her eye on the charming Oscar while she scribbled on her pad.

"Uh-huh." As she preened for Oscar, Janet never looked at Grady. "Anything to drink?"

"A beer for me," Oscar answered.

"Iced tea," Grady said, images of Melinda and their afternoon ritual springing unbidden into his mind. He swallowed down the softness swelling in his chest once more.

"Coming right up." Janet sashayed away, and Oscar shook his head appreciatively at the sway of her hips.

"I thought you and Gloria were engaged," Grady teased.

Oscar held his hands up in mock surrender. "Hey, I'm not touching, man. I'm being appreciative of the view. Nothing wrong with that. Gloria knows there's no one else for me." Oscar gulped most of the water in his glass. "She's grilling chicken for fajitas tomorrow. Want to join us?"

"No, thanks anyway."

Oscar's eyes twinkled with mischief. "You could bring Melinda."

"What makes you think I'd want to bring her?" Grady's hand tightened around his glass.

"Because she's got your guts twisted inside out."

"Where'd you hear that?"

"Didn't believe the grapevine till I saw it with my own eyes tonight."

"What'd you hear?"

"Old Lena Strong told Kerry at the Winn-Dixie how you've been stopping by Melinda's house every afternoon. Kerry told Tracy at the beauty parlor, who told Mrs. Mallory. And you know what happens when Mrs. Mallory gets hold of juicy gossip."

"The whole town knows in about five and a half minutes."

"You got it."

With one hand, Grady twisted his glass around and around, watching the circle of condensation widen with each turn. "Which means Brasswell knows."

"Maybe not. She hasn't been in town much. She's been awfully cozy with that lawyer Ely Amery lately, trying to smooth his ruffled feathers over his daughter's jailing."

Grady blew out a frustrated breath. "Great."

"About Melinda—"

"You're wrong." Grady knocked back half his iced tea. "She's a witness, that's all."

"Yeah, I can see that." Oscar laughed, then paused to ogle Janet as she brought their meals to the table. As if there had been no interruption, Oscar took up the thread of conversation where it had ended. "You know deep in your gut she's nothing but a lady."

"My guts have been wrong before."

Oscar carefully set his knife and fork on the edge of the plate. "I saw the way you looked at her when we came in. You never looked at Jamie the way you look at Melinda. Jamie was hormones. Melinda is soul." Oscar grinned and wriggled his eyebrows. "Like me and Gloria."

"I think, *hombre,* you inhaled too much burning petrol in those Arab oil fields during the Gulf War."

"And maybe you know I'm right. And maybe that's what's got you so scared."

"I'm not scared." Grady pushed his plate away.

"You can lie to yourself if you want to, but you can't lie to me. You never could." Oscar dug into his meal and rubbed a satisfied hand over his stomach. "So, do you believe her?"

Grady stared at Oscar for a moment. There was no use pretending he didn't understand his friend's question. They knew each other too well. "I don't know. She seems to be exactly what she says she is. But we both know appearances are illusions. She was there. You saw her.''

"I saw a frightened woman, not a drunk. Your focus is too narrow, and that's not like you.''

Grady ran a hand roughly through his hair. "What else have I got? Angela's ex was helping his new wife deliver their baby the night of the murder. Mike was on his way to Nashville to launch their new career. Everyone loved Angela.''

"Maybe that's it. Maybe someone loved her too much.''

And everyone who claimed to love her had a solid alibi. Grady took a long drink from his glass. Except Melinda. She'd been found at the scene. Time to start from square one again. Check and recheck. Basic procedures.

"Passion,'' Oscar said. "It's tough to explain the things it drives people to do. Know what I mean?''

Thinking of Jamie, Grady snorted. "Yeah, too well.''

"Take a word of advice, my friend. You got to decide where you stand and stick to it. You either believe her, or you don't. You can't seesaw on top of the fence like that. You'll end up with nothing if you do. No woman. No promotion. Myself, I'd go for the woman.''

"I ended up in trouble the last time I took a stand.''

"So you're gonna spend the rest of your life with Jamie's shadow hanging over your head? How's that gonna help solve Angela's case? I thought you had more sense than that.'' Oscar reached into his gym bag, drew out several bills, and secured them with the edge of his plate. "I gotta go. Gloria's waiting for me. Wants me to rent her another one of those tearjerkers she likes to watch after her shift at the hospital.''

Oscar rolled his eyes to the ceiling, but Grady didn't believe him for a moment. Oscar loved tearjerkers. They brought Gloria into his arms and into his bed. Grabbing his bag, Oscar slipped out of the booth. As he passed Grady, he paused and squeezed Grady's shoulder.

"Take a stand and stick with it. Hear me, man?"

"Yeah, I hear you."

Slipping bills onto the tabletop, Grady realized he'd come to care too much for Melinda in the past week. Her honest goodness, her soft strength and the pain she so carefully bottled away had gotten to him. Not being able to reach her, to get at the truth, to dislodge the memories trapped inside her mind was driving him crazy.

He stopped at the counter and ordered an assortment of goodies for Seth.

Take a stand and stick with it.

It would require trust—in her, in his muddled hunter's instincts.

The last time he'd trusted, he'd taken a hard fall. Balancing the take-out box in one hand, he hitched his bag over his shoulder and waved goodbye to Maggie and Janet. He was getting too involved with a case, again. Too involved with Melinda.

Trust.

That was the crux of it all.

Did he believe the sea of shades of gray in her eyes, or the black-and-white concrete evidence?

A leap of faith.

Jamie had taught him there were worse things than losing his promotion. He let out a silent burst of ironic laughter. If he was going to screw up, he might as well do it royally.

He had two weeks left before Brasswell announced Seth's replacement. Two weeks to find Angela's murderer. Time enough to stack up the dominoes and see which way they fell.

For now, he'd err on Melinda's side.

He'd rent a monkey suit, let her drag him to her father's

highbrow shindig, and see where this particular path of the maze led.

AFTER A LONG DAY OF irritating nuisance calls, Grady had finally signed off duty. He'd gone through his chores at the ranch with rapid precision, which Ironsides—with a quick cow kick to the shin—had let him know he didn't appreciate. Even with his rushing, he'd found himself with less than half an hour to shower and dress in his rented tux.

As if seeking to irritate him, his answering machine blinked with two messages—one from Aimee, wanting him to return the salad bowl he'd borrowed. The other was from Harold Hobart. It was the third of the day. Finding his daughter's killer had become an unhealthy obsession with Harold.

Grady ignored both messages and struggled with the length of black silk that should, he'd been assured, knot into a bow tie. All of his fingers seemed to have suddenly turned into thumbs.

The house was quiet. Too quiet. Quiet was dangerous, because his mind tended to fill the silence with thoughts. And these days, any thoughts sooner than later turned to Melinda. He cranked on the radio to a classic rock station.

The uneasy quiet had nothing to do with her. He liked quiet. It had never bothered him before. He liked his life the way it was. Few complications besides the usual office politics.

Why was this tie giving him so much grief? He was tired, he decided. Which had nothing to do with Melinda.

"And if you believe that," he said to his reflection in the mirror, "I've got a bridge to sell you."

He'd long ago decided he didn't want a family of his own. His childhood hadn't painted him a rosy picture of marriage. His work had drilled into him the declining well-being of the institution. How many fellow officers had taken the plunge only to find they couldn't beat the odds? Serving the law and marriage just didn't mix.

As a cop, he saw the worst side of people, the damage people could wreak on each other. But he had to admit, if grudgingly, that even with all the misery he saw every day, there were pockets of happiness. Seth and Rita Mullins had been happily married for over forty years. His sister Aimee had found a loving husband in Colton Rangel.

He still didn't want marriage. Desiree was right, he did get too involved in his job. Few women could put up with that. No, he didn't want marriage. Didn't even want love. Just one particular woman.

The one he couldn't have if he wanted his promotion to chief.

He pulled on the loops of black silk and they fell apart in his hands. Swearing, he tried the knot once more.

The quicker he got to the secret hidden in Melinda's memory, the quicker she could get back to her life and he to his. It was a good, simple life, and he liked it that way.

Yeah, right. Tell yourself that often enough and you might actually believe it.

He yanked at the lopsided bow and was about to throw the thing across the room, when he heard a knock on his front door through the pounding beat of rock music. On his way to the door, he snapped the stereo off.

In all the time he'd spent with Melinda, nothing had prepared him for the vision that stood before him. She took his breath away.

Her black hair was twisted up in a sophisticated chignon. A few loose tendrils curled around her face, accentuating the elegant curves of her neck. Her dress—a simple, spaghetti-strapped sheath of black in a soft material that shimmered dark blue when she moved—swirled exquisitely around her knees. Sheer black stockings hugged her shapely calves, and three-inch heels encased her dainty feet. A diaphanous shawl skimmed her shoulders.

And, he noticed, as his gaze lingered on the soft curves of her breasts, she wore no bra beneath the dress. As if reading his instant and painful hunger, her nipples hardened beneath the material. He stifled a groan and invited her in.

"You found me," he said, while he sought to reengage his brain.

"I told you I would. It's really not too hard in a town like this."

Grady sidestepped to the small mirror in the entryway and fumbled with his tie.

"Here, let me." Melinda reached for his collar, stood it up, then picked up the strip of black silk. With practiced ease, she started the knot.

"I don't like ties," he said gruffly.

"Then don't wear it."

"Isn't it expected?"

She chuckled and the sound tickled through him. "And you wouldn't want to breach proper etiquette, would you?"

"Are you laughing at me?"

"No, I could never do that." Her smile erupted through him with a speed and a power so great, it surely surpassed nuclear fusion. Her painted lips, so close and bright, begged to be tasted. He stuck his hands in his pants pockets to keep them from touching the creamy expanse of skin her dress exposed. "It's nice to know you're human, that's all. I was starting to wonder."

Her fingers at his throat had the strangest effect on the rest of his body. Her touch rippled down his limbs like warm water. He swallowed hard. "Human? What did you think I was?"

"Don't move." She bit her lower lip, but he saw the corners twitch up. "A computer."

"Really?" If only she could feel the havoc her flowery perfume created, she'd think twice about her description.

"Yes, really." She patted the bow in place. "There. You're all set and presentable." She looked up at him, her dark eyes shining.

"You *are* laughing at me."

"Only a little. Are you nervous?"

"Of course not," he lied. A shindig with lots of pompous people, pretentious mutual admiration and pointless small talk. The type of people who thought nothing of using others, then throwing them away like used tissues. Yeah, just how he loved to spend a Saturday night! If he wasn't so desperate to have access to her repressed memories, she couldn't have gotten him within a ten-mile radius of the Van Horn home tonight. "Why did you ask me to come with you?"

She shrugged and turned away. Her gaze took in his surroundings, and Grady found himself wishing he'd bought a plant to liven up the place. For himself, of course, not for her. Her hand trailed the back of the recliner and tangled in the soft wool of the red-and-white afghan Aimee had given him last Christmas. He'd forgotten to fold it and return it to the foot of his bed after spending the night in the recliner.

"I want you to see what kind of world I grew up in. I want you to understand...." She shrugged again. He saw the caged-animal restlessness he'd observed so often return. "I'm not sure what it is I'm expecting." A pained look crossed her delicately made-up face. "There's good and bad, Grady. I want you to see the gray. If everything were black-and-white, there would be no monster. It exists because of the gray." Her forehead wrinkled. "Do you understand what I'm trying to say?"

"I think so."

She gave him a tentative smile. "I've got something to confess."

That perked his attention. "What?"

"I hate these chichi affairs, too." Her smile widened. "Are you ready?"

He offered his arm and she placed her long-fingered hand around his elbow. It looked so right there—as if it belonged.

"You know," she said, giving him a coy look, "for a country cop, you sure fill a tux well."

Laughter rumbled through him. "For a stuck-up social-ite, you don't look half-bad yourself." The evening might not prove so bad after all.

As they went through the front door, the phone rang. Knob in hand and key poised, Grady listened while the answering machine whirred on. Hearing Harold Hobart's voice demanding an update on the case, Grady shut the door with a definitive click.

Chapter Nine

Though it wasn't dark yet, more than a dozen golden luminaries lit the bricked path to Roger and Emily Van Horn's house in Fort Worth's posh Rivercrest area. At the curb, two valets waited to park the car. One opened Melinda's door. The other came around to take Grady's place in the driver's seat.

"Jackson. What are you doing here?" Grady asked. He barely recognized Carson Crews's father clean and sober.

"I was doing some carpentry work for Mr. Van Horn's office and he asked me if I'd be interested in some extra money. Not that it's any of your business."

Grady moved out of the way and allowed Jackson to sit in Melinda's Volvo. He leaned over the open door. "Does he know about your little problem?"

"He knows what he needs to know." When Jackson looked up at him, murder shone in his eyes. "Don't you go ruin this for me. It's bad enough you've got Carson's head filled with that scholarship crap."

"He's a good enough pitcher to get a baseball scholarship to any college he wants next year."

"He's needed at home."

"He's got the chance to get a good education."

"Carpentry's good enough for me. It'll be good enough for him." With that, Jackson slammed the door and roared off. Grady watched him drive away, pondering Carson's future. If he stayed at home, he'd end up no better than his father, and Carson had too much potential to waste this way. Grady knew for a fact that a college scout had been invited to watch the Mustang-Trojan game at the Fall Festival. Carson would get his chance. When he turned back to Melinda, Grady decided he'd make sure Carson took advantage of it.

Curiosity danced in her eyes, but Grady chose to ignore her silent question. Smiling at her, he took her elbow and led her to the house.

They were among the first to arrive. Emily Van Horn fluttered by for a quick welcome before she zipped away to check on last-minute details.

Drink in hand, Ely stood outside on the patio deep in conversation with Melinda's windmill-handed partner. Those hands were working overtime at the moment and the expression on the petite woman's face wasn't a pleasant one. In the midst of her tirade, she noticed them approaching, stopped abruptly and smiled worriedly at them.

Interesting.

Melinda greeted Dolores and touched her father's arm. Coiffed hair and red rose in place on his lapel, he turned toward her with a warm smile and gave her a hug.

"I thought you were going to get here early." With an exaggerated motion, Ely checked his watch and tapped the glass with one finger.

"I am early." Her pretty smile didn't waver, but Grady sensed the tension winding itself through Melinda's beautiful neck and shoulders and all the way down her slender back. He almost reached for the knotted triangle between her bared shoulder blades to soothe the tightness away.

Ely's gaze cut over Melinda's head and aimed straight at Grady. "The hired help is to report at the kitchen entrance."

"He's my guest, Daddy." As if to show the truth of her statement, she wrapped a hand around his elbow. Her long fingers dug into the folds of the jacket's material. To his dismay, his body answered her touch with a sharp flash of desire. Adrenaline, he decided—from being on guard in this unfamiliar territory. Nothing more.

"Why on earth would you want to do that?" No one could have missed the derision in Ely's voice. Was he putting on the thick act for the hick cop? Bitterness slid down Grady's throat and tightened his stomach, but he didn't let any sign of it show.

The tightening of Melinda's fingers around his elbow told him she wasn't pleased with the conversation—because her father was questioning her judgment, or because he was putting down her date? *You're getting much too cynical.* Or was she using him, too, for her own ends? As Jamie had?

"To prove a point," she said.

"You don't have to prove anything, and certainly not to the likes of him."

"Not to him, Daddy. To me." She turned deliberately to Dolores, and Grady had to admire the way Melinda kept her cool and hung on to her dignity. "I didn't know you'd be here tonight."

"Emily's an old friend." Waving her hands, Dolores snorted, "Don't know why she thought I'd enjoy such a crowd. Let's get you something to drink." With a stern look in Ely's direction, she linked her arm through Melinda's and led her back inside. Before they'd even turned away, Ely had prowled on to more stimulating conversation with a hyena-grinned cohort.

"It's good for you to be around people your own age once in a while," Melinda teased Dolores.

"Maybe you're right. It's hard to keep up with all those energetic hunks whose hearts you insist on breaking. I'm

not as young as I used to be.'' She glanced at Grady over
Melinda's shoulder. Her eyes crinkled with mischief. ''I'm
glad to see you're following your own advice.''

''It's not what you think.''

Dolores sighed with exaggeration. ''It never is.'' She
reached back and hooked her free arm around Grady's,
pulling him forward. ''I think, Lieutenant, that you ought
to take Melinda on a real date sometime.''

''Is that so?'' Amused, Grady looked at Melinda who
was blushing a pretty shade of pink and rolling her eyes
back in exasperation.

''You both look like you need a dash of life injected
into your existence,'' Dolores insisted. ''You're too young
to be this serious.''

''Don't listen to her, she doesn't believe in minding her
own business. If you're not careful, she'll line up half-a-
dozen dates for you before the evening's out,'' Melinda
warned.

He liked seeing her this way—all soft and warm, her
smile radiant and bright. There was no doubt she loved
the older woman at her side. Was this how she'd been
before the incident brought the shadow of fear into her
dark eyes? Seeing her like this, he wanted to believe she
was as innocent as she appeared.

Take a stand and stick to it, Oscar had told him. It
wasn't like Grady to waver, and he didn't like it one bit.
Was he erring on her side to unravel the lies, or was he
falling for those deep, dark eyes?

The pretty people had turned out en masse to honor one
of their own. At any given time, it took Grady less than a
second to spot Ely Amery among the press of people in
the living room that was growing more crowded by the
minute. He had to admit the man had style. Ely worked
the throng, acknowledging the most and the least of them
with a touch or a word, making them feel special, yet

somehow keeping a distance. He'd seen that same invisible wall around Melinda often enough to recognize it. So charmed and honored were they, most of them didn't notice the screen the "king" drew around himself. Didn't these people see how he used them? Didn't they realize that every day, he put their safety in jeopardy by setting the guilty free without a blink of conscience?

A sour taste filled Grady's mouth. Power. Ely Amery oozed it. Even the law had to bend for it—the kind of absolute power Grady had fought to keep his family together after his parents' death. He turned sharply away and concentrated on the woman on his arm.

Melinda worked the crowd with equal ease, making introductions and polite conversation in a practiced way, including him every chance she got. She fit in perfectly. Grady had to admit he was out of his element.

He wanted to rip the tie off his neck and loosen his collar button. The atmosphere in the room was stifling. It reminded him of the first time he'd walked into a courtroom. So much had hung in the balance then. He focused on Melinda's dark eyes. So much hung in the balance now. He needed to pay attention and set his unease aside.

Watch and listen.

Did the Van Horns realize the guy promenading puffs on a platter was a con? His walk gave him away. It couldn't have been long, either, from the look of things. The middle-aged blonde with a bad face-lift had sticky fingers. He'd seen her glance unobtrusively at the gold cigarette case on the occasional table more times than for mere curiosity. He'd bet his boots it would end up in that large purse of hers before the evening was over. And the guy trying to kiss Roger Van Horn's butt was lying through every one of his capped teeth. Body language gave him away as surely as a color magazine ad. Amazing. And they called themselves the "cream" of society.

A set of red nails touched his arm and brought his attention back to the semicircle of people around him.

"You're the officer who testified in the Waller case, aren't you?" the woman with the red hair and purple dress said. He'd missed her name. "Remember, Melinda? Two years ago when Jamie Waller was accused of killing her brother John, he's the one who helped get her off. That was an incredible piece of courtroom drama your dad pulled off."

The incredible part, Grady sneered silently, was that he'd fallen for the scenario hook, line and sinker without even realizing the reputation he'd spent a lifetime building was the bait. He glanced at his watch. An hour and a half had trickled by since their arrival.

Someone tapped a crystal glass with a spoon, causing a ripple of noise. Mrs. Van Horn announced that dinner was about to start.

He glanced down at the liquid in his wineglass. For once, he wished it held something stronger than water. It was going be a long evening.

DRONING SPEECH AFTER droning speech muddled Melinda's mind. A dull ache throbbed on one side of her head. Since her father's return, she'd had more headaches than she'd had in the past two years he'd spent in the Northeast. Was there a connection? she wondered idly. Of course not. She loved her father dearly even if he did manage to make her angry every time they spent more than a few minutes together.

This was his day. She'd try her best to remain composed. She studied the crowd and spotted Dolores deep in conversation with Emily Van Horn. Once again, Dolores's presence here twitched at her curiosity. There was no love lost between Dolores and her father. Ever since her mother had died, Dolores had not had one good word to say about the man. Knowing how much Melinda cared for him, Dolores more often than not chose to change the subject rather than talk about Ely. So why was she here at a party honoring someone she couldn't stand?

Melinda caught Grady's eye and smiled at him. He smiled back and returned to fighting off Kaitlin Carter's not-so-subtle under-the-table come-ons. He was holding up well. The taut lines of his face told her he hated every second of this ordeal, but to most people, he'd look as if he were paying rapt attention to every word uttered by the speakers. She was starting to know him well enough to realize he was looking, always looking, for something out of place. Did he ever relax?

Of course, in a place like this, no matter how used to it she was, neither could she.

With the meal eaten and the speeches finished, the assembled guests once again returned to the living room and spilled onto the outdoor patio. Grady was discussing the merits of various woods in flavoring smoked meat with the owner of the busiest upscale barbecue restaurant in town, and Melinda took the opportunity to excuse herself and visit the ladies' room.

As she reached for the bathroom light switch, she heard her name being called. Pausing at the door, she saw Dolores hurrying toward her. Dolores darted a look back into the living room, then gently pushed Melinda inside the cavernous bathroom and closed the door.

"I wanted to talk to you for a minute," Dolores said.

"Is anything wrong?" Melinda asked, curious about Dolores's odd behavior. Shotgun blunt she was, and not given to behind-closed-door discussions.

Dolores leaned against the door and smiled. "I just wanted to ask how you were holding up."

"Me? I'm fine." Melinda laughed softly. "Why

wouldn't I be? I hate these functions, but I've been to a million of them, and could handle them in my sleep.''

Dolores shrugged, her hands uncharacteristically still, flattened against the carved wooden door. "People aren't giving you a hard time, are they?''

Melinda turned from Dolores and perched her purse on the marble counter. "About the murder?''

Dolores nodded, anxiety pulling her pencil-thin eyebrows together. The intensity, too, was uncharacteristic of this usually easygoing woman. What was going on?

"No one's mentioned it directly.'' Melinda fiddled with the tiny purse's contents, looking for her lipstick, and shrugged casually. "There've been a few awkward silences, that's all.'' But she'd heard all the questions behind the lines, seen the speculation in glances held just a bit too long, and sensed the doubt couched in polished politeness.

"That's good. I was afraid—'' Dolores sank onto the bathtub's edge. Earnestly, her gaze intercepted Melinda's in the mirror. "That's why I came tonight. So you'd have a friend. In case an awkward situation came up.''

"Like what?''

"Indelicate questions. Accusations. Do the police have a lead yet?''

Just me, she started to say, then changed her mind. She would have to explain too much she herself didn't understand. Dolores was her friend; she worried too much as it was. She didn't need to know about the terror, the dreams or the unnerving tension that filled her whenever Grady Sloan was near. Melinda didn't want anyone to know about the fear humming on the edges of her consciousness and her own lingering doubts about the missing time and what might have happened. She noticed how tight her grip on her lipstick had gotten and forced herself to relax. "Not that I know of.''

"I hope, for your sake, they arrest someone soon.''

"Thanks, Dolores. For caring." Carefully, she filled her lips with red color she didn't really need. With a casualness she didn't feel, she dropped the lipstick back into her open purse.

"You can stay with me for a while, if that'll help. I don't like the idea of you being alone in that house of yours. It's too secluded."

As she leaned closer to the mirror to check the rest of her makeup, Melinda laughed dryly. What was she? A poster child for the dysfunctional adult? "I'm a big girl now. I can take care of myself."

"I know. I just worry about you."

"Ever since my mother died, you've been there for me. If I needed anything, you're the first one I'd go to."

"I'm glad." Dolores picked at nonexistent lint on her light coral dress. "Your mother..."

Melinda glanced into the mirror at the reflection of Dolores jumping up from the bathtub's edge. "Yes?"

Dolores gave her a watery smile. "Your mother would be proud of you." She reached for the knob and opened the door. "I'm here for you, Melinda. Always. Remember that."

Before Melinda could swallow the choked-up knot in her throat, Dolores disappeared, softly clicking the door shut behind her.

Moments later while she still pondered Dolores's unusual show of emotion, Melinda was intercepted by her father.

"You look pale," Ely said, handing her a glass of white wine. "Is everything all right?"

"I'm fine, Daddy." She accepted the glass and took a sip.

"I've got a great idea." Ely wrapped an arm around her shoulders and led her slowly into the buzzing living room.

"Why don't you let me take you to St. Thomas? We could both use a little vacation."

"No, really, Daddy. I can't take a vacation right now. I've got too much going on at the office."

He quirked his head and gave her a roguish grin. "It would be like old times. We could rent a villa on the beach and relax. Just the two of us. I'm worried about you."

"You worry too much. Really, I'm fine." The fingers of her left hand found the clasp on her purse and squeezed the decorative beads open and closed. "Between you and Dolores wanting to put me behind glass like some sort of fine china, it's a wonder I can function independently at all."

"We care for you."

"I know you do." She relaxed her head against his shoulder. "I'm lucky to have both of you in my life."

As her father glanced at Grady's approaching figure, his features hardened. The genial face acquired a subtle edge. "He's not giving you a hard time, is he?"

"No, he's actually making this evening half-enjoyable." She watched Grady's long, confident steps as he approached. A zing of electricity trilled through her. Her skin tightened in anticipation of his nearness and an ache that was becoming familiar settled low in her belly. She didn't understand her reaction, wasn't sure she liked it. But there it was, and becoming stronger with each step closer he took.

Her father frowned down at her. "When did you become so friendly?"

She wondered at the agitation she sensed beneath the calm surface. "It's not what you think."

"He's using you."

She looked up at him, a mischievous streak she didn't know she had bubbled to the surface. "Maybe I'm using him."

"That's a dangerous game."

The surprised glint in her father's eyes pleased her. "I've had the best teacher, so you can stop worrying about me, okay?"

"How's the investigation on the Petersen case coming along?" Ely challenged Grady before he'd even quite reached them.

"We're making progress."

"So you've got a suspect?" Her father's voice held just the right touch of incredulity.

"You know I can't talk about an ongoing investigation." Grady stood close to her, close enough to touch her, if she could manage to take a full breath. His heat rippled into her, and suddenly, she had an overpowering urge to leave, to feel wide-open spaces around her, to hear the quiet sounds of night in her garden.

"Ah, yes, the rules," her father mocked. "You were very good at those, weren't you?"

An adversarial tension crackled between the two men, making her feel once again as if she were a boat about to enter a storm-tossed sea.

"I prefer the truth these days."

"That's good to know." Like a dog who'd found a meaty bone, her father practically salivated at the confrontation he was building.

Okay, enough was enough. She didn't intend to get shredded, trapped between two dueling dogs, when they started taking bloody chunks out of each other's hides. She handed Grady her wineglass. "Grady, please, could you get me my shawl?"

Reluctantly, Grady took her glass, nodded and left.

"You've got to stop seeing him, Melinda. It's not healthy." His fingertips bored into her shoulder. She swiveled around to face him and free herself from the uncomfortable grip. "I don't like the idea of him pushing you so hard."

"It was my idea." She wadded her purse's long silken strap in her hand.

"Your idea?"

"Yes." Slowly she released her grip on the string, watching the little pouch swirl in a mad arc down to her ankles. "I—I've had memory blanks, nightmares, ever since I can remember. I haven't had a life, Daddy. Not a real one. That's what I want now."

A shocked look momentarily crossed his face. "Nightmares? Memory blanks? Why haven't you said anything about this?"

"You're not exactly the easiest person to admit a weakness to."

"And a bumbling country cop is?" Disbelief lit his face in a grotesque distortion, like an old-fashioned mask in a play.

"I trust him."

"But not your own father? I don't like it one bit, Melinda. If you need help, I'll get you some professional help. This man couldn't find a clue if it was handed to him on a silver platter."

From where she stood, Melinda became conscious of raindrops pattering the pool's surface. A feeling of being suffocated overwhelmed her. She gasped, disoriented. The night spun. Her hand sought something—anything—for support and found Grady's arm.

"There, you see what I mean. Look how pale you've gotten. You look positively sick. Let me take care of you, Melinda."

She hated the feeling of being manipulated by her father's soft, cajoling voice. Hated the feeling she was failing him once more. Hated herself for doubting his motives. He loved her. He wanted what was best for her.

"Can't you give your old man the pleasure of taking care of his little girl? One week, Melinda. What harm can it do?"

It was easy to see why he was so effective in court. He was playing the guilt card now, and it was having the desired effect, rumbling through her, cracking her self-confidence, eroding her determination.

Grady handed Melinda her shawl. Their fingers touched. In that small point of body contact, of heat, of breathless desire, she found her strength again. "If you'll excuse us, Daddy. Grady's got an early shift in the morning and I promised him I'd get him home early." Lying was coming to her with an ease she could never have imagined.

"Call me when you get home." It was an order, no doubt about it. Daddy had been left out of the loop, and that was something he wasn't used to.

"I will."

As she made her way across the house and said her goodbyes, she felt her father's sharp-as-a-knife gaze between her shoulders. Maybe he was right. Maybe she was playing a dangerous game with the persistent lieutenant. Maybe her father was right to worry about her ability to take care of herself. Her record in that department wasn't exactly a shining example of feminist self-reliance. On the other hand, maybe she was just getting downright paranoid. Not a pretty thought.

"What was that all about?" Grady asked as they waited for her car to be brought around. They stood side by side, not touching, yet she was aware of every solid inch of him.

"Nothing." She pasted on a pleasant smile and turned to him, putting extra space between them and finding it didn't diminish at all the strength of his presence. "What did you think of the party?"

"There's enough gray here to paint a barn," he said wryly.

She chuckled. "Buckets and buckets."

A fat raindrop splattered against her face and dripped down her cheek like a large tear. Her laughter faded. The rising wind caught the hem of her dress and swirled it around her knees. She looked up at the sky. And as black clouds churned into the sky, she knew her quest for peace was far from over.

"YOU'RE GOING THE WRONG WAY," Melinda said to Grady as he turned into Laurel Court instead of continuing straight to his own home.

"A gentleman always sees a lady home."

"Don't be ridiculous. It's raining. How are you going to get home?"

"I'll call someone when we get to your place."

He slowed the car and turned into her driveway. The windshield wipers slapped the pouring rain away from the glass, giving alternating views of wavy night and the stark clarity of dark glass.

"What's wrong?" Grady asked.

"I—I thought I left a light on." She shrugged her shoulders. She was going to drive herself nuts if she kept on like this. There was nothing wrong. It was just the rain making her tense again. Would September ever end this year? "I must be mistaken."

"Are you sure?"

"Of course." She reached for the handle and opened the door.

"I'll walk you in."

Pausing, one foot out of the car, she looked at him. "That's not necessary."

"I've got to make a call anyway."

"Yes, of course." She handed him her house key, and

pulling her shawl over her head, she made a dash for the front door.

As Grady pushed the door open, an orange streak shot out. Melinda gasped. Her hand went to her heart. Grady shoved her against the house, shielding her body with his.

"Rusty?" she said as she watched Angela's cat skitter around the corner of her house. "What was he doing inside?"

Grady tensed. "Did he sneak in before you left?"

"No, he refuses to come inside. Always has." She started forward, but he stopped her, once again pushing her flat against the outside wall.

"Stay!" Not looking at her, he edged forward. "I mean it. Don't come in until I give you the all-clear. Got it?"

"But—"

"Got it?"

"Yes."

He eased into the house, reaching under his jacket. For his gun? Of course, he was a police officer. Never really off duty.

With one hand, he reached for the light switch by the door. The rigid lines of his back made her uneasy. Gun ahead of him, he took one step in, and swung his arms in an arc as he swept the room for an intruder. He tilted his head, and scanned the inside of her living room as if he were seeing it for the first time. Dripping wet, Melinda wedged herself between the doorframe and Grady's hard body.

"I said, stay outside!"

At the sight of spilled pots and general chaos, she gasped. Quietly, he made a quick round of the rest of the house. She barely noticed. With zombie-like steps, she crouched to pick up the mangled Chinese evergreen closest to her. Rain from her hair dripped onto the scattered earth, turning the edges of the pile into small puddles of mud.

"Don't touch anything," Grady growled as he slipped his gun back in its holster.

She glanced up at him and found his gaze focused on the big dracaena knocked on its side, its terra-cotta pot a jigsaw puzzle of shards around its roots. One piece of pottery was missing. From the hole, came the glint of metal.

Grady carefully bent over the pot. With the tip of a pen he extracted from his pocket, he plucked a few more pottery pieces aside. He moved a hairbreadth, giving her a clear view of the object of his focus.

A knife lay tangled in the plant's roots.

"Is this yours?"

There was no use pretending. They both knew the answer. "It's the knife that's missing from my kitchen." She could clearly see there were the remains of rusted blood on the blade and embedded deep into the hilt. A shiver of horror unraveled through her.

Once more, he scanned the living room. "There are no open doors or open windows. Is there any other way the cat could have made its way into the house?"

Goose bumps trooped up her arms. "No."

"He never comes inside."

Her fingers turned to ice. "No."

"Why not?"

She wanted to jump, to run, to move, but found herself paralyzed to the spot. "He's always been shy."

"Would he have been scared enough to cause this much damage?"

Grady crouched beside her, blue eyes blazing with intensity. Her heart beat a mad race. Her thoughts grew more chaotic by the moment. Fear, sharp and bitter, snaked its way through her limbs, leaving her shivering at the possibilities. "I—I really don't know."

"Someone went through a lot of trouble for me to find

the knife here. Almost as if someone didn't trust me to find it on my own.''

He seemed to expect an answer of some sort, but she could make no sense of the thoughts scrambling through her mind. Except for one. *Get out. Now. Get out.* It took all she had not to run outside like a madwoman, to hide, to shrink, to disappear—as she'd done the night Angela had been murdered.

"How did the knife get in your plant?'' he asked.

Faraway thunder sounded like phantom footsteps. Closer. Coming closer. "I don't know.''

"Convenient amnesia, or—''

"Are you insinuating—''

"No, simply making a comment.''

She jumped up, no longer able to stand being still. Pacing a tight arc around the fractured remnants of her oasis, she ground potting soil into the green weave of the carpet. "Why are you going out of your way to make me suspicious of my own actions?''

"Most murder victims are killed by someone they know. Someone they care about.''

Rain pattered against the roof, added a layer of edginess to the fear thrumming through her. "What does that have to do with me?''

"You have secrets.''

"I didn't kill Angela.'' She wrapped her left hand around her waist, nibbled the nail of her right thumb. "I cared about her. But I didn't know her very well. I had no reason to want her dead.''

"When we found you, you'd lost track of reality.'' Voice like a metronome, he was hypnotizing her. "Could you have mistaken her for a monster, too?''

"No.''

"Are you sure?''

She wasn't sure of anything right now.

"Who has a key to your house?" he persisted.

Wind lashed against the house, driving sheets of rain against the windows. Her thoughts slowed. "No one does. Angela did. But she's dead."

"Is there any other way to get in?"

The rain drummed harder, seeming to fall in all directions at once, surrounding her in scrabbling sounds. The swirl of thoughts came down to a few. "I don't know. You're the cop. You tell me."

"Nothing visible."

His line of thinking finally dawned on her. He didn't really think the knife had been planted. He thought she was guilty of preventing him from finding the knife, of hiding the evidence, of killing Angela. He didn't believe her. Never would unless she could prove her innocence to him. And there was only one way to do that. Fingers shaking, she looked up a number in the phone book, picked up the phone on the counter in the kitchen, and dialed.

"Gail, this is Melinda Amery, we met a couple years ago when you did a piece about *The Essential Gardener*. Your paper carried an article about the Petersen murder in Fargate. My name wasn't mentioned in the article, but I was a witness. If you'd like an interview, please give me a call."

When she hung up the phone, he was right behind her. Rain pounded at the roof like monster fists battering to get inside. A strange calmness filled her.

"Why did you do that?" he asked, his voice a soft rasp against her skin, but the soothing tone didn't fool her.

She turned slowly to face him, her hands instinctively gripping the edge of the counter, crowding away from the man who'd returned to being all detective. "It's the only thing I could think to do to make you believe I didn't kill Angela."

He touched her face, his callused finger sliding down

her cheekbone. Her skin hummed. She longed to lean into the heat, draw comfort from his hand, to take a step forward and curve her body into his strength—to end the constant fear making her want to scream. The rain redoubled its rhythm. *Believe me. Please, believe me. I didn't kill her.*

"Someone did. My gut says it's not you. But my gut's been wrong before."

"Jamie." She swallowed hard, remembering the betrayal he'd suffered.

"And now I've got this hard evidence staring at me in the face. There's a bloody knife in one of your plants. Hidden there. Can you see my dilemma?" He whispered the words into her ear. His voice, low and hot, slid deep inside her and resonated, sending a shiver of pleasure—of fear—rippling through her. Flickers of lightning streaked in her peripheral vision. "If you didn't kill her, then someone else did."

"Yes," she said, her mouth dry. Thunder rumbled, its power stifled by the force of the downpour. "That's what I've been trying to tell you all along."

"If you do the interview, that someone will think you truly saw something." Lightning split the night sky. His face blinked half dark, half light. Her spine prickled. The fine hairs on the back of her neck rose. His voice became lower, huskier. "Do you understand what you've done?"

Thunder rocked the small house, making the windows shudder in their casings. Her breathing went shallow. His blue, blue eyes burned into her.

"Yes," she murmured, shifting from him, only to find the void in the middle of the living room even more frightening. "I've set myself up as the next victim."

Chapter Ten

He'd scared her, Grady knew. He'd had to. As he walked to stand beside her in the middle of her fragmented living room, he saw how hard she tried to control the trembling of her limbs. Angela's murder had been vicious, savage. If Melinda wasn't the murderer, then she was placing herself in danger of suffering the same fate. He'd had to make her aware of the possibility, had to make her understand the extreme consequences her action could have.

"If you go through with this interview, you won't be safe," he said, trying to soften the harsh blow he'd had to deliver. As the thunder again rumbled outside, her shoulders hitched up. He pointed to the knife tangled in the plant's roots. "You may not be safe now."

Her face was pale. The light had died from her eyes. Fear hummed tangibly from her skin. He had the insane urge to kiss some color back into her cheeks, the mad impulse to caress the smolder of desire back into her eyes, and the crazy notion to love warmth back into her body.

She's definitely getting to me. Not good. This wasn't supposed to happen. Not this time.

"Given the evidence, I can't rule out the possibility you planted the knife there yourself, but honestly, I think it's just a little too convenient."

"Thank you for that, anyway." Her shoulders sagged

as some of her tension eased, but her eyes remained whirl-pools of emotion.

Against his better judgment, he pulled her body against his chest, pushed her head against his shoulder and held her loosely. "It's all right," he whispered into the damp softness of her hair. Her hands crimped around the material of his jacket on his upper arms. That tiny gesture of need moved him more than a bucket of tears could have. "I won't let anything happen to you. Pack a bag. I'll take you somewhere where you'll be safe."

"No, I need to stay here." Her voice was thin, but rang with determination.

"It's not safe."

Her head turned into his neck. When she spoke, her breath fanned in intimate little bursts against his collar. "The first time I ended up in jail not remembering who I was, I ran away. I buried myself in this little town, thinking I'd be safe."

"This isn't the same thing." He stroked the back of her head, and her chignon, loosened by the rain, fell apart in his hand, spilling through his fingers like silk ribbons.

"I've tried hiding. It doesn't work. The fear…it follows me wherever I go."

"Deliberately placing yourself in danger isn't the ans—"

"Neither is pretending this isn't an option."

He sighed wearily. "We're not dealing with an imaginary monster, here. We're dealing with a murderer who won't be too happy to know someone saw him in action."

"I should have done this years ago."

"There'll be time later—

"But not a better opportunity."

"Melinda—" He took her by the shoulders and forced her to look at him. "Don't do it. Don't set yourself up as bait. The kind of person who did this is deranged, evil. He's killed once. He could do it again.''

She shook her head and gave him a weak smile. "I have to. It's got to come to an end. All of it.''

Gently he reached up to stroke her jawline with his thumbs. She might be Ely Amery's daughter, but she was also a beautiful, brave, vulnerable woman. Grady was having a hard time focusing on his hatred of her father, on the case and on this new development that blazed many more trails to this maze.

Before he could stop himself, he kissed her fiercely, protectively. She tasted of wine and innocence, of sadness and spring; and the improbable combinations sent a jolt zinging through him like an arrow on fire. He heard her murmur his name against his lips and he deepened the kiss. He wanted more of her...all of her....

What am I doing? I don't want this. I don't need this. Not now.

He released her, backing up one step until his hands cupped only her elbows. Her dark eyes were wide with confusion, with longing. If he drew her back into his arms, she would let him. If he led her to her bedroom, she would offer no resistance. It would be easy to take advantage of her now, to seduce her the way Jamie had him. But looking into her eyes, he found his taste for revenge dampened. This shadow of Melinda wasn't what he wanted. He wanted the warm Melinda of the garden, filled with life and color; the one whose fathomless eyes promised paradise. Blurring the lines of his boundaries with the investigation was one thing; sleeping with the primary witness was quite another.

They stood there for a while, not speaking, just looking at each other.

"Your father's not going to be happy once he finds out what you've done.''

A half smile wavered on her lips. "Then we'll have to keep it our little secret until it comes out in the paper."

"You won't be safe, Melinda. Do you understand that?"

She nodded once and went to the front door. "I think maybe it would be best if you left now." In the yellow glow of the outside light from the open door, rain intermittently dappled the cement stoop. "I'm tired. I just want to go to sleep. Tomorrow—"

"There are procedures that have to be followed," he said, loathe to leave, needing in spite of everything to protect her.

Her gaze shifted to the mess on her livingroom carpet, but she didn't let go of the door. "Yes, of course. How long will it take?"

"A while."

She nodded and closed the door. Rubbing her arms, she went to inspect a mangled plant. She crouched and started to right the pot.

"Don't touch anything just yet. I'll need to take some pictures first and gather the evidence for the lab."

With a resigned nod, she moved toward the back of the house, then hesitated. One hand on the corner of the wall, she looked back over her shoulder. "Is it all right if I take a shower and change?"

"Go ahead."

As he called Oscar and arranged for a car to be dropped off, he listened to the rustling of her dress falling in a heap at her feet, heard the slide of drawers, the creak of a closet door. To the soft patter of the shower, he checked and rechecked the locks on the windows and doors of the little house.

And questioned his decision.

He heard the phone ring, then Melinda's restrained voice

reassuring her father she was fine. She didn't mention the incident.

By the time the two squad cars pulled up to the house, impatience tainted his mood like a slow-acting venom. He didn't wait for a knock to open the door.

"I've got the evidence kit you needed," Oscar said, his body half in, half out of the house. A gust of wind drove rain through the open door and peppered the floor mat at the entrance.

Grady took the kit from him, grumbling his thanks.

"Hey, man, want me to handle that for you?" Oscar asked, his thick brows creasing together on his forehead.

"No, you go on." Grady placed the kit on the rattan footstool and flicked the metal tabs open. "I'll take care of everything."

"It might be better—"

"I said, I'd take care of it."

Oscar lifted both his hands in surrender. "Sure, man."

Realizing he was turning his nameless anger on his best friend, Grady softened his voice. "Thanks."

Oscar shrugged. "No problem. Want me to make sure extra patrols cruise by tonight?"

"That won't be necessary."

Oscar started to say something, then changed his mind. Shaking his head, he closed the door and left.

Grady tugged on the bow tie at his neck, pulled the strip of silk from under his collar and stuffed it into his jacket pocket. Walking carefully around the scene, he noted everything he saw, drawing on logic to drown out the instincts he'd come to mistrust. The department wasn't large enough, and so far, hadn't warranted a separate crime-scene unit. As the officer on the scene, he was responsible for making sure everything got done right. He photographed the green "victims" with their twisted limbs and smashed pots, distancing himself from the feelings tangled inside him. Then he combed the area once more, measuring, mapping, sketching, taking latent fingerprints—for all the good that would do—and bagging evidence. No one, not even Brasswell, would be able to fault this part of his procedures.

He did the best he could to straighten the plants and clear away the broken pottery and loose soil. The man in him didn't want her to go to sleep with this destruction only a few steps away; the hunter in him thought maybe that was exactly what she needed to shock some sense back into her. As he swished the last dustpanful of dirt into her kitchen garbage can, he knew he was getting too soft.

Her bedroom door opened once more. She came out wearing a baggy sweatshirt and a pair of shorts, her hair loose and wet around her shoulders, looking stronger than before. Only her eyes betrayed the turmoil still tumbling inside her.

"You're still here," she said as she examined his attempt to clean up. He knew that as soon as he left, she would probably beat the rug, repot the viable plants and do what she could to rescue her haven from the hell it had become.

"Just finishing up." He secured the broom and dustpan in her hall closet.

"You didn't have to clean up."

"I thought it might help you get a good night's sleep."

Her eyes glittered, erasing the fear for a moment, then she nodded and walked him to the front door. Opening it, she silently urged him out. She stood there, small and vulnerable, in her home that was no longer an oasis. But even with the remnants of chaos under her feet, her shoulders were straight and her gaze held his steadily.

Stay, an insistent nudge urged. But he could think of no logical reason to obey the disturbance in his gut, so he picked up the evidence kit he'd placed by the threshold. "I want you to lock the door behind me."

"I will. Good night, Lieutenant."

For half a moment, indecision kept him rooted to the spot; then, with a tap on the doorframe, he turned and left.

He sat in the car parked across the street from her house, watching—he wasn't sure for what. The bait hadn't been offered yet. There was no reason to believe Melinda would be anything but safe in her home tonight. But something held him back.

For all her brave front, Melinda was afraid. Every light in her house blazed. Just as he'd suspected she would, through the lightweight shades, he saw the outline of her figure busily rearranging her living space. He knew she would get little sleep tonight. And like a fool, neither would he.

THE ROOM SWIRLED WITH color. Black, red, green, yellow. Noises came in layers. Rain, thunder, a swish, a hiss. As the colors formed into a vortex settling above her, the stench of blood and sulfur permeated Melinda's senses. She willed her eyes to open. They wouldn't. She was powerless to avoid the cloud of color descending on her. The colors slowed and blended, then stopped. A crash. All was black once more, but she couldn't relax. The darkness clung until shards of light broke it apart, shaping themselves into something resembling a photo negative. Panic struck her, sharp and raw. The picture shifted once more bringing into focus one corner.

"Lindy, what are you doing up?" A smiling face beamed down at her.

She recognized the voice. Her eyes sprang open. "Mama?"

The image faded and disappeared.

"No! Come back!" she yelled with all her might. Her

body shot straight up. As she sought to regain use of her limbs, her breath ripped through her lungs. She felt bruised and battered. Her nightdress clung to her sweat-drenched body. Her head pounded as if all the blood had been squeezed out of it, then allowed to rush back in.

Great forks of lightning speared the sky, casting tortured shadows on the walls. She watched the darkness, tensing past endurance. The persistent sound of rain on the roof pecked at her brain. Her body shook. Thunder rumbled through the countryside. She had to escape. She couldn't breathe. She had to be free.

Barefoot, without thinking, Melinda raced across the house to the screened-in patio. Drops of rain crashed through the screen onto the white wrought-iron table, pinging a warning. Lightning struck the sky, making her jump and gasp. Every fiber in her urged her to run, to leave, to disappear—anywhere, it didn't matter, as long as it wasn't raining.

But she couldn't. Not this time. She had to fight.

She shoved through the screen door and ran over the stones arranged in a curving pathway to the front of the house. She'd go to the park and sit on the bench and watch the ducks float on the pond. That wasn't running. That was making a conscious decision. The ducks loved the rain, and watching them always took the edge off the apprehension making her feel as if she should apply as a circus sideshow attraction. *Come one, come all! Come see the September Storm Woman. She goes crazy each and every September just from the sound of the rain!* She'd watch the ducks swim for a little while, then everything would stop swirling, and she'd be okay.

Tears of frustration blended with the rain on her cheeks. "It's okay. You'll be okay. It's okay, you'll be okay. It's—"

"Melinda?" The voice came distorted and ugly across

the static air. A blob took shape black against the shifting shadows of the night.

A scream rent the air. *"Hide, Lindy, hide!"* Primal fear, instinct, took over, flooding her body with adrenaline. The hammer of her heart filled her ears. Hands grabbed at her. Her throat vibrated raw. She pushed away, scrambling in the opposite direction.

The monster—he was close, so close. Fear pulsed through her, pounding louder with every beat of her heart.

Hide, Lindy, hide.

Then he had her.

Mouth open wide, she froze.

"Melinda?"

Holding her breath, she waited.

For a reprieve from the horror.

Or the next move, which would catapult her into terror.

"It's me, Melinda. It's Grady. I won't hurt you."

"It's okay," she said between ragged breaths. She couldn't hear the rain anymore, or the thunder. She couldn't feel the night, or the monster holding her. She couldn't smell the damp earth, or the winey breath. A fuzzy warmth suffused her. "You'll be okay—"

"Melinda, look at me!"

An insistent weight lifted her chin and she found herself looking into vivid blue eyes. Familiar, that blue. Safe. The rain stung her skin through the gauzy layer of her clothes. The stiff grass poked into the soles of her feet. A solid body pressed against hers.

As the landscape of her nightmare shifted back to reality, a sob of relief escaped her. "Grady."

"You scared me."

"I scared myself." She'd done it again. She'd gone over the edge—let an old nightmare completely take over her present. Twice in two weeks. Shivers racked through her. Miniature eels of dread made her skin crawl. Was she going crazy? At least she still knew who she was this time. At least she hadn't woken up in jail. At least there was no fresh police tape flapping in the wind. She wanted to cry in frustration, but drew in a long breath instead and leaned her head against Grady's shoulder.

Solid. Strong. Warm.

She wrapped her arms around his waist and pressed herself closer. One of his arms rose to cocoon her shoulders. His free hand stroked her hair in long, soothing motions. Gradually her heart calmed, her body stopped shaking, and her mind slowed. Between the rain's gentle wash and Grady's reassuring caresses, the panic trickled away. She sighed.

"After the power went out, I heard you scream," he said. "How are you feeling?"

"Black with splashes of red and pinpricks of purple."

"What?"

She laughed mirthlessly into the sodden material of his shirt. "I told you not everything was black-and-white. Or gray. Feelings come in color. We should go inside. You're all wet."

"So are you. What happened?"

"An old nightmare caught me off guard."

Reluctantly, she took a step back, disengaging her hold on his waist. With his arms still wrapped around her shoulders, she placed her palms against his chest, lifted her head and sought his gaze. "Grady?"

"Um."

"Your sister… What kind of psychologist is she?"

She felt his chest stiffen beneath her hands, saw caution mask his features. "She deals mostly with children."

"Oh." Her gaze dropped to a pearl button on his shirt. "Why are you asking?"

She traced the button's shape around and around with a finger. "Could she…could she hypnotize me?"

"Why?"

"I don't want to deal with a stranger. She seemed like a nice person." She looked up again into the intense blue of his eyes. "I need to know, Grady."

His fingers curled tightly around her shoulders. A muscle in his jaw twitched. His brow furrowed. "Are you sure?"

"Yes."

He nodded once. "I'll arrange it."

AFTER THE STORMY NIGHT, the day dawned steamy and hot. Not a puff of wind stirred the sheers covering the front windows. The cicadas' violin plagued the morning's quiet, and the sun baked the stone wall and reflected into the house. Coffee mug hot in his hand, Grady moved to open the door at the first sign of Desiree's car coughing up the sleepy street.

His sister had grumbled about the ungodly hour he'd woken her up, but holding a large coffee, she'd shown up at Melinda's house anyway.

"Thanks for coming," Grady said.

Des thumped him on the side of the head. "You owe me one."

"You name it."

"You cook dinner on Sunday. You know how much I hate cooking, even for you guys." She dumped her huge purse on the floor. Lifting the plastic cover off her cup, she took a long, appreciative sniff of the coffee, then a deep sip.

"It was my turn last week."

With caffeine now streaming through her, she was looking more her normal self. "Sisterly acts of devotion come at a price."

"I'll have to remember that." He paused, uncertain as to what he wanted to say. "Really, Des, thanks."

She watched Melinda, dressed in a light denim dress and white canvas sneakers, pacing the patio nervously. "I'm not sure I'm doing you a favor." She took another big gulp and placed her cup on the kitchen counter. "Ready?"

He nodded and waved her ahead toward the patio.

"Why don't you sit in the hammock chair?" Desiree said to Melinda after greeting her warmly. She sat opposite Melinda on the stool she'd dragged out from the kitchen.

Grady leaned against the stone wall, not sure this was a good idea at all. Melinda looked pale. She'd refused to eat anything. Hadn't touched the cup of tea he'd brewed for her. And she'd paced that blasted garden of hers for hours, keeping him at bay as if he didn't exist. *Well, what did you expect after the way you scared her?*

"How do you feel about hypnosis?" Desiree asked.

Melinda twisted her hands in her lap and shrugged one shoulder. "I'm a little scared."

"What do you mean?"

"I...I mean, I'm afraid...of what I might find." She gave a quick look in his direction. A stab of guilt poked him in the gut. Was he pushing her too hard? Was he allowing this in order to satisfy his own needs? Or was he affording her a safe way to remember?

"That's normal with the memory blanks you have. Those are probably very painful memories you've buried. But isn't it worse to have your life disrupted to avoid knowing something? Because, even if your mind pretends it doesn't know, what happened, happened. You can't change that. But you *can* deal with the painful reality rather than hide it in a different world. What hypnosis can do for you is restore those memories instead of erasing them. It's up to you. Do you want to continue?"

Melinda hesitated, but her features cemented themselves in a determined set. "Yes, I do."

"Now there're a few caveats I want both of you to be aware of. Sometimes it takes more than one session to get to the heart of things." She turned to Grady. "If Melinda remembers seeing who killed Angela while under hypnosis, you'll still have to find a way to prove it without using her testimony. Memories regained under hypnosis may not be acceptable in court."

He'd understood that from the start, but knowing where to look made all the difference.

"What are you expecting from hypnosis?" Desiree asked, turning back to Melinda.

"I want to know who it is I'm so afraid of. I want to help Grady find Angie's murderer."

"Okay. Let me go over a few general things with you. The first thing you'll notice is that you'll start to feel relaxed and a bit drowsy. Don't try too hard. Just let things happen."

The toes of Melinda's shoes turned toward each other and her gaze was fixed pointedly at the nail of one thumb she busily scraped with the other. "What if it doesn't work? What if I can't be hypnotized?"

"Dissociation takes practice. You've probably hypnotized yourself many times already without knowing what you were doing."

Melinda's head jerked up and a touch of panic flitted across her face. He wanted to go to her, to hold her, but Des had warned him to stay in his corner and not interfere.

Desiree leaned forward and touched Melinda's hand. "Don't worry. You'll be in constant contact with me. You don't have to answer any questions you don't want to answer. And you'll remember everything that happened when you come out of your trance."

"Really?" she said in a relieved puff.

"Yes, in general, most people remember everything. It's

important to remember not to push yourself too hard. If things don't happen, well, they just don't happen.''

"Okay.''

Desiree sat squarely on the stool and flipped her braid behind. "Now, I want you to sit back and relax with your feet on the floor and your hands comfortably in your lap. Turn your eyes to a spot high on the patio ceiling. Keep your eyes fixed on that spot and focus. Take a deep breath. Hold it…then let it out slowly. Feel the relaxation flow into you. Nothing bad will happen to you. You are safe here. Listen and concentrate on my voice….''

Desiree spoke in a singsongy lullaby. Melinda's eyelids fluttered. His hands tightened around his biceps.

"Imagine yourself floating, drifting, gliding down a gentle current. Notice your left hand. Picture a large helium balloon attached to your wrist, lifting it up and up.''

Melinda's wrist drifted upward. How could she be under so fast?

"Try lowering your hand. It stays up. Right now it's too hard for you to lower it.'' Desiree paused. "Okay, bring it back down now. The balloon is gone. The hand is becoming very heavy now as though lead were attached to it, pulling it down, down, and down. As that arm is pulled down, your eyelids become heavier. You can't keep them open. It's okay to close them. Relax now.''

Melinda's eyes closed. Her body looked limp and relaxed. Even the frown between her eyes had melted. His jaw hurt and he forcibly tried to relax it.

"I want you to imagine yourself on a stairway now—a long, winding stairway. As you go down the stairs, you go deeper into hypnosis, deeper and deeper.'' Desiree's voice got softer, gentler.

"Remember, then go back into the past to a pleasant day when you were a child.''

A wide smile spread over Melinda's face—a wonderful,

bright smile that magically transformed her and managed to twist his gut.

"Where are you, Melinda?" Des asked.

"I'm in Mama's garden. I'm chasing butterflies. Yellow ones."

"How old are you?"

"I'm four. Mama's chasing butterflies with me. She catches me and whirls me around." Melinda's head tipped back and she laughed in the carefree way only a child could. "Then we fall down on the ground and look at clouds. Mama's so soft. She smells so pretty."

Could this be real? Could she really think she was four again and playing with her mother? If he didn't trust Desiree implicitly, he'd be inclined to think the whole thing was a hoax.

"Go forward now. Go to when the blanks started to come. What do you see?"

A frown creased Melinda's forehead. "I'm in my bedroom. I'm drawing a picture for Mama and Daddy."

"How old are you?"

"I'm six. Mama gave me George-the-monkey for my birthday. He's got a silly grin and makes me laugh. He's got a key in his back and when you turn it, music comes out of his tummy. Mama says the music is 'The Greatest Show on Earth.' But the cymbals won't work. I open the door, and I hear a noise. Mama's upset. She's crying. I can hear her. Mama, don't cry. I run to hug her. Then somebody yells."

"Who's yelling?"

"I don't know." Her frown deepened and she shook her head in frustration. "I can't see inside the room. 'Keep your voice down, Lindy will hear.' 'She's asleep like a good little girl. Wish I could say the same for her mother. Who was it this time?' 'How many times am I going to have to tell you, there is nobody else?'" Melinda jerked as if someone had slapped her. "He hit her! 'Don't talk back to me, you whore!' Mama's crying, she's crying and he's hitting her and hitting her."

"Who's hitting, Melinda?"

As if she'd dropped something, Melinda looked down to her left. "The cymbals. They're fixed!" She scooted to a corner of the chair, hunching her shoulders, bringing up her legs. Then, as if she held some paper and a pencil in front of her, she drew.

What's happening? Grady desperately wanted to ask, worried that the experiment wasn't going the way it should.

Carefully, Desiree placed a pad on Melinda's knees and a pencil in her moving left hand. Childish lines appeared on the paper.

"She's right-handed," Grady whispered as he crouched beside Desiree's stool.

"Shh."

"Tada-da-da…"

"What are you doing, Melinda?" Des asked.

"I'm drawing a picture for Mama and Daddy."

"Do your parents fight often?"

Melinda flinched, then scrunched her forehead in concentration. "I like to draw."

"Does it scare you when they fight?"

She made a fist around the pencil and slashed at the piece of paper. Grady thought of the sketches he'd found at the bottom of the closet. Was this how she'd produced them? During a stint of self-hypnosis? But what was the trigger? She dropped the pad and reached down for something. She brought this invisible thing to her chest and hugged it.

"I like the music." She moved her head from side to side while rocking herself gently back and forth. "Tada-da-da… It's okay. You'll be okay. It's okay, you'll be okay. It's okay.…''

Grady touched Desiree's arm. ''That's what she said last night before she spaced out.''

''It's her trigger phrase. What she uses to hypnotize herself. She's fine.'' Desiree didn't give him a chance to argue. ''Melinda, where are you?''

''Away.''

She looked dreamy and definitely not here. Could someone really escape within their own mind? He wanted this to end, yet he wanted to access those repressed memories. He had to trust that Des knew what she was doing; that Melinda would be all right.

''Away where?'' Des asked.

''Some place far inside. George taught me how to go there. There's lots and lots of space, and the light—it keeps me warm.''

''Melinda, go forward. You're eight. Imagine yourself right before your mother died. Where are you?''

Her head jerked up.

''What do you hear?''

''I don't know. Rain. Thunder. I'm scared. I want Mama.''

''Did you find your mother?''

She frowned, looked around. ''No, she's not anywhere. Oh, there she is.'' Relief washed over her face. ''I see her through the living-room window. She's in her greenhouse. The wind, it's strong.'' She put one arm up to protect herself. ''My pj's are getting all wet. It's hard for me to walk. Mama! Mama!'' She gasped.

''What's happening, Melinda? What do you see?''

''The monster, he's hurting Mama!''

''Look at his face, Melinda. It's okay. He can't hurt you. You're safe. Look at his face. Who is it?''

Her eyes opened wide with terror. Her breaths were quick and shallow like a pursued animal's.

Grady found himself tense and ready to jump. "What's happening to her?"

"Shut up! She's in too deep. I'm losing her."

"Do something!"

"I'm trying!" Desiree leaned forward. "Listen to me, Melinda." Her voice was once again calm, steady and soothing. "He can't hurt you. He can't touch you."

Melinda jumped up from the chair, and as if something hampered her efforts, she tripped backward to a corner formed by the wall and a side of the house, where she cowered into a tight ball. "No! No! No!"

Grady sprang toward Melinda, but feared touching her and interfering with Desiree's ability to bring her back. He could see the pain, feel the struggle. He wanted to protect her, but knew he had to let her go through with this—for herself as much as for the case.

"Come forward now. Come back to today. You're comfortable and feeling relaxed. You're aware of the memories you just relived. You see them like a movie. These memories cannot hurt you. In the past, you've run from the fear. Now you go to it. Stare at the fear. Face it. It hurts, but it doesn't scare you anymore. You can remember."

Grady swiveled back to his sister and questioned her silently.

"I'm just making a posthypnotic suggestion." Desiree focused back on Melinda, sitting limply in the corner. "I'm going to count backward from three, and at one, you'll open your eyes and be fully alert, feeling relaxed and refreshed, and your usual sensations and control will have returned. Three, take a deep breath. Two, let it out. One! You're fully alert. How do you feel?"

Melinda blinked, looked down at herself rounded up in

a ball. A little wobbly, she pushed herself up. He reached to help her, but she ignored his hand. "A little groggy."

"What do you remember?"

"I…I…I remember your voice. I remember floating like in a dream."

"What else?"

"Pieces and parts of a nightmare I've had ever since I can remember. I was…frightened."

"Would you like to discuss what you saw?"

Melinda shook her head. "I'm not sure I can. It still doesn't make much sense."

"That's all right. Take your time. Don't try to solve the whole puzzle at once."

She looked at him, uncertainty dancing in her dark eyes. "I think I saw Angela's window…."

"What did you see?" Grady urged gently.

She turned from him to finger the leaves of a plant on the wall. He sensed the internal war being waged. With a little push, could he help her face her monster?

He came up behind her and put his hands reassuringly on her shoulders, felt them curl forward against his touch. "What did you see?"

"Grady, don't—" Des said in the background.

"Tell me what you saw, Melinda," he whispered into her ear, willing her to understand that she wasn't alone, that he was her friend, not her enemy.

She pivoted on her heels, glanced at him with doleful eyes, and gave him a sorrowful smile. Her hand reached up and caressed his jaw once. Then, with back stiff and shoulders straight, she marched into the house.

"What'd you do that for, you jerk?" Desiree punched him in the arm.

"She saw something. It was right there. I thought maybe I could help her put an end to this nightmare."

"Yeah, well, you've chased it right back into her sub-conscious. Good going, Grady!"

The front door slammed. Both of them turned to look in that direction.

Grady scraped a hand through his hair and kneaded the base of his neck. Des was right. He'd really messed up, this time. "That sure would put a crack in Amery's reputation if the world knew he abused his wife."

"He wouldn't be the first to lead a double life."

"You're probably right on that count. Can I borrow the sketch she made? I want to compare it to the ones I found in her house."

"Sure." Desiree picked up the sketch pad and slapped it into his hands. "Better go after her. This has been a traumatic experience. Keep an eye on her. Make sure she doesn't drift off."

Grady frowned, worried. "If she does?"

She looked at him over her shoulder. "Bring her back."

"How?"

"Any way you can."

Soon after, he heard the front door snicking closed and the rough sputter of Desiree's car starting.

He leaned back against the wall and closed his eyes. The cicadas' hiss jeered at him. The sun grilled the exposed skin at the back of his neck. He could see Seth, Brasswell and Angela all shaking their heads at him. He knew without a doubt he'd failed. He'd alienated his witness, and hadn't gotten the information he needed. As bad as that was, he also knew he'd broken the tentative trust forged between him and Melinda the evening before. She wouldn't go through hypnosis again. Not for him. Maybe not even for herself.

She'd go through with the interview, though. He'd seen that fact hidden beneath the soul sadness of her eyes. There was nothing he could do to stop her, and little chance she'd let him keep her safe.

He punched the top of the wall and swore hotly.

Maybe the town council was right. Maybe he wasn't ready to fill Seth's shoes.

Chapter Eleven

Melinda stomped through The Essential Gardener's parking lot. She kicked at the door when her key hesitated in the lock. After finally getting the stubborn thing opened, she wrenched the door locked again. As she made her way to her cubicle, she allowed the low growl of pent-up frustration to escape.

Blurred shadows, bits and pieces of memories that refused to collate themselves into a concrete whole fluttered on the edge of her consciousness like hummingbird wings. She needed work, mindless busywork, to let them think they were safely hidden in her mind. Then, when they least expected, she'd turn around and face them frankly; face the truth and find a way to deal with it—on her own, without leaning on her father, Dolores...or Grady.

She'd always felt different, and now the returning memories of a forgotten portion of her childhood made her feel even more like a freak. Emotionally vulnerable and seeking reassurance, she'd almost succumbed to Grady's silent invitation to let herself be soothed by his strength and solidity. When she'd turned to him, she'd almost leaned into him, almost let him take over, almost let him take care of her. It would have been so easy to hide in his self-assurance. But when she'd seen the warm, yet insistent look in his eyes, she'd known she couldn't.

She needed to know she could rely on her own inner fiber to sort through this mess, or she'd always wonder if it was the man, or the strength that was so much a part of him, that she was falling in love with.

Collapsing into her chair, she groaned. How could she possibly be falling in love with someone like Grady Sloan? What had he done for her, except make her life miserable?

Her gaze sought the watercolor of the rose arch still pinned to her cubicle wall. She fingered the couple kissing beneath the cascade of morning glories.

He could be gruff, determined. He was self-assured, strong. But he could also be gentle. And it was when he was gentle, when he whispered softly into her ear, that the essence of him infiltrated her, wound itself deep inside her, reaching her soul. He could touch her in a way no one else ever had. And the frank desire she'd seen in his blue eyes made her feel very much like a woman.

But the thought of caring for him so much, of wanting him in a way that came close to a need, frightened her.

A loud, determined knock on the glass door startled her. When she looked up over the partition, she was not at all surprised to see Grady standing there.

"Go away," she said, not daring to get too close to the door, as if he could reach through the glass, if he wanted, and bend her will to his. "I need to be alone for a while."

"We need to talk."

"Later."

She started to turn away, but his authoritative bark stopped her. "Now. Open the door, Melinda!"

She shook her head. "I'll call you."

"Open the damned door!"

With a resigned sigh, she reached into her pocket for the key and cranked the lock open. It was easier to deal with things as they came up rather than let them build in importance by putting them off. If nothing else, she was learning that lesson clearly. If she talked to him now, he'd go away and leave her alone. For a while, anyway.

"What's going on down there?" Dolores's voice carried to them from the top of the stairs.

"It's nothing, Dolores," Melinda said, looking over her shoulder. She hadn't realized anyone else was here. Grady pushed his way in while she was distracted.

"All that racket doesn't sound like 'nothing' to me." The metal stairs rattled beneath Dolores's feet.

Melinda grabbed Grady's sleeve and tried to usher him back out the door, but he proved as immovable as the bronze statue she'd once wished he was. "I've got it under control."

"I don't want you to do the interview," he growled into her ear. "It's too dangerous."

She opened the door wider, and whispered back, "I'll keep your opinion in mind."

"And do whatever the hell you want anyway."

She shrugged. "I need time alone, Grady. To think."

And time, she knew, was the one commodity Grady had little of when it came to this investigation.

He scraped a hand through his hair. His jaw tightened. He blew out a huff of frustration, then relented. "I'll be back to pick you up after my shift's over."

"That's not necessary."

"Maybe so, but if you're going to insist on setting yourself up as bait, I want to make sure you come out of it alive. Don't leave the building."

She jutted her chin up. Her fingers tightened around the door handle. "I have a business to run."

"Run it from your desk today." She could tell the action cost him, but he softened his voice. "Okay?"

If he could give an inch, so could she. "It was my plan all along."

"Is there anything wrong, Lieutenant?" Dolores asked as she came to stand next to Melinda.

"No, everything's fine. Are you planning on being here for a while?"

"Until I can put that darned hydroponic system together." Hands in constant motion, Dolores waved in the direction of the stairs. "Why?"

"I don't want her left alone."

"I—" Melinda started.

"She'll be fine," Dolores said, wrapping an arm around Melinda's waist. "I'll look after her."

Melinda leaned her head back and shook it in short, sharp strokes. "I wish both of you would stop treating me like a naughty four-year-old."

"I'm beginning to think a four-year-old would be easier to handle," Grady said. "At least I could send her to her room." With that, he left, rattling the door behind him.

"What was that all about?" Dolores asked.

"A simple misunderstanding about my ability to take care of myself. So, which system are you putting together?"

"Come up and I'll show you."

The second floor was laid out in two sections. One held a large conference table that was presently littered with competitors' catalogs and information packets sent by suppliers for their spring tool and seed catalog. On the other half were dozens of projects in various stages of assembly and testing. In the middle of it all was a huge cardboard box marked Deluxe Pumping Hydroponic System with Stand.

"You didn't carry this up all by yourself, did you?" Melinda asked, giving Dolores's small frame a disbelieving look.

Dressed in jeans, sneakers and a sleeveless turquoise shirt, Dolores struggled with the large box. Small muscles bulging, she manhandled the box into the position she wanted and ripped open one end. "No, I had a couple of the warehouse boys carry it up yesterday."

"Want some help with that?"

"No, according to that worthless engineer you hired, someone dumber than a box of rocks is supposed to be able to set this up on his own in less than an hour. With the instructions written in 'geek,' though, I'm expecting you'll have a lot of rewriting to do. So, why is the lieutenant worried about your ability to take care of yourself?"

Leaning against the doorway, Melinda shrugged. "It's a long story."

"I've got the time." Dolores laid out the various pieces of the wooden frame.

"Do you remember two years ago when you came to pick me up at the police station?" During a September storm when thunder and lightning had battered the house, she'd heard her father arguing with someone. She'd ended up wandering the streets of her neighborhood and had been picked up by the police. She didn't remember much of anything, except waking up scared to death in a jail cell.

"I knew something was wrong when you didn't show up to sign the partnership papers. I had to find you. And your father—" She shrugged and squinted at the instructions.

"What about my father?"

Dolores turned away and reached for the toolbox near the conference table. "He had a court appearance that morning."

There was no need to mention that court dates took precedence over everything. How many times had Melinda been disappointed by her father's absence at important times?

Her mother's death had taken all the warmth out of her world. After her death, a series of nannies had paraded through Melinda's life. Most of them had seemed more interested in her father's money than in taking care of her. None had stayed around long enough to form a lasting attachment. Dolores had proved to be the only constant in her life. She'd been her mother's best friend, and was now hers. How often she'd searched for her father in the crowd and found Dolores's smiling face beaming at her instead!

Melinda shook the sad memories away. "The same thing happened the day Angela died. They hadn't brought me to the station for questioning about Angela, like I told you, but because I couldn't remember who I was."

"Oh, hon, why didn't you tell me?" Dolores looked up from her pretzeled position on the floor.

"Because you worry too much about me as it is. I wanted everything to go back to normal."

"And it hasn't, has it?"

Melinda shook her head. Gazing intently at her twining fingers, she took in a long shaky breath. "What do you know about my mother's death?"

Dolores looked up from her task and silently stared at her for a moment. "It was an accident. Lightning struck her greenhouse. There was a fire and she was caught inside."

Like dabs of paint thrown at a canvas, the bits and pieces in Melinda's mind flecked with color and feelings. Green, black, red. The look of horror on her mother's face. Her dead eyes. Ancient feelings of helplessness, of knowing, climbed up Melinda's spine like a poisonous vine. She fought the anxiety tightening her chest, making her palms sweat. "I—I don't think it was an accident."

"What?" The screwdriver Dolores held slipped and gouged into the fingers of her opposite hand. She shook her hand, then stuck the tiny wound into her mouth.

"I think something else happened," Melinda said,

searching the ceiling tiles as if they held an answer. "I remember—"

"'Remember'?" Dolores grunted, and looked once again at the directions. "You were eight and asleep—what can you possibly remember?"

"Do you know anything about my father...hurting my mother?"

Dolores snorted. "Your father's main goal in life is to hurt people."

"No, I mean, you know, did he physically abuse her?"

Dolores sighed and put aside the instructions. "When things were going well for him business-wise, he was good to her. When they weren't, he took it out on her."

Though Dolores's words confirmed her memories, Melinda found little comfort in the truth. Because if that was real, was the suspicion beginning to form in her mind also true? The possibility dropped a ball of lead into her stomach. "Why didn't she leave him?"

"She had her reasons."

"I don't understand," Melinda pleaded.

"Which is probably best." Dolores resolutely turned her back on her and hefted the frame into position. She tested the stability, adjusted the wobbly section, then proceeded to tighten all the screws.

"I need to know, Dolores. Please, tell me."

"Ely was your grandfather's choice of husband for Abigail. She was in love with someone else. When she tried to defy him, your grandfather cut her off. She didn't have any money, no skills. Gardening was a hobby to her, not something to be exploited." Dolores shook her head sadly. "She had no choice but to bow under his demands. She was going to leave after your grandfather died, but her inheritance went straight to your father. And there was you to consider. She didn't think she could take care of you on her own."

"Why would my grandfather do that?"

"Who knows why men do anything?" She slapped the wooden tray parts together and reached for the screwdriver once more. "I'm really not sure. In the last few years, your mother got depressed a lot and closed in."

"I don't remember ever seeing her sad." Melinda had heard her cry, but she'd never seen anything but a large smile on her mother's lips and the shine of happiness in her eyes. "Why didn't you say anything before?"

"Because I thought your present happiness was more important than a painful past."

Melinda digested the information, not quite knowing how to react. The feelings, rolling inside her like tides, crashed and ebbed before she could label any of them. "I went through hypnosis this morning."

Dolores's screwdriver stopped, then seemed to move at double speed. "Why did you do that?"

"I found a bloody knife buried in one of my plants."

Eyes wide, Dolores spun to face her. "Oh, Melinda, no…"

Melinda saw the unasked question, the fear, the worry, in Dolores's pale blue eyes. She averted her gaze to the artificial light shining on a bunch of African violets in the corner. "I don't know. Maybe violence is genetic…."

Saying the horrifying thought out loud actually brought a measure of relief.

"Of course it isn't," Dolores said, uncoiling a length of tubing. "There's not a mean bone in your body."

"That's why I tried the hypnosis. I had to know."

"Did you… I mean…" She shrugged and twisted the tubing in her hand. "Did you see the…murder?"

"Not yet, but I know I will."

Dolores's brows knit in worry. "Does your father know about this hypnosis thing?"

"He will when he sees tomorrow's paper."

"What do you mean?"

"I'm going to let Gail Goodwin interview me."

Dolores cleared her throat. "Are you sure that's wise?"

"No, but I've got to do it."

It would be so easy to give in, to let someone else take charge. She now knew she shared her mother's weakness of spirit, but she wouldn't make the same mistake her mother had. Not with Grady. Though she wanted him, she didn't want a skewed relationship like the one her mother and father had shared. She wanted to be able to come to him as a equal, solid on her own two feet. She cared about him too much to settle for less.

"Melinda…"

She lifted her gaze to the older woman standing beside the frame holding a heavy wooden tray in her hands. "Don't think ill of your mother," Dolores said. "She had her reasons. Do you understand?"

She didn't, but she nodded anyway. The truth would come out soon, and this time, she would face it squarely. Time to stop hiding. Time to act.

"I've got a call to make."

The sound of the tray falling into place on the stand sounded like a gunshot. "And I've still got to finish wrestling this system into place."

"GRADY, A MOMENT OF YOUR time, please," Betty Braswell commanded as she charged into his office. She slapped a copy of the *Fort Worth Star-Telegram* on his desk, scattering papers in its wake. "I want an explanation about this. Why wasn't I informed that Miss Amery had recovered her memory?"

"Because she hasn't," he said, leaning his chair back and crossing his arms beneath his chest. "She's taken it upon herself to set herself up as bait."

"And you let her?" Her eyebrows arched in surprise,

then crimped in a frown. "What were you thinking of? Do you know how much trouble I've gone through to make sure Ely Amery wouldn't cause our town any grief?"

"Yes, ma'am, I'm well aware of it."

She leaned forward, poking one stubby finger at the top of his desk. "Then why didn't you stop her before she committed this grievous act?"

"Mayor Brass—"

"Now I'm going to have to call for extra help." She swiveled away, pacing the small confines of his office.

"What? You think Wayne can do a better job than me?" Grady asked sarcastically.

"That's exactly my thought, but I wasn't thinking of Wayne. He's busy with the rash of car thefts we've had lately. The State Police have more resources than we do—"

"They don't know the people of this town like we do." Grady's chair slammed back to the floor.

"That doesn't seem to have gained you any advantage so far."

"I'm—"

She leaned across his desk one more time, both hands flat against the top, glaring at him straight and square. "I know you like to buck the system, but sometimes, to get what you need, it's best to play the game. I want this settled before the Fall Festival starts—whatever it takes. Am I making myself clear?"

"Crystal."

"If I see no new development in the next few days, I'll call in reinforcements."

She turned on her heel to leave, then paused. "One more thing. I've heard rumors that the relationship between you and Miss Amery has crossed the lines of propriety."

"It's business, not social," he said, knowing how blurred the lines had become.

"Let's make sure it stays that way. Do I need to remind you of your duty—"

"No, ma'am, that won't be necessary."

She gave a sharp nod. "If anything untoward should happen to this witness, I will hold you personally responsible." She didn't wait for a reply, but left, heels clicking away on the hallway tile. There was no mistaking her threat—produce or vamoose.

"Yeah, sure. No problem. The impossible is my specialty."

Needing to move to help himself think, he decided to pay Halloran's Ice Cream Parlor a visit. Rumor had it that Mike Bishop, Angela's music partner, was in town and back at work. Shielding his eyes against the bright sun with glasses, he headed for the shop, which was located only a block down in a strip mall that also contained the Winn-Dixie, a dry cleaner, a video rental store, and a card shop. As he opened the door, the bell above it clanged. At ten-thirty on this Monday morning, the place was empty. Mike, his light brown hair tied in a short ponytail, wearing a white apron over his jeans and T-shirt, looked up from the table he was wiping down.

"In for your regular iced coffee?" Mike asked, smiling genially.

Grady removed his glasses and stuck them in his shirt pocket. "For starters."

Mike nodded, stuffed the cloth into the pocket of his apron and rounded the counter. "Kerry Merrill said you'd probably want to talk to me."

"You understand I have to ask these questions." Grady took a seat on one of the striped stools in front of the counter.

"I know. I want to help Angie's case. I'll do anything I can."

With eyes as clear and bright as a puppy's, delicate

peach fuzz on his chin, and his slight frame, Mike looked more like a fifteen-year-old boy than a man of twenty-four.

"How'd your trip work out?"

"I did okay for the first time out. Two stations were gonna play our song." The brightness on his face melted away. "Not that it matters now."

"When did you get back?"

Mike grabbed a glass from the mirrored shelf. "Last night around nine or so."

"When did you last see Angela?"

The glass in Mike's hand hovered an inch from the counter. "Around six the—*that* night. I stopped to get the publicity information she'd gotten printed out for us."

"Then what did you do?"

"I got some gas, and started driving. Toward Nashville." Mike released the glass, then fumbled through his pockets and pulled out several receipts, which he slipped across the counter. Grady noted the hesitation, the nervousness. He'd let it go for now and return to it later. "This one's from the Texaco across the street. It says I got gas at six thirty-three. This one's from the motel in Arkansas where I spent the night."

Grady examined the receipts and handed them back, saw the relief in Mike's eyes as he stuffed them into his pocket. His gut told him that although Mike was speaking the truth, he was also holding something back.

"Were you and Angela romantically involved?"

A bright red flush crept up Mike's face. He shoved a scoop into the ice bin and let the cubes clank into the glass. "No, of course not."

"Do you know if she was involved with anyone else?"

"She wasn't." Coffeepot in hand, he spun to the far end of the counter and the small fridge that held the cream. "Tommy Lee's leaving really hurt her and she wasn't ready to try again."

"Do you know of anyone who would have a reason to want to hurt her?"

"No. Everyone loved her." Mike choppily finished mixing the drink. It took him two tries to stick the straw into the glass. He searched the counter, then finally found the cloth he was looking for in his apron. Wiping the dribbles from the glass, he handed it to Grady.

Grady let the silence stretch, knowing full well it was human nature to want to fill it. He sipped at his drink, never taking his gaze off the nervous young man as he busied himself with cleaning up his mess. Broom in hand, Mike rounded the counter and started sweeping the restaurant floor. Grady swiveled on the stool, keeping watch. Mike's movements became choppier and choppier until he finally collapsed into a chair at a nearby table.

"What's wrong, Mike?"

"It's my fault." Mike dropped his head into his upraised hands. "It's all my fault."

"What's your fault?"

He shook his head sadly. "She tried to warn me, but I thought she was just exaggerating. You know, one of those things people say, but don't really mean. I told her I'd keep her safe, but I never thought I'd actually have to. That he'd actually do it. I let her down."

"Who did what?"

"The reverend." Mike looked up at him, his eyes filled with anguish. "Angie said if her father ever found out about what she was doing, about her singing with my band, he'd kill her."

Chapter Twelve

Melinda dreaded going home tonight to see what new surprise awaited her. She walked out of The Essential Gardener and looked around for Grady's black truck. When she didn't see it, she walked to the live oak near the warehouse entrance and sat in its shade. The sky was eye-squinting blue; the heat, dry and blanketing despite the constant breeze. The scent of parched grass and dust wafted to her in spurts. She pulled several blades of yellowed grass and absently braided them. Leaning her head against the tree trunk, she thought back over the week and wondered if she'd ever get a good night's sleep again. Waiting for something to happen was proving worse than whatever might eventually come to pass.

On Monday she'd found a dark-haired, Barbie-like doll wearing only a gag inside her mailbox. The intended message to keep quiet had been obvious.

Grady had spent the night in his truck outside her house.

Tuesday, a message had waited for her on her answering machine. "Calumnies are answered best with silence," the voice had said. It could have been a man or a woman; there was no telling from the static. Again, the message's intent had been clear.

Grady had spent the night patrolling the grounds.

Wednesday, she'd found a page torn from a Bible on

her kitchen counter. The passage, "Let your women keep silence: for it is not permitted unto them to speak," had been highlighted in lime green. How had the messenger gotten in? How had he snuck by the patrols Grady had set up? How had he known this simple intrusion would stir more fear in her than a direct confrontation?

And though she hadn't shared her growing restlessness with Grady, he'd insisted on spending the night prowling the inside of her home.

As much as she hated to admit it, she'd been glad to know he was right there, glad she didn't have to face the fear alone. But this dependence on him also stirred feelings of weakness, of inadequacy.

She glanced at her watch, then scanned the road for his black truck. There was nothing in sight, except the red-and-white Office Master van pulling in for its regular delivery. Since the first incident, Grady had insisted on dropping her off at work and picking her up. Today, he was late. She'd give him five more minutes, then she'd head home on her own. It would be good for her to handle whatever little surprise awaited her on her own. After all, there was no real physical threat, just simple intimidation calculated to bring on fear—which was working much too well—and silence—which was easy to comply with because the memories were still like mud stirred in a pond; nothing was clear.

It wasn't good to be so dependent on Grady—for either of them.

At the sound of churning gravel, she jerked her head up. The Office Master van barreled past the warehouse doors. As if the world suddenly ran in slow motion, Melinda watched the silver bumper heading straight at her. The sun caught the bumper's rounded edge, glinting off it like a headlight, and like some helpless deer, she sat mesmerized.

Then her heart hammered, loud and insistent. Her blood whooshed frantically past her ears. Adrenaline flooded her bloodstream, screaming for action.

Instinctively, she rolled to one side. Looking over her shoulder, she placed her feet beneath her to jump up. The van blurred past her back. The material of her dress whipped madly, stinging her skin.

As she leaned forward to run, hands on the ground for balance, the van crashed into the tree. The creak of crumpling metal boomed in her ear. She lunged forward; boomeranged back, falling in a heap on the ground.

Then everything sped forward. A door grated open. Footsteps rushed away. Others raced forward. Voices shouted.

"Melinda? Are you all right?" It was Grady, kneeling beside her, checking her limbs for damage. Dolores and most of the staff peered anxiously over his shoulder. "I thought he'd hit you."

"I'm fine." Except for the uncontrollable shaking of her body.

One of the warehouse workers raced over to Grady. "Sorry, he got away. Had a truck waiting for him a ways down the road."

"Did you catch the tag number?"

Resting his hands on his knees, he breathed hard and shook his head. "No, I was too far back."

"Thanks." Grady spoke the information into the radio strapped to his shoulder, then turned back to Melinda. "Are you sure you're okay?"

Melinda nodded and tried to sit up, but felt a tug at her waist. Turning, she saw the hem of her dress crushed between the metal bumper and the tree. The tiny white flowers on the burgundy material were pressed painfully into the bark. Gently, she tried to extricate the challis from its prison. When she couldn't, she yanked on it, tearing a rip that would reach from knee to ankle. She stroked the frayed edges over and over again. A few more inches and it could have been her leg. A few more, her torso. A few more.... The dire possibilities mushroomed into a full-blown horror picture show in her mind.

Deliberate, deadly intention. She shuddered.

Eyes narrowed, Grady shifted his gaze from the shredded material crimped in her fist to her face. ''That's it. I'm taking you some place safe until this thing is resolved.''

She wanted to argue, but couldn't find her voice. She let Grady deal with the chaos around her, let him take her shaking hand, let him lead her to his truck. When he drove her home and ordered her to pack a bag, she complied without a word. Sitting tensely beside him as he drove, she tried to ignore her awareness of his frequent glances in her direction, of the questions he wasn't asking, of the tension growing palpable between them.

She was angry with herself for being aware of him; angry at the fear that was making her once more dependent on his strength; angry about her weakness. She wanted to hate him for opening doors that had long ago slammed shut, for shattering the illusion of safety she'd worked hard to create for herself, for making her feel again. But she knew she couldn't. All of it was long overdue. And by not facing it sooner, she had brought these consequences onto herself.

His profile was grim and tight-lipped; angry, but in control. She found resentment building in the pit of her stomach. Did his control ever crack? Was his self-assuredness ever shaken? Did he ever have a moment of weakness? Just once, she'd like to see that. But she knew he wouldn't let it happen. So she needed to let the resentment flower, needed it in order to find her own strength again.

And as much as she would like to wait and pretend the whole situation didn't exist, she knew she would have to force a confrontation between herself and the mysterious messenger. Only then would the truth come out. Only then would she be free…to live.

She glanced once more at Grady's fierce profile.

And maybe to love.

MELINDA JUST SAT ON THE living-room sofa, not moving. Something about her too-quiet manner troubled Grady. She should be upset, alarmed. Instead, she showed no emotion. She avoided his gaze. Her answers to his questions, when she even bothered, were clipped, one-word replies. He could almost hear her mind churning and wanted to calm her worries, but she kept a thick wall around her as if he were somehow responsible for her situation.

And maybe he was. He'd pushed her and pushed her and hadn't let her draw back into the illusion of comfort she'd created for herself. He'd held a mirror and forced her to look into it. He couldn't expect anything, least of all gratitude. Not when he'd allowed her life to be placed in danger. But he couldn't just stand by and watch her spirit ebb out of her, either.

Then he remembered how she'd brought the outside into her house, and he thought of the horses in their paddock and the fields and wooded hills behind his house. His suggestion of a ride brought a visible relaxation of her shoulders and a puff of relief, as if she'd been holding her breath. Within minutes she changed into an oversize rust-colored silk camp shirt and a pair of faded jeans at least a size too big, and in the time it took to brush and saddle the horses, a bit of color returned to her cheeks.

She sat on Red as if it were the most natural thing for her to do, following the mare's movements with unconscious grace, and doing things to his body he never thought such a simple sight could do. Shifting in his saddle to ease his discomfort, he scanned the horizon, then checked the barbed wire along the fence they were following—anything to distract his attention from Melinda's gently swaying hips.

"It wasn't an accident, was it?" she said, breaking the silence.

"Doesn't look like it." Dull acceptance was written all over her face, and Grady wasn't sure he liked this harder edge etched into her delicate features. "It wasn't the regular driver. His van was stolen when he stopped for a soda."

"Was the other driver caught?"

They reached a gate and Grady hopped down to open it. "He got away. We're working on it."

She nodded, indifferent.

As he mounted again, the saddle leather creaked. They walked along slowly, the rhythm of the horses' hooves on the dry grass creating a relaxing shushing sound.

"A penny for your thoughts," Grady said as they crested a small hill and stopped to watch the sun's still-bright rays paint the small pond's surface in a living watercolor.

"I'm trying to put the pieces together." She twisted in the saddle and looked at him. "That's what you do, isn't it? Take pieces and try to make a whole. Nothing seems to make much sense."

"No, it doesn't," he agreed, the frustration of it tensing his muscles. He squeezed his calves, urging Ironsides into a walk again.

Melinda trotted Red to catch up, then let the mare's gait match Ironsides's. "Angela had no enemies. *Everyone* liked her."

"Which doesn't rule out anybody. With the murder weapon being a knife, it's likely the murder wasn't premeditated. It was an impulse, not planned. It probably happened in the heat of passion."

"She didn't have a boyfriend."

"They're not the only ones who can kill."

"I know. I'm trying to picture the…suspects and think of any possible motive." Her fingers fiddled with the reins. "Tommy Lee, her ex, didn't have a reason. She let him go without any obligation on his part."

"He was helping his wife deliver their child at the time Angie was killed."

They skirted the pond's edge. When they reached a narrow trail heading into the woods, Grady took the lead.

"Mike was a friend, but they weren't involved," Melinda continued. "She was worried about crossing her father's wishes, but excited about the prospect of singing the songs from her heart."

"Watch out for the branch," Grady said as he ducked beneath a low-hanging oak limb. The reverend's dislike of country music was common knowledge, but had Angela really thought her father would kill her for singing it? He'd checked and rechecked the alibi. It seemed solid. Neat. Tidy. "Mike's holding something back, but we can place him away from the scene at the time of the crime."

"He doesn't seem like the type, anyway."

"They never do."

The woods opened onto a field where a dozen head of cattle grazed. Knowing Red's fear of the horned beasts, Grady let Melinda come up alongside him, putting a barrier between Red and the cattle. The mare's ears perked and swiveled, her eyes grew wide. She snorted. Melinda reached for the mare's neck. Petting the chestnut hide in calming circles, she crooned softly to the horse. They passed the danger, and Red relaxed once more.

"Kerry was Angie's best friend," Melinda said. "They had a good relationship. In the evening, I could often hear them gossip and giggle in Angie's yard. There's no motive there."

"That's the way it looks."

"Her father..."

"Was leading a youth Bible group."

"Her mother?"

"Baby-sitting Angie's sister's kids."

"Siblings?"

"All accounted for."

"A total stranger?"

Grady shrugged. "Seems unlikely. The evidence points to the fact she knew her killer and let him in willingly."

"A hired killer?" Melinda suggested, but her voice held no conviction.

"Would have used something neater, more efficient, more removed."

The frustration knotting her brow mirrored his own. This whole case was a mess; and with no progress, and further complications growing like warts on a toad, he knew Brasswell had put a call in to the State boys. Tomorrow, he would have the dismal pleasure of sharing his failure with someone who, like Ely Amery, regarded him as no more than a bumbling country cop.

"But someone killed her," Melinda said in a thin voice. "Someone who's afraid I saw something. If it was a crime of passion, not premeditated like you say, could he really kill in cold blood?"

"Hard to say. People react to fear in strange ways. We can't rule it out."

They'd come onto a wide-open space with a long line of electric towers. The sand between the posts and the good care provided by the electric company made the footing safe. What Grady needed to release all this sticky tension was a good run. "Want to race?"

A smile lit her face. "Where to?"

"There's a stone wall with a gate up a ways, but you'll see it in plenty of time to stop."

Sensing the coming excitement, Ironsides bobbed his head and pawed at the ground. "Ready?"

She nodded, and taking a more forward stance, she gathered up the reins. At his signal, Ironsides burst into a gallop. Red followed.

As they reached the gate at the top of the hill, a single shot rang out. Something hot slashed at his jeans. Beside him, Red's hindquarters hunkered down. She whinnied in terror, then bolted sideways toward the woods, away from danger.

Reflexively, Grady whirled Ironsides around in the shot's direction. As he ducked for cover, he scanned the growth of small trees along the rock wall, searching for movement. Breathing hard from his run, Ironsides trembled beneath him, waiting for a command.

Another shot cracked, whizzing past to their right, missing both horse and rider. The gelding jumped sideways. As Grady settled his horse, a glance over his shoulder showed him Melinda was once again in control of Red and protected by the squat mesquites at the far end of the field.

He inched Ironsides along toward the spot where the shot had come from. The sound of running steps caught his attention, then a blur heading for the dirt access road. The shooter was getting away. Grady urged Ironsides into a gallop. He didn't intend to let this would-be murderer get away twice.

A stone wall stood between him and the road. Without missing a beat, he jumped it in time to see an unfamiliar rusty pickup speeding away, a cloud of dust obstructing his view of the license plate. Slowing Ironsides to a halt, Grady swore hotly.

He whirled back over the wall, and headed toward Melinda. On foot and leading the mare, she was walking in his direction.

"Are you all right?" she asked, a bit breathless and eyes wide with worry.

"Fine. He got away."

"Red's hurt," she said, pointing at the top of the mare's hindquarters.

Ignoring the burning pain in his own thigh, Grady drew alongside the mare and examined the bleeding wound. "Looks like it's just a scratch." As was his own injury. "Hop back on and let's get her home."

Deliberately keeping his left side hidden from Melinda's view, Grady led the way home. She had enough to worry about. He glanced at her. She looked pale and scared, but seemed to be handling the second attempt on her life in one day with amazing calm. He, on the other hand, burned with rage. He wanted—needed—to punch something, someone. But he didn't want to scare her with the magnitude of his anger. So to control himself, he ground his jaw until his back teeth hurt.

He'd promised to keep her safe and he'd almost lost her. Right in his own backyard.

Melinda tied the reins around the hitching post, then examined the torn flesh on Red's backside. Grady tied his own horse and disappeared inside the barn. First-aid kit in hand, he came back out and plopped it at her feet.

"Can you handle putting the horses away?" he asked, using Red's neck as a shield. "I've got to call this in."

Already busy at work untacking the mare, she nodded. "Sure. No problem."

"The hose is around the side." Although the gunman was long gone and probably wouldn't be back anytime soon, he hated leaving her alone outside. But he also sensed that keeping busy would help her deal with the trauma.

Her gaze met his across the horse's back. "Do what you have to do, Grady. He's gone. I'll be okay."

HIS CALLS COMPLETED, Grady was struggling to get out of his bloody jeans when he heard Melinda walk into the house. "I'll be out in a minute."

Threads of the ripped material had stuck in the drying blood, and when he yanked the denim from the wound, a grunt of pain escaped him.

"Grady?" she called from the hallway. "Is everything all right?"

He tried to close his bedroom door, but wasn't fast enough; she spotted the blood on his thigh.

"You're hurt!" she gasped, pushing her way into his room.

"It's nothing." He shrugged, turning away from her toward the closet.

"It needs to be looked at. Who's your doctor?"

"I can handle it." He pulled the closet door open and yanked out a fresh pair of jeans.

"Oh, yes, whatever was I thinking! Of course, a macho man like you can handle a little thing like a bullet. I'll bet you like cold showers and raw steak, too."

"On occasion."

He thought she would back down and leave. Instead, she took the jeans from his grasp and flung them on the bed. With both her hands on his chest, she pushed him backward. When his knees hit the back of the bed, he swayed, trying to hold his ground, then toppled into a sitting position.

"First-aid kit?" she asked, moving to the foot of the bed at his side for a closer look at his bloodied thigh. Her tone left no room for argument, and he found he didn't have the will for one. Besides, with the angle of the wound, it would be easier to have some help.

"In the bathroom."

She came back out armed with a package of gauze, medical tape, a tube of antibiotic cream, a wet cloth and a dry towel.

Kneeling at his side, she washed the raw flesh with the cloth as if tending a half-naked man were a normal task. This, from a woman with a house built for one! He tried to ignore the brush of her fingers against his skin, the maddening tingling surrounding the throbbing flesh that spread through him like a fast-moving infection. He was thankful the long tails of his shirt hid his stirring reaction, and fervently hoped she wouldn't look up.

"Red's going to be fine," she said, seemingly unaware of the chaos she caused with her diligent nursing. "I think she was more surprised than hurt. She's grazing peacefully now."

"Good," he said, aware of his pulse quickening with each brush of her skin against his.

"Ironsides, on the other hand, is going to be a mess."

The spring scent of her teased his nostrils. "He rolled as soon as you let him into the paddock."

"You got it. His coat was still wet, so now he's caked with mud."

"Typical." Sweat beaded along his forehead.

"Does it hurt?" she asked, frowning down at the side of his thigh.

"No." It burned like hell—the wound, his whole body. And his determination to remember he was a cop and she a witness was fast smoldering into a pile of ashes.

"I still think this should be looked at by a doctor." She dabbed around the wound with the dry cloth, then slathered antibiotic cream, its coolness a foil to the warmth of her touch. And suddenly, a roomful of high-priced lawyers hell-bent on cross-examining his questionable testimony seemed a cozy alternative to her alluring proximity.

"Was the bullet meant for me or for you?" she asked, seemingly unconcerned.

Her gaze was concentrated on his wound, but he felt her hesitation, her guilt, and her question acted like a bucket of ice water, bringing him back to the reality of their situation. She was in his care. He had promised to protect her. And had failed. This house was no safer for her than her wrecked haven. "Hard to say. He wants to silence you. I'm in the way."

She gingerly covered the wound with a gauze pad, anchoring it with pieces of medical tape. As she looked at her handiwork, a deep frown formed on her forehead. Slowly, deliberately, she traced the flesh around the bandage with the tip of her finger, then leisurely bent down and kissed the same area of sensitive skin. His reaction was instant, fiery and heavy. His fingers curled into the comforter and he sucked in his breath. His skin grew hot and damp despite the ceiling fan whirling above him.

Her hair fell forward in a blue-black cascade, causing a tortuous satiny tickle against his leg. He couldn't decide whether he was in heaven or in hell.

With one hand, he cupped the nape of her neck and with his thumb under her chin raised her face to look at him. "Melinda?"

She grasped his hand in one of hers, frowned at the healing bite mark she'd inflicted. She lifted his palm to her mouth and kissed it. Her mouth slid to the inside of his wrist. Her lips warm against his thrumming pulse turned his thoughts to mush. The room narrowed to just her and her touch and his growing need. The sweet curve of her breast was only a breath away from his forearm. A simple wish would place its peak against his flesh. As if reading his thoughts, her nipple strained against the thin material of her silk shirt, branding him with fierce desire. Closing his eyes, he swallowed his frustration.

He wanted her. But it couldn't happen.

Not for him.

Not with her.

She gently let go of his arm and stood. Helpless, he opened his eyes and followed her movement. A sensual fire burned in her dark eyes. His chest rose and fell in hard, deep breaths as he fought to retain his control.

Bending forward, she brushed her lips lightly against his…took his face in both her hands…put her lips on his…and pressed gently while looking full into his eyes. There was no mistaking the invitation, the naked desire.

He knew then, as he'd instinctively known from the first time he'd seen the mystery-deep darkness of her eyes, that he could get lost in them. And when she closed her eyes to kiss him with heightening passion, he followed—a willing prisoner. There was nothing he could do to stop himself. With a groan of surrender, he gave in and let her carry his better judgment away.

As Grady returned her kiss, Melinda's stomach quivered. A ripple of pleasure purled through her, ignited by the desire so raw and intense in the blue of his eyes, so sweet and hungry under the crush of his lips.

He put his hands on her legs, spread his fingers wide, and slid them heavily, slowly upward. The heat of his touch penetrated the thick layer of denim covering her skin. When his hands reached her waist, he tugged her forward until she was thrown against his chest. Desire coiled hot inside her, making her soft and pliable against him. She slid down his body until her knees touched the floor.

Holding her possessively, he trailed his lips down her throat, deep into the open vee of her shirt to the rise of her breasts, and back up again. She moaned her protest. Hands strong on both sides of her jaw, thumbs stroking the corners of her mouth, he tilted her face to his and held it. There in the burning blue of his eyes, in his silence, in his held breath, was her chance to turn back.

This was stupid, foolish, for both of them. But she needed this—the warmth of another human being touching, loving and affirming life. She needed him, his strength, to fill her completely. She wanted to forget about nightmares and blank spaces and death suddenly so close and constant. She craved him, yearned to melt against him, feel the hard solidity of his body. Running her hands into his thick, brown hair, she kissed him as fiercely as he'd kissed her, giving him his answer.

He groaned and shivered. Pulling her up onto his lap, he held her tightly and rolled sideways into the downy softness of the black and navy comforter.

He peeled the layers of her clothing away like the petals of a daisy, his gaze intense, his fingers sure. *He loves me, he loves me not…*it didn't matter as long as he didn't stop. The last scrap of cloth fell away, leaving her skin exposed to his admiring gaze.

She reached for the silver buttons of his chambray shirt. He trapped her fingers and pushed them away. As he lay propped on one elbow, the fingers of one hand wound themselves in her hair while the other hand explored the female landscape he'd just uncovered. Never would she have guessed that the simple stroking of her hair could be so erotic. Never would she have thought a touch could engender such an ache of need. Her insides coiled tight like a wound spring of boundless want.

"Grady." How easily the name rolled off her tongue, how comfortingly it rumbled in her chest. "Please…"

"Are you sure?" he asked, his big hand paused on her belly.

"Yes." Her voice quavered, her need as open as his in the single word.

"Why?"

She reached up and stroked the edge of his face, feeling the rasp of five o'clock shadow on his jaw. His pupils dilated further, making her body feel jittery in the distance separating them. *Closer,* she wanted to say. *Come closer.* "Because I need to feel alive."

"Is that all?"

"Because I trust you," she said, holding his gaze steadily. "Because I choose to."

"What do you want?" he asked, his voice raspy and low.

For a moment the question took her aback. Then she understood the power he was handing her, the determined strength it took to tamp his hunger and give her a choice. He'd shown her his need, shown her she had the ability to shatter his control. A potent thrill quivered through her. She curved toward him. Inhaling the spicy scent of his male muskiness, she pressed her breasts to his chest, her hips to his hips, her lips to his ear. "I want you," she whispered. "Inside me."

He shuddered. The thunder of his heart beat strong against hers, drowning the whir of the fan. The flat, golden light of late afternoon glowed on his glistening skin. "One night," he said huskily. "That's all."

No empty promises. No sheltering. No lies. Honesty, pure and simple. She could deal with that. "I'll take whatever you want to give me."

And with those words, the control she'd so longed to see shatter did. With a growl low in his throat he shed his clothes, reached for protection, and rolled onto her. As she stroked the solid muscles of his back, he thrust inside her, driving her with his rhythm to the edge of insanity. Eyes closed, rocking to his thrusts, she arched back in passion, reaching with yearning for the release he promised.

"Look at me, Melinda," Grady said, his voice gruff.

Tremors tightened, torqued inside her at the unexpected

pause, at the gritty fierceness of Grady's voice, at her own unforeseen intense passion.

She opened her eyes, meeting the deepening blue of his gaze. He moved inside her again. Slowly at first, then faster and faster, he restoked her fire, driving her closer and closer to the golden explosion of release.

"Let yourself fall, Melinda."

And she did, becoming nothing more than a contented, heated river, flowing at the mercy of his whim. When his own release came, she felt their skins meld together, their spirits touch, their souls unite, and knew without a doubt that one night would never be enough. Forever she would yearn for a repeat of this moment of perfection.

When she could refocus on him, his face told her he hadn't expected to fall so hard himself. His stomach rose and fell in a rapid kneading rhythm against hers. She held him, feeling completely and utterly sated. Completely and utterly secure. And for the first time in twenty years, she didn't see the nightmarish explosion of colors as she fell asleep—only the golden glow of their spent passion. Securely spooned into the cocoon of his arms, she was safe from the rest of the world—for now.

Chapter Thirteen

The beeper bleating on his night table jarred Grady awake. The noise sent his heart thundering and his mind racing. For a moment, in the darkness of night surrounding him, he couldn't remember where he was. Then Melinda snuggled closer to his side, her hand sliding proprietarily across his belly, firing a primitive hunger he thought had been completely sated. And he remembered. Eyes closed, he fumbled for the beeper. Squinting at the small plastic square, he cursed under his breath at the number in the window.

The station.

The effect was a shocking wake-up call he hadn't expected to have to face until morning.

Even as Melinda's curves fitted more snugly into his side, a mixture of anger and regret had him slipping away from her. A small whimper of protest escaped her. He tucked the sheet around her shoulders. Away from the warmth of her body, he shivered under the air-conditioning's rumbling blast.

What he'd done was unforgivable, unprofessional, unethical—not to mention very, very stupid. He was a cop; she was a witness under his protection.

Once again, he'd let his lust for a woman affect his judgment.

As he punched the numbers into the phone and waited for the ring to be answered, he realized he'd crossed a dangerous boundary. He looked at Melinda's sleeping features softened by the moonlight streaming through the window. Yet, even knowing this could cost him his promotion to chief, he knew he'd take the risk again, and blasted himself even more for his weakness where she was concerned.

Glad for the pain in his thigh that burned with each of his movements, he reached for his jeans on the floor and gave himself a mental bracing.

Jamie had proved to him that thinking with his heart instead of his head could be dangerous. And without a clear head, not only was his future at stake, but so was justice for Angela, and possibly even Melinda's life. To keep her safe, to catch this elusive killer and solve this case, he had to push her away, had to curb his feelings, had to concentrate.

"Sloan," he barked when the phone was answered.

"We just got a call about trouble at the Jackalope Acres. Thought you might want to know," the dispatcher said. She hesitated. "The Crews kid called it in himself."

Grady swore. Carson would never call unless the situation was out of control. "I'm on my way."

"Get dressed," he said to Melinda more tersely than he'd meant as he shook her awake.

"What?" Stretching out, Melinda rubbed her eyes.

Her unconscious movements caused the sheet to move, exposing her creamy skin. The sight of it was like a feast to a hungry man, making Grady salivate, though he knew he couldn't eat. And knowing he couldn't have her again brought an aching sadness more poignant than he could ever have imagined.

Steeling himself against the need for her growing strong again, he turned from her and reached into the closet for a clean shirt. But not even the scent of fabric softener on the garment could mask the spring freshness of Melinda's perfume still clinging to his skin. He could never get enough of her; not in one lifetime. "There's some trouble I've got to take care of. I can't leave you here alone."

Her head fell back to the pillow. "I'll be fine."

"After those shots this afternoon, I can't take the chance." He reached for her and drew her up. "Up you go. You've got less than a minute to get dressed."

When they reached the trailer park, Jackson's drunken rage could be heard three rows down. Grady shoved the truck into neutral, jerked on the parking brake and left the engine running. "Stay here and don't move. Got it?"

Melinda started to protest, then wisely nodded.

A group of neighbors, in various states of dress, huddled near the Crews' trailer, speaking in urgent whispers. At the sight of Grady getting out of his truck, there was a collective sigh of relief.

A gray-haired matriarch pushed forward toward him, tightening the too-short belt of her pink terry robe. "It's been goin' on for near half an hour. You've got to stop him before he kills the kid. Don't understand why it hasn't been done already."

Rules, Grady wanted to explain, but didn't. There was no point.

"Police, open up!"

"Get lost!"

"Open up, Jackson, or I'm coming in!"

As Grady opened the trailer door, he heard a police unit screech into the park. With a scanning glance, he spotted Carson huddled beneath the kitchen table against the wall, and a raging Jackson only a few feet away, holding an empty wine bottle by the neck in one hand and an aluminum baseball bat in the other. In the harsh light from the fluorescent tube over the sink, Jackson's face was etched with stark lines of fury and hatred.

"Get outta here!" The bottle flew in a weak arc and exploded against the wall not a foot from Grady's head. Jackson, swaying as he turned, searched for another missile to launch. Finding none, he charged at Grady, brandishing the bat like a mace. "Stay out of this, you bastard!"

"Put the bat down, Jackson." Glass from smashed bottles and fractured dishes crunched under Grady's feet.

Jackson took a swing at Grady and missed. Grady caught the drunk by the collar and shoved him against the wall.

"It's your fault the son of a bitch wants to leave." Jackson aimed a punch at Grady's stomach. Grady moved aside and the punch connected with air, throwing Jackson off-balance. With a twist, Grady wrenched the bat free from Jackson's grip and threw it out of reach. Standing straight, he waited for Jackson's next attack.

"You ain't never gonna mess with my business again." With the maddened grunt of a bull seeing red, Jackson launched himself at Grady. A uniformed policeman stepped into the trailer in time to witness Jackson's assault.

"I've been waiting a long time for this," Grady muttered as Jackson neared. Venting all his frustrations, Grady swung at the man and flattened him. Sprawled on the floor, Jackson looked drunkenly up at Grady, then passed out.

"He's all yours," Grady said, flexing his smarting knuckles. There wasn't as much satisfaction in the punch as he'd expected, and he instantly regretted stooping to a drunk's level. Was it any wonder the town council had no faith in him? With a disgusted shake of his head, he turned his attention to Carson, who still cowered under the table.

"He broke my pitching arm!" Carson sobbed, edging out from the table's protective cover at Grady's urging.

"He broke my pitching arm! The big game's next week and the bastard broke my pitching arm!"

"Let's take a look at it." Gently Grady examined the swelling arm, feeling Carson's heartbreak as if it were his own. He remembered being that young and watching his world shatter around him, remembered the helplessness and the fear. "Can you move your fingers?"

Face contorted in pain, Carson shook his head. Grady went to the small refrigerator and pulled out a tray of ice. There was no need to ask what had happened. The broken wine bottles and scattered beer cans told the story clearly enough. Time enough later for details. All that mattered now was Carson. He dumped the cubes onto a dishcloth and tied the ends of the cloth in a knot. Kneeling once more beside the boy, Grady placed the ice on Carson's arm.

"I love him, Grady. But no matter how hard I try, I can't do nothin' right by him."

"I know." Grady tied a makeshift sling over the arm. "We're going to take you to the hospital now, then we'll file a report."

A frightened look crossed Carson's too-white face.

"It's got to be done, Carson. He's got to take responsibility for what he's done to you. It's the only way he can get the help he needs."

Jackson moaned in the background. After a fearful look in his father's direction, the boy nodded and struggled to his feet.

"I'll be right beside you every step of the way." Grady would stand by Carson the way Seth had stood by him. "Come on, let's get this arm looked at."

Outside, the whirling blue and red of the police unit's lights added a macabre effect to the sick yellow of the sodium bulbs high on their safety perches around the park, giving the curious crowd an unhealthy complexion. Grady spotted Melinda poised half in, half out of the truck and didn't know whether to be mad at her for disobeying his orders, or take her in his arms and smooth away the deep frown of worry creasing her forehead. He did neither.

"Why don't you settle Carson into the truck," he said to Melinda as he headed back to the trailer. He came back out with the officer, Jackson's weaving body supported between them. Melinda's arm circled Carson protectively.

"Kids," Jackson muttered sluggishly as the officer guided him into the unit. "They're all morons. They don't appreciate nothin' parents do for them. All the sacrificin'. Here…" Jackson reached into his jeans pocket and drew out a fistful of change. Most of the coins fell through his thick, uncoordinated fingers. He threw the rest in Carson's direction. "Here's a quarter. Call someone who cares."

The unit's slamming door cut off the rest of Jackson's litany. The officer stooped over an object on the ground. "Grady, you might want to take a look at this."

On the dry red clay, highlighted by the flashlight's strong beam, was a heart-shaped locket. The fall from Jackson's pocket had jolted it open. Inside was a small picture of Tommy Lee Petersen.

It was nearly two in the morning when they returned to Grady's home and to separate beds. Carson Crews, arm in a cast, had been settled in a hospital room until something more permanent could be arranged in the morning. Because of the danger stalking Melinda wherever she went, Grady hadn't been able to see to Carson himself. Jackson Crews had fallen into the blissful oblivion of the drunk in a holding cell, and questions would have to wait until morning for answers.

Melinda had longed for the comfort of Grady's arms, but the incident at the trailer park seemed to have left him wearing the mask of the terminally polite. It irritated the

stuffing out of her, but she wasn't about to beg for a hug—
no matter how badly she needed one.

She tossed and turned on the small mattress in Grady's
spare room, alone under the cool white sheets. She kept
picturing him on the other side of the wall, wondering if
he was as sleepless as she was. Finally, the constant flap-
flap of the ceiling fan's paddles allowed her to relax and
the tiredness in her limbs migrated to her mind.

But when she slept, the nightmare returned. The
splashes of color electrified her brain into overdrive. Melinda had to get up. It wasn't a choice, but an overwhelming need—a need to release the potent energy swirling
through her like a tornado of wind, fire and lightning.

She didn't bother wiping the sweat from her brow.
Didn't bother getting dressed. Her mind was focused on
the urgency of the need to draw. Her heart told her it would
unlock the gates of her private hell.

She snapped on the overhead light. With frantic movements, she scrounged the night table for paper and found
none. As she ransacked her suitcase, the monster's feral
growl pounded in her head. Tears of frustration strangled
her throat. Biting her trembling lower lip, she swiped at
her eyes with the back of her hand.

Sketchbook finally in hand, she dumped the contents of
her purse on the sand-colored carpet and snatched a pencil
from the debris. Drawing her knees up, she used them as
an easel.

Fast and furious pencil lines appeared on the pristine
white sheet of paper. Then came the painstaking layers of
detail. One after another, creating a transparent effect of
images within images. They made no sense, even to her.
But she didn't analyze. She sketched, guided by an unknown internal force, and trusted that in time she'd understand.

She drew until her cramped hand could no longer hold the pencil and the rush of explosive force died.

Hands flat by her sides, she stared at the feverish lines until slowly a picture took form. Flames, high and hungry. A knife large and sharp. A body, felled and falling. And there in the midst of chaos, a glint of recognition. A cuff link, plain and simple, with an *A* etched on its face.

Sensing she was no longer alone, she looked up.

Grady stood at her bedroom door, his face pale, his eyes crinkled with worry, his mouth a thin line, but he offered no physical contact. She could taste his loneliness across the space from bed to door, could feel his inner turmoil in his knuckle-whitening grip on the knob and jamb, could hear the hesitation in his breath. Some sort of demon had stolen her memory, but she sensed that a different kind of monster had stolen something from him, too.

They were kindred souls.

Except kindred souls didn't look at each other as if they were strangers—not after what they'd shared that afternoon. And lovers didn't hold each other at icy arm's length.

Slowly, he turned away.

"Grady…"

He hesitated, then continued on. The soft click of the door closing sounded like doom. He was back to being a cop, and she a witness.

Distance—maybe it was best.

She'd known there was a risk in giving in to her physical need for him. She'd thought it would be all right, had thought she could keep heart and body separate. She hadn't known the union would be one of soul and spirit, too, and would touch them both so deeply. She wanted to go to him, wanted to hold him until morning, wanted to feel the peace that came with contentment in his arms. But her body seemed incapable of movement.

With his loving, he had taken a part of her that would never belong to anyone else. With his quiet leaving, he was marking boundaries. With his silence, he had pushed her away. She curled her fingers around the nightgown fabric over her heart, trying to hold the jagged pain from spreading.

It was too late. Already her limbs were numb, cold and shaking.

MELINDA DIDN'T BOTHER trying to sleep again. She showered, changed, and stared at her mad drawing until the steely light of a cloudy day filtered through the curtains, until the lines blurred and the feeling of betrayal had deadened into nothing more than a slow throb. When she heard noises from the kitchen, she joined Grady.

"I don't have tea or English muffins," Grady said as he placed a glass of orange juice and a plate of toast spread with peanut butter on the small table. Dressed in his uniform blues, he looked neat and pressed and very remote. "Coffee?"

"That'll be fine." Her smile was brittle. She was touched that he even remembered her preferences, yet hurt by the distance his stiff body language proclaimed. Had she been wrong to think their lovemaking had affected him as deeply as it had her?

"It'll have to be a quick breakfast. I've got to get to the station." Grady handed her a mug of coffee and settled in front of the sandwich he'd set on the counter for himself.

"That's all right. I can find my way to work on my own." If being around her was so painful, she wouldn't prolong his agony.

"It's not safe."

"Neither is this house," she said looking pointedly at his covered thigh. "At least at work I won't be alone. There'll be plenty of other people around."

"I'd rather have you where I can keep an eye on you."

She fidgeted with her glass. Having him so close and yet so far would be a torture she wasn't sure she could endure. "I'd go stark raving mad with nothing to do all day. I've got a business to run, Grady. I *need* to be there."

His cool, blue gaze raked her intensely, but she didn't recoil. As if he were weighing two sides of an equation, his jaw flinched.

"You'll stay inside," he said finally.

"Yes," she said, her relief evident in her sighing of the word. She looked away, concentrating on the contents of her glass, her fingers feeling jittery, her muscles twitching for action.

"You won't go anywhere alone?"

She smiled, countering his seriousness with a light tone. "Not even the ladies' room?"

"Not even there." His expression remained grim.

"Isn't that a little extreme?"

"So was that van nearly making you the stuffing of a deadly sandwich."

Her smile faded. Was it her personal safety or her well-being as a witness that worried him so much? A kernel of anger settled in her stomach and as prolific as a weed in mulch, it took root and wouldn't let go. "You're right, of course," she said stiffly. "I'll be careful."

After a silent ride in his truck, Grady saw her settled at her desk at The Essential Gardener, and after giving her a set of safety instructions rivaling a clearance application for a secret military project, he left.

Her police escort had naturally drawn plenty of attention and it wasn't long before Dolores showed up at her cubicle, hands flying, asking oblique questions. Not in the mood to deal with anyone, Melinda answered evasively.

"So what's really going on?" Dolores asked, perching on the corner of Melinda's desk.

Melinda opened a drawer, then closed it again. "Nothing."

Dolores's grin was Cheshire-cat wide. "After all the dates I've tried to arrange for you, you've gone and fallen for the starched cop!"

Shrugging, Melinda searched the top of her desk, she wasn't quite sure what for. "Of course not. Grady's just a cop doing his job, and I'm just someone he thinks is a witness."

"Uh-huh. Well, you'll get over him soon enough. He wasn't right for you, anyway. What you need is someone who can add some fun to your life. Stiff upper lip and whalebone corsets are fine, hon." Dolores's voice softened. "But sometimes, you've got to let down the wall to see the view. It might surprise you."

Melinda found a file and shuffled the papers inside. "I have no idea what you're talking about."

"Tonight, I'm taking you out. I've got two very handsome young men who are dying to meet you."

With a firm slap, Melinda closed the file. "I doubt that idea's going to sit well with Grady. He's determined to keep me under lock and key until Angela's killer is found."

"For how long?" Dolores leaned forward. Irritation showed in the thinness of her voice. "It could take a while before the killer's found. Are you going to let him keep you prisoner like that, keep you from having a life?"

"Dolores—"

"Or have you remembered anything more that's given him a solid lead?"

"Not really." She shrugged again. "Not about Angela's murder anyway." She frowned down at the hands twined in her lap. "I'm starting to get the really bad feeling my father is responsible for my mother's death, though."

Instantly, Dolores perked up. "What makes you think that?"

She hesitated, then leaned back in her chair, looking intently into Dolores's eyes. "Did my father own a pair of gold cuff links with the letter *A* etched into them?"

As she nodded, a pained look crossed Dolores's face. "They were a wedding gift from your mother."

"I saw one last night in a...memory."

"Oh, Melinda." Dolores reached for Melinda's hand and pasted on a bolstering smile. "Then you need this evening out more than ever." She squeezed Melinda's fingers gently. "Your mother would want you to laugh, to enjoy life, not to dwell on this painful past like you are."

"If he did kill her, then he needs to face the consequences of his actions."

As Dolores hopped off the corner of the desk, her face pinched. "Men like your father don't have to. That's something I learned a long time ago. You'll only make your life miserable by pursuing this. If you really want to hurt him, what you need to do is divorce yourself from him."

Melinda didn't answer, couldn't think of what to say. But hiding once more from the truth felt wrong.

"About tonight—" Dolores started.

"I'll think about it," Melinda said, but the idea of going out with one of Dolores's boy toys held no appeal. Not with so much weighing on her mind. Not with Grady's loving still imprinted on her body and soul. Not with her heart so heavy from Grady's forced distance.

"You do that," Dolores said, "and I'll arrange everything." With that, she left, and Melinda's tension deflated like a balloon that had lost its tie.

Melinda drummed her fingers on her desk. She'd never asked questions about that night so long ago. Instead she'd accepted what she'd been told and hidden in the comfort of surface reality. But even that hadn't buried the truth. Her checkered dreams had visited her every night to remind her of the past. And while she'd been pretending everything was normal, her nightmare had slipped from the misty folds of nighttime dreams and invaded her daytime life, destroying the illusion of safety she'd created for herself.

She'd made her own prison. It was up to her to set herself free.

Chapter Fourteen

The old house with its red bricks, thick trees and homey English ivy climbing the chimney looked inviting. But the doorbell echoed eerily inside the house and an icy blast of air-conditioning was her welcome when Melinda opened the door with her key.

"Daddy?" she called as she deactivated the alarm. Her voice carried across the marble-floored hall, but her father's answering boom didn't follow.

She'd spent most of the day at her desk, making phone calls between editing copy for the spring catalog. One of those calls had been to her father who'd agreed to meet her here at five. Another had been to Grady who'd seemed relieved to hear she'd be tied up at work until late. But before he'd agreed, he'd made her promise that Dolores would be there to keep her company, and the doors would be double locked and the alarm would be set.

Lying to Grady had been harder than she'd expected, but with him as her shadow, her father would never speak openly, and she'd grown weary of lies, of nightmares, of fears. Finding the truth, finding peace, had become worth any price. Grady had shown her how much of life she was missing. With her past known and faced, maybe she'd feel safe enough to allow her current repressed memories to return. Then she could help Angela receive justice and Grady solve his case.

She wandered into the living room with its triple set of French doors. The lure of the outside garden was too much to resist, so she opened the middle doors and stepped into the greenery.

Gray clouds frothed in the sky like a brew from a witch's cauldron. The wind swirled the rayon of her dress against her ankles, made the tree limbs shake and shiver, the flowers bend and bob. The scent of rain tainted the air. And edginess crept into her limbs like tiny hungry spiders.

Sitting on the stone bench where her mother's greenhouse had once stood, she absorbed the surroundings. There was nothing left of that night, except her memories. Crossing her arms beneath her chest, she rubbed at the sudden chill and started rocking her body slowly back and forth.

"It's okay. You'll be okay...."

Realizing she was falling back on her habit of self-hypnosis, she stopped rocking, unfolded her arms and took a deep breath. Superimposing Grady's strength onto herself, she straightened her spine, closed her eyes and forced herself to look at the images forming on the edge of her consciousness.

"Lindy, what are you doing up?" Her mother smiled down at her.

"I can't sleep."

Mama stuffed a foam block into a vase shaped like the tops of the white pillars at the front of the house. "Well, why don't you help me for a while, then?"

Melinda happily hopped onto the worktable. Kicking her slippered feet, she picked up a frond of fern and tickled her mother's cheek. They both laughed. "What're you doing?"

"I'm making some pretty pots for Daddy's office. Red roses and white chrysanthemums."

Roses. A whole vaseful of them. Perched on her mother's worktable, she buried her nose in the fragrant blooms. Twelve. Mama had once told her that the best arrangements held an odd number of blooms. Her chubby child's fingers reached for a pair of pruners. Wouldn't Mama be pleased when she saw Melinda had remembered the lesson?

"Going back to bed?" Mama asked.

"No, it's a surprise." She giggled as she headed for the bushes just outside the greenhouse for a thirteenth blossom.

The ledge protected her from the worst of the rain, but her nightgown was tight around her legs, and she couldn't move well. She tripped and fell into the rosebushes. Thorns from the roses held her trapped in place. She opened her mouth to yell for help, but when she turned her head to look at Mama, nothing came out.

The silent tape, like a horror film in a black, doorless theater, continued to play in exaggerated slow motion, showing every movement, every detail in perfect color and surreal vividness.

The monster's shadow crept across the entrance. Too scared to cry, too scared to move, too scared he'd get her, Melinda shivered helplessly.

"Melinda? What are you doing out here? For heaven's sake, it's raining!"

At the sound of her father's voice, Melinda jumped and gasped. "You scared me," she said, hand over her heart.

As she looked at her father's stylish figure, the rapid hammering of her heart increased. The monster of her nightmares? Could someone she loved so much have killed his own wife, the mother of his child?

"What's wrong, Melinda?" Her father sat beside her

and hugged her close. "You look awful. I really wish you'd see a doctor."

She edged away, turning on the stone bench to face him. The time had come to face the truth. The time had come to face her mother's murderer, the monster from the closet, the thief of her memories. "We need to talk...about my mother."

Her father gave an exasperated sigh. "What's brought this on this time? The cop again?"

"The lies, Daddy. I'm sick of them."

"I've never lied to you."

"But have you told me the truth?"

He had the decency to look away, his gaze faraway in the deepening gray of the sky, uncharacteristically unfazed by the slow raindrops staining the jacket of his suit. He turned a fond expression toward her. "I guess it's time I accept you've grown up."

"I have been for quite some time now."

He smiled. "I expect you're right. Let's get out of this rain."

Taking her hand, he led her inside to the living room. "What can I get you?"

"Nothing. I'm fine."

Her father headed for the small bar and poured himself a glass of Chivas Regal—neat. "What do you want to know?"

There was no point dancing around the issue. As much as her father liked taking the long way around, she'd take the short-cut today. "I remember you...hurting my mother."

"'Remember'?" He cocked an eyebrow, making her feel small and stupid. It had never taken much for him to be able to do that. She bristled inside, but kept an impassive face. "As in those nightmares you told me about?

Those are surely false memories. There's been a lot in the news about that lately.''

Melinda stepped behind a wing chair, putting something solid between her and her father. ''What about all those late-night arguments?''

He puffed his chest and adopted his courtroom pose. ''Your mother and I—''

Melinda saw straight through the transparent gestures. ''The truth, Daddy.''

He took a sip of his drink and shrugged. ''Every couple has disagreements now and then.''

''But not every husband chooses to beat his wife. I heard you, Daddy.'' She mimicked her parents' voices as she remembered them from her hypnosis session. '' 'Keep your voice down, Lindy will hear.' 'She's asleep like a good little girl. Wish I could say the same for her mother. Who was it this time?' 'How many times am I going to have to tell you, there is no one else?' Then I remember you slapping her, Daddy, while you called her a whore. Is that a false memory, too?''

Her father took several steps forward, but when he saw her hands grab hold of the back of the chair, he stopped. ''Melinda, sometimes children exaggerate what they think they see and hear—''

Melinda shook her head, and the tightness in her throat made it hard to speak. ''And sometimes they pretend it isn't happening because they love the people involved so much. I pretended for twenty years, Daddy. Isn't that long enough? All I want is the truth, so I can put that past behind.''

The harder he tried to cajole her out of her memories by calling them false and confusing her, the more she knew the memories were true. She found she could stand toe to toe with him and not back down. Loving her father hadn't been wrong. Making him into a god to rationalize that love had been her mistake. He was human, after all. And that simple humanity became clearer as he lost his courtroom composure. His face crumpled from the weight of his guilt.

"I'm not proud of what I did," he said, downing the drink and reaching for the bottle for a refill.

Melinda gripped the back of a wing chair. "Why, Daddy? Why?"

The bottle paused in midair, creating a painful silence. "Because…because I loved her, and she never loved me."

Although such a simple reason shouldn't make sense, somehow it did. Her father had never liked losing. Not at anything. And her mother's refusal to return his love must have been impossible for him to endure. Had it driven him to do the unthinkable?

The sky opened up and a rush of rain battered the French doors. "Did you kill her? Did you kill my mother?"

The glass he raised to his lips shook in his hands. He closed his eyes and took a deep breath. "Yes."

GRADY HATED COMPROMISE. Contrary to popular belief, it didn't lead to a win-win proposition, but more likely to a lose-lose one. Especially when the law tried to compromise with a lawbreaker. Even more so when the criminal had courted the law so often he knew every slippery loophole and didn't hesitate to demand them.

After reviewing his file on the Petersen case, Stanton and Maury from the State police had taken over Jackson's interview, and Jackson had held court all day, with Grady forced to do no more than observe. Finally, a deal had been struck. For showing them the place where he'd found the locket, Jackson would get no more than a slap on the wrist for what he'd done to his son.

Still seething with anger, Grady picked up the phone ringing on his desk. "Sloan."

"I've heard you've apprehended someone for Angela's murder." The Reverend Hobart's cowed and tired voice on the other end did nothing to cheer him.

"I'm sorry to say you've been misinformed." Grady curbed his impatience. "We may have a new lead."

"Who? What? Where?"

"We still need to check it out."

There was a long pause. "Of course. You'll let me know what happens?"

"I'll do that."

Before he followed the little caravan out on its field trip, he wanted to check up on Melinda, hear her voice. Just the thought of her brought back a strong, unexpected longing. He jabbed in her office number. No answer.

Stanton popped his grizzled head in the door. "Ready?"

"Be right there."

He tried the number again. When he got no answer, tension knotted the back of his neck and twisted his gut. One thing at a time, he reminded himself. She was safe. Had to be. The pressure in his gut increased. *It's just your feelings for her getting in the way,* he chided himself as he closed the office door. If anything more was discovered at the site where Jackson had found the locket, this whole thing could be over soon.

Jackson led them on a course as crooked as one of his drunken binges. First the local bars, all three of them, then the liquor store, and finally to the place where the railroad crossed the Forlorn River, where weeds grew tall, but the river's twist and the railroad's pilings made a cozy corner to imbibe with nature. Half-buried on the riverbank, partially hidden by weeds, was a black gym bag.

"I didn't take nothin' else, just the locket."

Nope, just contaminated the evidence in a murder investigation, Grady thought wryly.

"What about the knife?"

Jackson became belligerent. "There was nothing else worth pawning in there."

Crouching, Grady took one look inside the stained gym bag, and a flicker of fear plucked at his chest. It had never been a matter of black or white, or even shades of gray. It had always been a matter of black-and-white together, yet separate at the same time, with all the colors in between.

There inside lay the bloody remains of a pair of red jeans, a pair of size-six once-white canvas sneakers, and a sleeveless white blouse decorated with red embroidery.

The puzzle pieces slid together smoothly, offering a chilling picture.

Kerry was the only one in Angela's circle who was small enough to fit into those clothes. Kerry had a cut slicing the meaty part of her hand. Kerry, Angela's best friend, who became almost hysterical when the subject of Angela was brought up.

And as the final understanding clunked into place, his heart stilled.

Once again, he'd trusted the wrong person.

Shouting instructions to the stupefied state officers, Grady raced away and prayed he would get there in time.

"IT'S NOT WHAT YOU THINK," Ely said, watching his daughter edge away from him as if he were a monster. And maybe he was. He, after all, had the genes of monsters inside him. "I didn't kill her with my fists, but with my lack of trust. Your mother didn't want to marry me—"

"I know. Dolores told me."

He saw the sadness in his beautiful daughter's eyes, and wished he'd done something about it sooner. She might not have become a brilliant lawyer as he'd wanted, but she'd become more like him than she thought. All those feelings hidden inside. It was a wonder she'd never cracked. If nothing else, he'd taught her to be strong.

"I thought that eventually she would learn to love me." Ely downed another sip of courage from the liquid fire in his glass. "She was beautiful and so charming. I was from the wrong side of the tracks. The only reason she married me was because your grandfather insisted, to protect his reputation." Ely had been nothing. His mother had beaten the belief into him early. With every lick of the strap, he'd vowed he'd prove her wrong. "The only thing I had on my side was ambition and skill—two things your grandfather greatly admired. And those two qualities led to success, which your grandfather prized even more. It was my mistrust that killed whatever love your mother might have learned to have for me. And watching her eyes grow duller with each passing year made me feel helpless."

"I don't understand."

The sound of the rain outside turned more urgent and beneath its staccato beat against the glass came the low rumble of thunder. Melinda was right. He'd never lied to her, but he hadn't told her the truth, either. He hadn't seen the point of causing her pain. She'd looked so much like her mother. But the omission had hurt her anyway.

He squared his shoulders and looked straight into her dark eyes. "You are not my daughter. In exchange for marrying your pregnant mother, I received a partnership, and eventual ownership, of your grandfather's law firm."

"What?" Her face paled alarmingly. Her fingers on the wing chair's red brocade looked like bleached bones. He took a step toward her, only to have her shrink away from him. The tiny movement cut him deeply.

"Your birth father was an artist…like you. Ironic, isn't it?" He polished off the contents of his glass. "I worked so hard to prove to your mother that making a child and being its father were two unrelated events."

"That's why you wanted me to become a lawyer."

She'd always been smart. He'd loved his conversations with her even as a child. "Yes—"

"And I went and proved you wrong."

He placed the empty glass on the coffee table, then sank into the sofa, feeling defeated in a way that had never happened to him in court. He'd lost his beloved Abigail, and was now on the way to losing his daughter, too. "It really didn't matter, Melinda. I grew to love you as if you were my own. I was...illegitimate, too, and I wanted a better life for you than the one I had. I never wanted you to know the pain of being hated for an accident of conception."

Her grip on the chair back loosened. "That's why you gave so much to charity—the women's shelter, the Angel's Gate home, the abuse hotline."

"Penance," he said with a weak smile.

Melinda came around the chair and sat down on its edge. Hands on her knees, she leaned forward. "Why, then, didn't you let me be who I wanted to be? Why didn't you let me study art?"

"Why didn't you tell me it was so important to you?"

Her dark eyes shone with emotion. "Because I was afraid to let you down."

A lump of sadness landed hard in the pit of his stomach. "Melinda..."

"When you saw I couldn't become a lawyer, why were you so against my working at the catalog when it made me so happy?"

"Partly arrogance. Partly because I never liked Dolores. Did she ever tell you how she got the capital to start the catalog?"

"No." Melinda sprang up and wandered to the French doors. To escape from him? He'd really screwed everything up, hadn't he? And now he would erase her faith in the one person she'd always trusted. That trust had been the only reason he'd allowed Dolores to get away with blackmail.

"She threatened to expose my...abuse. She had your mother's diary to prove it. I had no choice. I had to give her the money she wanted. I had too much invested in my career to take a chance on seeing it ruined."

Melinda flinched at the lightning and backed from the thunder. Standing in the middle of the room, she looked so small and vulnerable. He could still imagine her as an eight-year-old, gazing up at him for comfort. With sadness, he realized that, she would not turn to him this time.

"I—I saw your hand with a knife. My mother fall. Blood all around her..."

He shook his head, feeling the blood drain out of his face. How could she even think he could perpetrate such a dire act? A piercing sadness filled his chest. Given her memories, what other conclusion could she draw? He wanted to deny everything. But he said nothing, knowing nothing he could say would alter her image of him. To her, he would forever be a monster.

"I saw the cuff links my mother gave you as a wedding gift."

"Your mother gave me no wedding gift. Why would she? She didn't want me and knew what I'd been promised for marrying her."

A frown furrowed her forehead. "Gold cuff links? The ones with the *A* etched into them?"

"Weren't mine. I, on the other hand, did give your mother a gift. A braided-gold bracelet with a heart-shaped charm. I had an *A* engraved on its face and Forever Mine on the back." He patted the cushion next to his on the sofa. He should have done this a long time ago. Talking had always been his best talent, and with the one person who'd needed his words the most, he'd been the quietest. "Come sit next to me, Melinda."

MELINDA SAT ON THE COUCH, leaving one cushion open between them. Hope and fear, love and hatred, mixed and curdled like a sauce gone bad. She didn't know what to believe anymore. Her father didn't feel like the monster of her nightmares, yet she knew what she'd seen in those returning memories. Dolores had always appeared soft and warm, yet she'd blackmailed her father to get what she wanted. Which was right? What to believe? Melinda's mind flickered to Grady, but she knew she couldn't lean on his strength this time. She was all alone—like she'd been twenty years ago.

"All those nights I heard you cry in your sleep after your mother died," her father said, "I let it go because I thought you'd get over it."

"I saw what happened, Daddy," Melinda insisted, refusing to believe she could have made up something she could see with such detail. "I saw my mother being murdered."

"Murdered?" Her father seemed taken aback. "No, the fire was an accident. It was sparked by lightning."

Melinda shook her head and closed her eyes. "No, there was rain, thunder, lightning. But someone was there, too. I'd gone to Mama's garden to get an extra rose and got caught in the bushes. I tried to call out, but nothing would come out...."

The slip of expensive wool against brocade reached her. Her father wrapped an arm around her shoulder, and she leaned her head against his. "Tell me what you saw, Melinda."

Fear kept her still and silent, trapped amid the thorns of her mother's beloved roses. The shadow moved across the space. Voices. Surprise. Anger.

"What are they saying?" he asked.

Melinda never got to answer the question. A crack shook the room. She startled. Her eyes opened wide.

Between the space of reality and dream, she saw her father crumple forward. Blood, red and bright, stained the white of his shirt.

"Daddy!"

As she held her dying father, she felt a chill climb her spine. The monster's aura was unmistakable. The hairs on her arms, on the back of her neck rose straight up.

Fear, raw and primal, churned through her. She was eight again and cornered. Helpless.

"Mama, Mama! Wake up, Mama!" Her sobs were so loud she didn't know the monster had returned until the slap of liquid from a bottle on her mother's workbench splashed on the ground next to her. The acrid smell filled her nostrils. Stunned, she sat frozen. She heard the swoosh of the match against the workbench. Still she couldn't move. Then an all-encompassing poof set yellow flames racing across the floor, biting, eating, devouring everything in their path. As she ran, her screams echoed in her head, but didn't make their way past her throat. Up the stairs she went, up into her bed. With the sheet over her head, she closed her eyes and the colors and the smells and the awful taste melded one into another. It wasn't until the blackness came that she realized she'd left her mother behind to be eaten by the flames. "It's okay. You'll be okay...."

It took all of Melinda's courage to turn around and face the monster. It stood in the doorway, frowning at her, both hands extended forward, the muzzle of a gun pointed straight at her heart.

With a simple squeeze of the trigger she could be dead. Like her mother.

Like her father.

"I didn't want to do it, but you left me no choice. I tried so hard to make up for everything. Why didn't you just let everything stand as it was?"

Chapter Fifteen

Grady tried to concentrate on the road, but his worry for Melinda constantly pulled at his attention. In his mind's eye he saw her face as she relived her nightmares under hypnosis, so vulnerable, in so much pain. He'd failed her just as everyone else in her life had. He swallowed hard. How would she react to the knowledge that the one person she'd trusted was the monster of her dreams?

The truck screeched to a halt in front of The Essential Gardener. Leaving the engine rumbling, he raced for the door.

Black. Everything inside was black. Rain dripping into his eyes, he pounded on the door. "Melinda!"

Forcing himself to calm down, he doused his runaway emotions. With his mind once again still, he searched for the thread of her presence, for the feeling that came over him whenever she was close. An echo of emptiness returned to him, cold and dark.

She wasn't here.

Once more in his truck, he searched his mind for clues. Where had she gone? To her home? To his? Then he remembered the picture he'd seen her draw—was it only this morning?—and panicked. Had she gone to face her past alone? Or worse, had her monster caught up to her?

"Why should she have trusted you with her plan? You

certainly did your best imitation of someone who couldn't care less," he said bitterly.

Morning seemed like a lifetime ago. But the ghostly whiteness of her skin and the pleading of her soulful eyes had nearly undone him. It had taken every ounce of strength he possessed to walk away from her. He'd thought he was doing the right thing, but now he wished he'd gone to her, held her, loved her instead. Maybe things would have turned out differently.

He'd made her only one promise—to keep her safe. And he was blowing it royally.

Mistakes—would he ever stop making them? he thought as he turned into his ranch-house road.

Finding Melinda's drawing still on the bedroom floor took no time. Seeing the form beneath the lines took a little longer. Understanding them brought a sense of relief. If she'd gone to face her father, she'd be safe enough. He reached for the phone.

MELINDA HADN'T EXPECTED to be this scared. But she hadn't counted on the rain or the thunder or the shadows, or on the way they played with the remnants of her nightmare fears like costumed ghouls on Halloween. As a child, she'd retreated, but she couldn't now. She'd tasted what life could be like without black dreams and monsters, and wasn't ready to give it up without a fight.

"Dolores?" She couldn't believe that the woman who, for all intents and purposes, had taken over the role of her mother, now stood before her, eyes wild and gun in hand.

Melinda heard a weak gasp. Reflexively, she leaned toward her father, reaching for the red stain spreading on his chest.

"Don't move," Dolores warned.

"H-he needs help."

"He's dead."

"No." Melinda pressed her hand to his chest, desperately trying to stop the flow of blood. He wasn't moving. He wasn't breathing. "Daddy?" He couldn't die. Not now. Not when they were just starting to understand each other. "Why?"

"It didn't have to end this way." Anger glittered in Dolores's light-blue eyes.

Slowly, Melinda released her hold on the bloody shirt. Her father was dead, and she would be next. The sharpness of Dolores's eyes told her so in no uncertain terms. How could she have loved someone with such cold eyes? Why hadn't she noticed their soulless surface before? How could she have trusted her with all her secrets? She looked closely at the weathered face and saw no trace of warmth, no trace of the friend she'd known, only icy determination. Panic replaced grief.

"Dolores, why?"

"Because he betrayed me—not once, but three times. This was one time too many." Dolores strode purposefully toward her. "If you hadn't been stupid, if you hadn't gone and fished in those damned memories of yours, all this could have been avoided."

As the lens through which Melinda viewed the world twisted, the sound of the rain became more acute, the shrill of the phone painful, the reds and golds of the room too vivid.

"Don't you see? I couldn't let you remember."

Watching the woman she'd trusted like a mother approach her, Melinda had no doubt Dolores meant to kill her. And the bitter taste of anger scorched her throat. She looked around her for a weapon. Dolores had killed her mother. She'd killed her father. Melinda had to stop her before she became the next victim. She lunged forward. On the coffee table she found her father's glass, a crystal ashtray, a vase of dahlias, and threw them all in close succession. They bounced off Dolores as if she were made of rubber and crashed on the carpet.

Grabbing Melinda's arm, Dolores twisted it back, then butted the gun's muzzle against her temple. "Stop squirming. I'm not quite ready for you to die."

Strangely, in the steely grip of her dreaded monster, Melinda's panic ebbed. The real monster, she realized, had been her own fear.

If she could keep Dolores talking, Melinda decided, she'd give herself half a chance to escape.

"This doesn't make sense," she said, mind churning for threads that would give her the truth without provoking Dolores into a premature carrying out of her mindless execution.

"Doesn't it?" Dolores said in a high-pitched voice. "Think, hon, think back to twenty years ago. You were in bed. I know you were. Your mother and I tucked you in together. Your father was working late."

Melinda twisted in Dolores's grip, hoping for a weakness in the wiry steel of her arms. Dolores tightened her hold and pressed the gun's cold muzzle flush against her temple.

"But you weren't in the greenhouse when I went downstairs again," Melinda said, swallowing to lubricate her dry throat.

"We'd had an argument. I'd left. Then I came back to apologize." Dolores gripped her tighter, pulling her once again toward the couch. "I was always the one apologizing. It wasn't right for pretty little Miss Perfect to lower herself to such a level."

"But why, Dolores, why did you kill her?" Melinda forced herself to relax and become a dead weight in Dolores's arms.

"Don't make this harder than it is, hon." Dolores kneed her in the kidneys. Melinda staggered forward, hoping to unbalance Dolores, but the older woman was prepared for the move and yanked her back up. Pain shot through Melinda's bent arm. "Owww!"

"Ely said he loved me, but he married her. Then he poisoned her mind. Slowly he turned her against me."

"It doesn't make sense, Dolores. She was your friend—"

Dolores whirled Melinda around and pushed her down next to her father's body. With her knee across Melinda's lap, the gun at her head, and a hand gripping her throat, Dolores pinned her captive to the couch.

"I loved your mother, you know," Dolores said, the truth of it carving deep lines of regret around her mouth, a scowl of sorrow on her brow. "But to her I was nothing more than the gardener's daughter, then the gardener. I never realized. And him. After all I'd done for him, he still told her all those lies."

"What could he have said to turn her against you? She was your friend." At first Dolores didn't respond. She seemed caught in her own memories of that awful September night twenty years ago.

"And she believed him," Dolores continued. "All those years we'd shared secrets like sisters. She still believed him. When she told me to leave, not come back, something happened. She'd taken Ely from me. And now she was turning her back on me. I'd lost him. Now I was losing everything else—my job, my friend, my goddaughter. Before I knew it, her work knife was embedded in her chest—"

Held prisoner by the rosebush's sticky arms, Melinda heard the monster screech in pain. Dolores, eyes wild, face red and contorted with hatred, plunged the knife into her mother's heart. "I won't let you. I won't let you!" Her mother's hand rose up in a protective gesture. The golden heart at her wrist winked in the light. The A scrolled on

its surface rocked back and forth against her skin. Her
mother fell to the ground with a dull thump. Blood spread
black over her dark green apron. Her head rolled. Her
frightened gaze caught Melinda's. "Run, Lindy, run."

"I knew that I'd just ruined my life."

"You ran away."

"But then I realized I had to make the mistake disappear."

"So you set the fire."

"I had to. I had no choice."

Hot tears burned the backs of Melinda's eyes. "And all
those years you pretended to be my friend, they were lies."

"I tried to protect you," Dolores said, her mouth droop-
ing at the corners, a frown deepening on her forehead. "I
loved you. Like a daughter. But did you ever love me?
No. Just like that, you're ready to condemn me, too."

"You weren't trying to protect me," Melinda accused,
her voice fading away. Dolores had done her very best to
confuse the images of Melinda's nightmares, to keep her
from remembering what she wasn't supposed to have seen.
"You were trying to protect yourself."

With surprising force, Dolores curled Melinda's reluctant fist around the gun's handle. "I tried to be the mother
you'd lost."

Melinda squirmed, strained, fought. She tried to kick.
Dolores's tough grip kept unerringly on its track, slowly
pointing the gun back in the direction of Melinda's head.

"And now I have to lose you, too." Dolores's finger
tightened on the trigger.

HE SHOULDN'T HAVE MADE love with her last night. By
doing so, she'd become a part of him as essential as
breathing. Letting her go this morning had been the hardest
thing he'd done. Now the chance of losing her permanently
was more than he could bear. When had she ceased to be

Ely Amery's daughter? When had she captured his heart? His soul? He'd give up his chances of promotion. He'd give up his career. *Anything* to see her safe.

Parking his truck two doors from Melinda's father's house, Grady focused his mind once more.

"Concentrate on what you want, son," Seth had told him more times than he cared to recall. *"If you concentrate on trouble, that's what you'll get."*

He wanted Melinda safe, and for that he needed a cool head. Assessing the situation, he saw three vehicles parked in front of the house. He recognized Melinda's Volvo, her father's Cadillac. The third must be Dolores's truck, rusted like the one that had sped away from him near his ranch.

Gun in hand, he circled the house, looking into every window. When he reached the tall French doors, the scene he saw chilled him more thoroughly than the rain. The great Ely Amery lay in a helpless heap, and Dolores held a gun to Melinda's head.

One wrong move and Melinda was dead.

No help. No backup. No radio. He was out of his territory. He'd have a lot of explaining to do, but he couldn't allow Melinda to die. If Dolores killed her, the sun would be eclipsed from his life.

Seth's voice spoke softly in his mind; *"You do what you gotta do, the rest takes care of itself."*

Through the rain-slicked door, he caught Melinda's gaze, and prayed she understood and could buy him the time he needed.

IN GRADY'S EYES, MELINDA saw life, love and despair, and knew she'd never give up fighting as long as she had breath in her body. She couldn't die—not when she'd just found life.

Screaming the scream of terror she'd repressed as a child, she startled Dolores. In that moment of surprise,

Grady burst through the French doors; Melinda pushed against the monster, throwing her back.

"No!" Dolores's head cracked against one of the wing chair's wooden claws. Gripping the gun with two hands, she pointed it at Grady and squeezed the trigger. The shot missed. She swiveled her grip to aim at Melinda's face. Before she could fire, Grady's bullet felled her.

In the next moment, Melinda was in Grady's wet arms. His strength held her up despite her buckling knees. He shielded her from the grizzly view, kissed her hair, her eyes, her mouth.

"My father…he's dead." She couldn't deal with this right now. It was too much. Later. She'd let the full impact of what had happened here sink in later.

His arms tightened around her. "I know. Don't look."

"Dolores." Her chest hurt and the words came out in sobs. "She killed my mother. She killed my father."

Sirens screamed in the background. "I know."

"I loved her. I trusted her." The feeling of betrayal cut through her, scalpel sharp.

"I know."

Melinda raised her head from Grady's shoulder. His face swam in the blur of her tears. As he held her, strong and warm, the final horror burst into her mind. She gasped. Her fingers curled into fists around the sleeves of his shirt. "That's what I saw that night at Angela's. It's all coming back, Grady. Kerry—she's the one who killed Angela. She killed her own best friend!"

"I know. We found her bloody clothes near the river."

Melinda's head fell forward once more against his shoulder. "It was just like the night my mother died."

"It's okay," he said in a choked voice and kissed her again. "You'll be okay."

Tense laughter bubbled in her chest at his use of her old mantra. She was alive. She was here. Holding his face between her hands, she kissed him back with all the fervor of a woman who'd cheated death and won. "I know."

AFTER DEALING WITH police and media, after the ordeal of burying her father and Dolores, Melinda sought solace in her garden. The waterfall gurgled over the rocks and splashed into the small pool where a pair of koi swam. The bird feeder swayed gently in the breeze, on the lowest branch of the pecan tree. Pipe wind chimes tinkled softly from the corner of the porch not far from the single hammock chair where Rusty lay curled in a tight ball.

She remembered those afternoon teas with Grady and how he'd asked her what she buried in her garden. He'd seen through a coping mechanism she hadn't even known she'd used. With every bulb she'd planted, she'd tried to bring her mother back to life; with every seed she'd sown, she'd repented for leaving her mother alone in the flames; with the beautiful haven she'd created, she'd tried to mask the ugly darkness of a little girl's guilt.

But she had no need for that now.

There had been no more dreams. Rain no longer set her on edge. Thunderstorms no longer caught her holding her breath, waiting for something awful to happen. She would miss her father's forceful presence. He might not have fathered her, but he had been her father. In spite of his faults, she had loved him. His actions might not have been the right ones, but his intentions had been based on love.

As for Dolores, Melinda wasn't sure what to think. She doubted the woman had ever truly understood the meaning of love—of what she'd had and destroyed. With time, the pain of betrayal would surely dull.

Raindrops fell gently on the pond's surface, creating a circle of ripples. The truth had been laid bare. No more ghosts would come to haunt Melinda, no more memories would hide in the fury of a storm.

With a sigh she rose. But as beautiful as her garden was, something was missing.

Grady and their afternoon teas. Grady's arms around her. Grady's love shining down at her from those intense blue eyes. She wanted him—not to lean on, but to love, and to create a blooming future richer than any she could build on her own.

Without him, she would be...incomplete.

GRADY RANG MELINDA'S doorbell. He'd had a lot of explaining to do in the past week. But the explanations had been nothing compared to the paperwork. And the paperwork had paled in comparison to the mental gymnastics he'd put himself through.

In the end, not only Seth but Brasswell, had stood one hundred percent behind him. Grady chuckled. That was Brasswell for you—town image first and foremost. In the wake of the positive press he'd generated, what else could she do but stand by him?

Ely Amery, despite his appearance of invincibility had fallen prey to the type of monster he'd freed with his glib tongue and persuasive politics.

Defending Jamie had not been wrong; distrusting his instincts had been his mistake.

He'd done his best in the past, and his best was all he could give—to anyone.

He loved Fargate. He loved the people he served. And most of all, he loved Melinda.

"Hi!" Grady said when she opened the door. Genuine pleasure shone in her eyes. Small ripples of joy fluttered all the way to the soles of his feet.

"Hi!"

He hesitated at the threshold. "Can I come in?"

"Oh, please do." He walked into the room that was an

extension of the outside, and she closed the door softly behind him. "Can I offer you some tea?"

"Please." His gaze trailed her every movement. He wanted to run his fingers through her hair, hold her tightly in his arms, make love with her until neither of them could move.

"It's over," Grady said. Melinda sat in the lone chair. He sat on the ottoman. Their knees touched, and warmth spread through his limbs. "All of it, except Kerry's trial. The knife was found in the river near where we found the gym bag. The lab tests proved the commingled blood on the clothes we found in the bag was Kerry Merrill's and Angela's. Kerry was arrested and spilled her guts."

"Why did she do it?"

"She was having an affair with Mike. He kept putting off marrying her because of the band. She tried to persuade Angie to quit singing and honor the reverend's wishes. She thought that would settle Mike down. Even when she confessed her true motive, Angie refused, and Kerry snapped. She hadn't planned on killing Angie. She felt betrayed. It just happened. Then she had to make it go away."

"Like Dolores." As Melinda handed him a glass, their fingers touched, held, then hesitatingly separated.

So civilized.

He wanted to scream.

Melinda took a sip from her glass. "She didn't seem like the type."

"They never do. A physical exam revealed an unsutured cut healing across the palm of her hand and one on her upper thigh."

Melinda placed her glass on the small table beside her chair. "The Barbie, the message, the note—they were hers?" she asked, her eyes darkening to impossible depths.

"Yes." He cleared his throat. "She got the key to your house from Angie's kitchen."

"I still can't believe she would do all that." Melinda shivered at the remembered horror.

"When she read the article in the paper, she was afraid you'd really seen something and wanted to scare you into silence."

"She did a good job." Melinda slid forward in her chair. "The knife in the plant?"

He flexed his fingers in an unconscious gesture of need. "Her, too. The blood on the hilt was from the meat department where she worked."

"That was a truly evil touch." Melinda shook her head. "She really had me thinking I'd killed Angie." She blew out a long, frustrated breath. "The van?"

"Driven by one of Dolores's young male friends. She'd blackmailed him into doing her the favor."

"One of the men she was always trying to fix me up with." She cocked her head, looking at his thigh with a saddened expression, and rubbed his healing wound beneath his pants in an infinitely tender torture.

"It appears she'd found out something he didn't want his family to know and used it against him."

Melinda shook her head sadly. "She was good at doing that. And the gunshot?"

"Dolores," he said hoarsely.

"What's going to happen to Carson Crews?"

"He's going to go live with his aunt in Oklahoma. The scouts who saw the season-highlights video we showed at the Fall Festival were impressed enough to want to give him another look when his arm heals."

"I'm so glad."

"Yeah, the kid deserved something good in his life."

She took his glass and placed it next to hers. The condensation on the glass that had pooled in the hammock of his thumb dribbled onto his palm.

"So, Chief," she said as she climbed into his lap. His

reaction was instant and strong. She wrapped her arms around his neck and snuggled her body close. The hard peak of one breast grazed his uniform pocket. "I hear there's a cold front coming through tonight."

The feel of her, so close and so warm, tripped the rhythm of his heart into high gear. He wrapped his arms around her waist, buried his face in the blue-black silk of her hair, and inhaled the spring freshness of her scent. "Yeah, it's raining already and the temperature's dropping." Everywhere except his body. There, a raging inferno burned.

"I don't have flannel sheets." She nuzzled his neck, setting his pulse at a maddening gallop.

"You don't need any." He kissed her chin. "I'll keep you warm." He kissed the tip of her nose. "Very warm." His lips paused a breath away from hers. He looked straight into her deep, dark eyes. "Tonight and every night. If you'll have me."

Lightning struck close by. Thunder shook the small house. There was no haunted look in Melinda's eyes, only one of heated promise; and a seductive smile that made him very hungry. He knew she would never again fear September storms, and as long as she was in his arms, there would be no more rainy days for him.

In the full bloom of her kiss, he heard her answer. "Tonight and every night."

Silhouette Stars

Born this Month

Sean Connery, Elvis Costello, Patrick Swayze, Coco Chanel, Bill Clinton, Robert de Niro, Madonna, Danielle Steel, Magic Johnson, Princess Anne

Star of the Month

Leo

The year ahead is full of opportunity. You will need to make changes in your personal life in order to reap the benefits of all that is on offer. Career moves later in the year should bring financial benefits. Travel is also well aspected especially if taken in the autumn when it could well be linked to new relationships.

SILH/HR/0008a

Virgo

Events of last month should have made you wiser about exactly who you can trust. Having learnt this you should feel ready to move on in a positive and forgiving mood.

Libra

With renewed optimism you enter a new phase in which many of the problems that you have encountered lately vanish. A romantic relationship brings an added glow to your life.

 Scorpio

Your love life may have led you to neglect other areas of your life, although now you will be able to get the balance right. There could be exciting job opportunities coming your way.

Sagittarius

You have sailed into calmer waters after the upheaval of last month. You should feel pleased with the way you have handled yourself. You should start to move onwards and upwards, putting yourself in a stronger and more positive position.

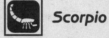 **Capricorn**

Changes in several areas of your life will cause a degree of tension. Take any offers of help and by the end of the month you should feel pleased with all you have managed to achieve.

Aquarius

Recently you have dealt with a great deal of upheaval. By mid month you should be reaping some of the benefits. A reunion with someone from your past may lead to a celebration.

SILH/HR/0008c

  **Pisces**

An excellent, positive month in which many of your plans will start to come to fruition. Friends and loved ones should be supportive and you may see a certain relationship in a very favourable light.

Aries

You should feel confident about the future and now that you have made the decision to move on you will be surprised how supportive those close to you are. Travel plans are well aspected, especially those connected with business.

 **Taurus**

There could be a few tricky moments as certain people seem determined to misinterpret what you are really saying. Take a break and allow the dust to settle and by the end of the month life will be back on track.

Gemini

Don't push yourself too hard as your batteries need recharging. This is an excellent time to take a break, catch up on family, or just relax at home pampering yourself. A lucky win late in the month gets you in the mood for celebrating.

   Cancer

After the upheaval of last month life quietens down and you can use the calm to assess what you do next. Your finances receive a boost and you may be able to buy something special.

Look out for more
Silhouette Stars next month

SILHOUETTE
INTRIGUE™

AVAILABLE FROM 18TH AUGUST 2000

SECRET ADMIRER Amanda Stevens

Gallagher Justice

Working with Detective Tony Gallagher is Eve Barrett's dream come true—and her worst nightmare. She's loved him since she was just a girl and now she has to hide both her secret desire and her real assignment: investigating Tony...

COWBOY JUSTICE Patricia Rosemoor

After years of struggling, Cash Abreu has everything he's ever wanted—except Reine Kendrick. Now in peril, Reine turns to Cash for help—and she's willing to do *anything* to convince him that she really needs him...

TO SAVE HIS BABY Judi Lind

Amnesia

Gil Branton disappeared suddenly from Valerie Murphy's life—and her bed—four months ago. But when he reappeared, unable to remember who he was or where he'd been, he knew they were in danger. He vowed to protect this beautiful woman—and her unborn baby.

BEHIND CLOSED DOORS Carla Cassidy

Lawman Lover

At first Ann Carson thought the notes were a prank. Then came more sinister threats. So rugged policeman Clay Clinton became her bodyguard. The summer nights were long and hot, and as the stalker closed in, the temperature was definitely rising...

AVAILABLE FROM 18TH AUGUST 2000

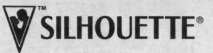

Sensation
Passionate, dramatic, thrilling romances

A PLACE TO CALL HOME Sharon Sala
IDENTITY: UNKNOWN Suzanne Brockmann
RIO GRANDE WEDDING Ruth Wind
FALLING HARD AND FAST Kylie Brant
THE MARRIAGE PROTECTION PROGRAMME
Margaret Watson
CULLEN'S BRIDE Fiona Brand

Special Edition
Vivid, satisfying romances
full of family, life and love

SURPRISE DELIVERY Susan Mallery
HUNTER'S WOMAN Lindsay McKenna
THE FATHERHOOD FACTOR Diana Whitney
THE HOME LOVE BUILT Christine Flynn
DR COWBOY Cathy Gillen Thacker
A FAMILY SECRET Jean Brashear

Desire
Intense, sensual love stories

TALL, DARK AND TEXAN Annette Broadrick
CINDERELLA'S TYCOON Caroline Cross
HARD LOVING MAN Peggy Moreland
SAIL AWAY Kathleen Korbel
STAR-CROSSED LOVERS Zena Valentine
TOO SMART FOR MARRIAGE Cathie Linz

0008/46b

FREE!

2 Books
and a surprise gift!

We would like to take this opportunity to thank you for reading this Silhouette® book by offering you the chance to take TWO more specially selected titles from the Intrigue™ series absolutely FREE! We're also making this offer to introduce you to the benefits of the Reader Service™—

★ FREE home delivery
★ FREE gifts and competitions
★ FREE monthly Newsletter
★ Books available before they're in the shops
★ Exclusive Reader Service discounts

Accepting these FREE books and gift places you under no obligation to buy; you may cancel at any time, even after receiving your free shipment. Simply complete your details below and return the entire page to the address below. **You don't even need a stamp!**

YES! Please send me 2 free Intrigue books and a surprise gift. I understand that unless you hear from me, I will receive 4 superb new titles every month for just £2.70 each, postage and packing free. I am under no obligation to purchase any books and may cancel my subscription at any time. The free books and gift will be mine to keep in any case.

10ZEB

Ms/Mrs/Miss/Mr ....Initials..............................
BLOCK CAPITALS PLEASE

Surname...

Address...

....

....Postcode ....

Send this whole page to:
UK: The Reader Service, FREEPOST CN81, Croydon, CR9 3WZ
EIRE: The Reader Service, PO Box 4546, Kilcock, County Kildare (stamp required)